Sun Seekers

Sun
Seekers

◆ A NOVEL ◆

RACHEL MCRADY

alcove
press

Published in the United States by Alcove Press, an imprint of The Quick Brown Fox & Company LLC.

Alcove Press and its logo are trademarks of The Quick Brown Fox & Company LLC.

Library of Congress Catalog-in-Publication data available upon request.

ISBN (hardcover): 978-1-63910-497-0
ISBN (ebook): 978-1-63910-498-7

Cover design by Sarah Brody

Printed in the United States.

www.alcovepress.com

Alcove Press
34 West 27th St., 10th Floor
New York, NY 10001

First Edition: January 2024

10 9 8 7 6 5 4 3 2 1

For my marvelous grandfather, John Dozier:
Yes, I know how much you loved me.

And for Caleb, Iona, and Isla,
my favorite adventures.

Gracie

"MAMA, WHAT'S A 'GRIT'?" I ask, watching the goopy globs falling off the wooden spoon. Mama is standing in the kitchen, stirring the pot with her hand on her hip. She's pinching her side like she does sometimes when she's cranky or nervous.

"For the sake of this conversation, it's breakfast, baby girl," she says with a small laugh, adding, "I can't believe I've never made you grits before."

The grit smells okay, but it looks so gross that I don't know what to believe. But Mama knows what I like, so maybe the grit won't be so bad.

"It looks like something the worm would eat," I say, and Mama goes quiet. Her back is to me, but she gets all stiff and still. I can tell she doesn't like that I brought up the worm.

Grandfather's had the worm in his brain for two years now. That's what Mama says. Most days the worm is sleeping, but it's always there. On the sleeping days, Grandfather tells me he loves me. He brushes my hair back and tells me I'm the most marvelous girl in the whole wide world.

But sometimes, when it's late and the sun goes down, the worm wakes up. When the worm is awake, Grandfather doesn't know my name. Sometimes it's even worse than him not knowing my name—he stares past me like his eyes are covered with a blindfold.

I covered my eyes with a blindfold once at Becky's birthday party. There was a giant horse, and her belly was filled with candy. I know the horse was a girl because only girls have things come out of their bellies. I wore the blindfold because Becky's mama told me that was the way to play the game. But I didn't like wearing it because I always like to see what's around me. How horrible it must be for Grandfather when he can't see.

Last week, after "the incident," Mama told me that the worm is invisible. She thinks the worm will always be there and there's no getting around it, but I know better.

"Mama, what does the worm eat?" I ask her, even though I know she doesn't want to talk about it. Sometimes I can't help it. There are too many questions in my head.

Mama keeps stirring the pot and pinching her side. She still won't turn around to face me. "Umm, brains, I guess?" she replies.

"The worm is eating Grandfather's *brains*?" I shout a little. I picture the invisible worm—or at least its squiggly outline that's shaped like Grandfather's twisty mustache—chomping through his brain. Maybe that's what made him look that gray color the other day. That day he had to sit in the wheelchair after his accident and Mama cried.

"Oh, sweet pea, I'm not sure. I guess the worm lives in Grandfather's brain, but we don't know what it eats," Mama says, turning around and giving me one of her special smiles that she only gives me.

My mama reminds me of the sun. Some days she is so happy and bright. On those days she is the tickle monster, tickling my tummy until I fall on the ground laughing so hard I can barely breathe. On those days, she plays music on her phone and spins me around the kitchen and even lets me wear some of her sparkly eye shadow. But other days it's like there's a storm cloud in front of her, blocking her light. On those days she doesn't wear any eye shadow. Sometimes I just see her sitting there, staring at the wall, and I have to call her name a few times to get her to hear me. One time I asked Mama if she had a worm in her brain too, and she looked surprised and said, "No, baby, I'm just tired. That's all."

But lately it seems like she's always tired. Some days she's too tired to take a shower and she just wears her pajamas all day, and I have to remind her to make me dinner. Some days I make my own dinner. I am very good at making peanut butter and jelly sandwiches. I can't cut the crusts off as good as Mama does, but I know what each side of the bread needs—two scoops of grape jelly on one and one scoop of extra crunchy peanut butter on the other.

On the sunshine days, Mama looks like a princess. When I get "old enough" I hope I look like her on her sunniest days. But Mama says looks aren't important.

"Looks can only get you so far," Mama once told me. "And in my case, they sent me in the wrong direction."

I know she's talking about Daddy when she says this, but I don't ask her any more questions, even though I have about one million. Mama says lying is bad and that's why Daddy went away, but Grandfather says some lies are necessary. Necessary lies are for when you don't want to upset people. I never want to upset people, so I'll probably have to tell many necessary lies.

Daddy used to live with us in a different house, but then we moved here to Grandfather's house when I was four years old, and now I don't see Daddy very much. We never went on adventures together or even talked about adventures the way Grandfather and I do. It seems like daddies are the kind of people you are supposed to miss, but I don't know if I actually miss him or if I miss being able to talk about him. Some days I forget I even have a daddy. Rowan Frank, from school, says her daddy is a soldier and is saving our country like a superhero. He lives far away and Rowan told me that she gets to call him sometimes on her mom's phone and that she can see him talking to her on the screen. One time I asked Mama if we could call Daddy like that and see his face, but she just got real quiet and then she said her phone doesn't work like that.

Mama scoops some of the grit into the bowl, and I stare at it carefully. I don't trust it yet.

"It doesn't have a very nice-sounding name, 'grit,'" I say.

"Well, why don't you just try it before you write it off?" Mama says, placing a bowl in front of me. She puts some cheese and butter on top and they melt into the grit. It sure does smell good.

Slowly, I dip my Mickey Mouse spoon into the bowl, picking up a few of the grit pieces. I'm a little scared, but I see Mama watching me, so I put the spoon in my mouth because I know it will make her happy. I might have to necessary lie about liking the grit. It slides in smoothly, and I roll the pieces around on my tongue. The grit is salty and thick, not like the watery mash I was expecting. I pause to swallow.

"Verdict?" Mama asks.

But I'm not ready to give it my approval just yet. I scoop my spoon back into the bowl, getting more grit pieces this time. Now I'm less afraid to put the grit in my mouth, and I open wide. I give Mama a big thumbs up.

"Can I have more grit for my birthday?" I ask her.

She smiles. I know she's happy I like the grit.

"It's 'grits,' baby girl, and of course you can," she says, bending down to give me a kiss on the top of my head.

I turn seven next week. My birthday is on July 5, the day after America was born. I hope by then I will be old enough. Mama is always saying I'm not old enough for things. Mama says she'll take me to Disney World when I'm old enough, and I can't wait because I have never been on an adventure before and that will surely be an adventure. Every year I ask if we can go, and every year Mama says, "When you're old enough." It seems like I'm always getting older, but it's never old enough.

But that's okay. I'm about to go on an adventure of my own. Grandfather says it only takes one day to have an adventure, though I think this one will take longer.

The washer beeps, and Mama flings the wet clothes over her shoulder and heads outside to hang them on the clothes-line. I can tell it's already sticky hot outside because Mama lets out a "Jesus!" as she hops down the steps off the back porch.

It's probably good that it's so hot outside. That means my dress with the daisies around the collar will dry in time for tomorrow. I need to look my best for my adventure, and the dryer broke a few months ago. But Mama says there's no use in spending all that money to replace it when you live in Reading.

"Most days it's hot enough to fry an egg on that sidewalk, Gracie Lynn," she says, wiping the sweat bubbles off her forehead. "No idea why I even bother putting on foundation in this town."

Last week was my last day of first grade. Next year I will go to second grade, which might also be an adventure. My report card is coming soon and Mama says if I get an "exceeds expectations" I can get a bonus ice cream—which means two ice creams this week instead of one. We go to Baskin-Robbins for my one ice cream a week because they have pink chairs and chocolate peanut butter ice cream. All ice cream stores should have pink chairs and chocolate peanut butter ice cream, but they don't. When we order, Mama always asks the person with the giant spoon to get me extra chunks of peanut butter because she knows that's my favorite part. Mama knows all of my favorite things.

I think I will get an exceeds expectations on my report card because Mrs. Hoyt says I'm very "advanced" for the first grade. I am already reading chapter books and some of them don't even have pictures—which I like, because that way I get to use my imagination. Mrs. Hoyt says I have an "overactive imagination," which sounds like a bad thing, but I know it's not. My favorite chapter books are called the *Magic Tree House* books. They are about Jack and Annie, who are brother and sister and get to go on adventures through time and visit all these different places. I wish I could go with them.

When Grandfather used to live with us, we would do fun projects and he would read me the comics. Now he doesn't want to do much of anything. He sits in his recliner chair and we talk, and sometimes on good days I ask him to tell me stories of his adventures. Those are my favorite days.

Even though chocolate peanut butter ice cream is my favorite treat, I told Mama that I wanted to go visit Grandfather as my treat for when I get an exceeds expectations instead. We used to visit him every other day when I didn't have swim practice, but we haven't been to see him in the home since the incident last week. That's what Mama calls what happened—"the incident." I tried talking to her about it the other day, but it just made her cry, so now I will call it the incident too because I don't want to make Mama cry. Mama makes me to go to Becky's house to play while she goes to the home and "handles things." I don't really know what that means, but I guess I'm not old enough yet.

"The home" is what Mama calls where Grandfather lives now. He used to live with us here in his real home, but then one day the police found him in the street in his underwear and he got in trouble because you're supposed to wear your clothes in the street. So he had to go to the home. A lot of people live in the home. It smells kind of gross in there, like the cleaning spray Mama uses when I wet the bed, which I only do sometimes when I have my pee dream. I know that can't be what it is because grown-ups don't wet the bed, but whatever it is, it doesn't smell so good.

Grandfather calls it "old people stank."

Aunt Sarah is mad that Mama and I live in Grandfather's real home now, but I don't know why because we take good care of it. I even planted flowers in the back garden and none of them have died even though it's the middle of summer. That's because I have what Mama calls a "green thumb." That is when you're good at taking care of flowers even though it is very hot. It doesn't mean my thumbs are actually green.

Mama says Aunt Sarah is family, but I'm not really sure she is because I thought families are always supposed to be together and we're never together. But I also know that Daddy is family too, and we're never together either. So I guess I don't really know what families are.

I pull my espionage notebook across the counter. It's where I keep all of my clues. "Espionage" is what spies do. They learn secrets just like I learn lessons at school. The notebook is getting pretty full. I write everything down in there. I write down what I have for breakfast—today I write down the grit—and I write down when Mama pinches her side. To a spy, everything is a clue. And since I'm not old enough to know things yet, I'll try to figure them out by putting the clues together.

Mama let me watch the *Harriet the Spy* movie a few weeks ago on Netflix, and ever since then I have been keeping my notebook. I also tried to eat a tomato and mayonnaise sandwich, just like Harriet, but it was really gross, so I'll just write in my notebook instead of eating those. I'm going to solve all of the great mysteries.

Gracie Lynn and the Mystery of Being "Old Enough."
Gracie Lynn and the Mystery of Grandfather's Worm.
Gracie Lynn and the Mystery of the Missing Daddy.
Gracie Lynn and the Mystery of the Hidden Brown Bear.

That last one was made up. I know where Brown Bear is. I gave him to Grandfather in the home so that he might help the worm to sleep. Brown Bear always helps me sleep. But I don't think that Brown Bear works for the worm, because a few weeks ago Mama got a call in the middle of the night.

Mama wouldn't tell me what happened, but I have written down the clues in my notebook so that I might be able to solve this case sometime soon.

So far I know that Mama got a phone call when it was very dark outside. I know because it woke me up. She said, "What?" and "Are you serious?" Then she said, "How much blood?" I couldn't hear the rest, but Mama didn't come into my room or leave the house, so I don't think it was that serious. The next morning I asked her, "Who called you on the phone last night?"

"It was someone from the home, Gracie," she told me. She looked very tired and didn't have any makeup on, so I wrote down that it was a storm cloud day.

"What happened?" I asked.

"Just some grown-up stuff, sweet pea," Mama said, using her fake happy voice. "Nothing for you to worry about."

"Ummm hmmm," I said very wisely, not letting her know that that made me cranky. Then I pulled out my notebook to take notes on what she said and gave Mama a very suspicious look, just like Harriet the Spy would.

"What'cha writing in there?" Mama asked.

"Just some kid stuff," I copied her. "Nothing for you to worry about."

Mama grinned and kissed the top of my head. "You got me there, baby girl."

The phone call happened exactly six days before the incident, but I don't know if they're connected. Mama said that the incident happened because Grandfather is sick with the worm, but I don't know if the worm has anything to do with the blood. Mostly I think the worm just makes Grandfather confused.

I still haven't figured out that mystery and a few other ones, but now I'm using my notebook for a different reason. I'm taking notes about my plan, so that when Grandfather and I go on our adventure, Mama will understand. I'm sad that

Mama can't go with us, but I know she wouldn't want to. She never wants to go on adventures, and she probably wouldn't be too happy about this one because it's about the worm.

Her flip-flops flap against the wooden floors as she comes back in, taking a long drink of orange juice straight out of the carton. I'm not allowed to drink out of the carton like Mama, but I guess I can when I'm old enough.

"Alright, girlie!" she cries, flinging her arms in the air. "Time to go show that pool who's boss."

I slap my espionage notebook shut because I don't want Mama seeing any of my notes, shove one last spoonful of the grit in my mouth, and grab my yellow backpack. My backpack is special. It's covered in patches of my favorite cartoon characters that Mama sewed on even though it was hard and it made blood teardrops on her fingers. She also pinned my swimming ribbon onto it from last week's meet. Maybe if I do well today, I'll get another ribbon. I'm not just an advanced reader—I'm also an advanced swimmer, and Coach Grant said I can be on the Purple Team this summer. Not only is purple my favorite color, but it's also the team for the best swimmers besides the high school kids, so I really want to be on the Purple Team. But I'm not sure if I'll be here this summer. I may not even be here for my birthday. I have to save Grandfather, and I have to do it tomorrow.

"Mama?" I say.

"Yes, sweet pea?" she replies, grabbing her keys and tucking a piece of hair out of her face.

"Thank you for my grit."

◆ 2 ◆

Dan

It's too bright out today. I wish I could hide in the shadows, but there aren't any in this parking lot. I can almost feel the heat steaming off the asphalt through my shoes—brand-new Allen Edmonds dress boots that Ashley says are on trend. As I look at the hand-crafted banners and the cars with elementary school bumper stickers, I don't think the latest fashions will work in my favor here. Suddenly dress slacks and a button-down shirt seem far too formal for a kids' swim meet, and I feel ridiculous as my shoes squeak with every step I take toward the pool.

What a terrible idea. I mean, I've had worse ones, but this one is up there. I adjust the collar on my shirt. It's stiff, crisp, ironed to perfection.

I wish Ashley hadn't signed up for the school emails. I could have lived in blissful ignorance, never knowing my daughter had a swim meet or that she was a top-ranked swimmer for her age group, or that she was starting to get the same dimple in her cheek that I have. Living in ignorance has been so easy until now.

I wasn't there for Gracie's first time in the pool. LeeAnn took her herself when Gracie was three, telling me as I was heading out the door to a work conference as an afterthought. I still remember that pang of being left out from yet another pivotal moment in my daughter's life, one I'd even dreamed about. But by that point, I had one foot out the door anyway, so I brushed it away, like I always did in those days.

I was a swimmer when I was Gracie's age—a fact I'm sure Saint LeeAnn forgot or she never would've signed her up. I remember flinging myself into the pool with a giant cannonball as the girls in my grade would squeal—that was me, already the star of the show. My parents would take me out for pizza after my meets, bragging about my medals while I pretended to be embarrassed.

The smell of chlorine wafts past me as I pass through the chain-link fence, taking me back to those days. Swimming was replaced with football, which was replaced with frat parties, which were replaced with after-work drinks, but I feel like I could cannonball back into the water all over again. I wish Ashley were here, or maybe Jack, our son. But she insisted they shouldn't come; she said Gracie and LeeAnn seeing me would be enough drama, and the day wasn't about Ashley. But still, it would be nice to have a security blanket of people who don't think I'm pond scum. Not that I entirely blame those who do consider me to be lower than the dirt beneath their fingernails, but that doesn't mean I enjoy the wave of shame that seeing or talking to LeeAnn always summons.

I approach a folding table packed with Stepford moms, all grinning back at me in unison. There's a blonde woman who looks like a former pageant queen whose face has since deflated, another woman whose hair is so light it's practically white in the midday sun and whose skin is lathered in an orangey fake tanner, and another one who has some of the biggest, whitest teeth I've ever seen. They blind me as I approach.

"Name?" Self-Tanner asks.

"Um, Dan," I offer, not wanting to give up my full identity; I was trying to come in undetected.

"No, silly!" Self-Tanner giggles as if I've just told the most hilarious joke in the world. "What's your child's name? Or are you here for a, er, friend?"

The women in the group exchange looks of concern, like I might be a creep stalking out kids' swim meets to get my jollies.

"Gracie," I blurt out, panicked by their false perceptions. "Gracie Clarmont."

Self-Tanner wrinkles her nose in exaggerated confusion. "We don't have a Gracie *Clarmont*," she argues. "Do you mean Gracie Abernathy?"

No, I think. *I mean Gracie Clarmont, daughter of Dan Clarmont. I was there the day she was born. We have the same dimple. Bring her over here, I'll show you.* But the moms are looking at me expectantly, so I just smile and nod.

"Dannnny? Is that the famous Dan Clarmont?" The woman with the big teeth steps forward, surveying me with scrupulous precision. She's wearing a hot pink tennis skirt that is half an inch shy of obscene and a crop top clearly designed for someone closer to Gracie's age than the grown woman before me.

"Err, yes?" I reply, feeling as if that's the wrong answer to give.

She flings her arms in the air with a squeal and lunges her heaving bosom toward me like she's throwing the shot put.

"I can't believe it's youuuu," she declares, drawing the last word out and accentuating the pout of her overly plumped lips.

I desperately try to place her, feeling sweat start to pool around my lower back where my belt sits snugly on my hips. There's definitely something familiar about her, but her name and how she might have once fit into my life completely elude me. There's so much about my past that haunts me, and clearly this woman hasn't made the cut.

Her bright smile falters one small tick as she realizes I don't immediately recognize her but recovers and playfully bats my arm. "Corrine, Danny! Corrine Carter! Well, Bryant now," she adds, wiggling her finger to flash a blinding diamond ring almost as shiny as her teeth.

Corrine Carter. Shit. I can see it now—just replace that tennis skirt with a cheerleading uniform and take her down a few bra sizes and the memory materializes like a Polaroid photo coming into focus.

"Oh, of course, hey," I reply, eager to end the conversation. "Gotta go find a seat," I add, though the bleachers are only a third full. This isn't exactly an SEC stadium.

"Grrrrreeatt!" Self-Tanner exclaims like Tony the Tiger as Corrine stands there dumbly, smile frozen on her face like it's painted on. "Feel free to sit in the second set of bleachers. Gracie's group will be going in about ten minutes. They wear the blue suits. And please do take a flyer for our book fair to raise money for the PTA in late July. Every little bit counts!"

She waves the piece of paper in front of my nose like she's trying to swat a fly away. I watch it dizzily for a few seconds before plucking it from her, as if I have a choice.

"Oh, and LeeAnn normally comes in right before the meet starts," Corrine tells me conspiratorially. "So she probably won't even notice you're here."

I haven't seen Corrine since high school and I barely remember her from back then, so I'm unsure how she knows I'm more than happy to avoid LeeAnn, but I don't question it. I just smile and quickly walk away from the group's super-glue gazes, past a much less polished woman wearing a cat shirt who looks almost as out of place as I feel.

Clutching the book fair flyer in my hands, I twist the paper back and forth as I walk past the other parents in the stands. I wonder how many of them know who I am.

Dan Clarmont. That name used to mean something around here. When I was a senior, and one of the football captains, I helped the team get its first championship in thirty years. There was a giant banner in the center of town that had my picture on it. I landed a partial scholarship to the University of South Carolina—my chance to get out of this hick town and make something of myself. Most people at college had never heard of Reading, South Carolina, even though it was only thirty minutes away, and I liked that. I had three glorious years where the only person from Reading in my life was LeeAnn, and she visited Columbia so often back then it was easy to feel like she was a part of this new life I was forging. While it might not be the most bustling metropolis, Columbia at least offered the illusion of progress.

Reading's biggest attraction is the Walmart Superstore, and that's five minutes outside of the actual town limits. It's a decaying place where the heat seeps through your clothes and clings to you like an unwelcome neighbor.

You hear people in Reading talk about how they wish they could restore this pit of a place to its "former glory." I sort of remember a time when it wasn't a wasteland, when there were monthly events and markets and bake sales. But sometimes I don't know if those things really happened or if that's just the image that comes up every time someone references "the good ol' days" in any small town in the South. After everything went down with LeeAnn, I moved back to Columbia with Ashley. I may not live far away now, but I cherish those twenty miles of highway that separate me from this place. They are necessary for my sanity. Being back here feels like watching a movie about my life, none of it real.

No one seems to recognize the old Dan, the town hero, except maybe Corrine. I've been rebranded now, as they'd say at the marketing firm where I work. These days Dan Clarmont is the absent father. I'm the cheater who can't be bothered to show up at his kid's school events, the lowlife who hasn't even earned the basic honor of sharing a last name with his child. I'm sure that's what they all think, especially if LeeAnn has anything to say about it.

The flyer is a sweaty wad of paper in my palm now. I make my way up the steps to the back row, my legs shaking slightly. I hope there aren't any sweat stains showing. I don't need any more signs of my weaknesses visible in this crowd.

They don't know the real story. Saint LeeAnn is Gracie's only real caretaker in their eyes—this perfect parent who has sacrificed everything, while I moved on to greener pastures. I used to think the same way, feel constant guilt for the pain I've caused, but over time I've learned there's more to it than that.

The bleachers scorch my legs, even through my pants. I wish I'd worn my Braves cap or brought a newspaper or something, anything to hide behind. The lingering shame of my poor life choices burns just as hot as the metal under my thighs.

"This seat taken?"

It's Corrine. Her sugary smile sickens me as she stands inches away, oblivious to the idea that someone might not want to be around her. She flicks her blonde hair behind her shoulder, fanning herself with her hand like it's some huge burden to have to stand there for the few seconds it takes me to respond.

"Umm, no, go for it," I say in what I hope is the least welcoming tone I can get away with while still sounding polite. The flyer her crony handed me back at the table now feels like a giant spitball between my fingers. She doesn't seem to notice, plopping down so close that her tennis skirt brushes my khakis. I fidget with my collar again, slightly queasy at the smell of the sticky stuff she's put on her lips. Her smile is stretched across her face as if it's taking all of its energy to remain perfectly in place.

"Gracie is a killer swimmer," she tells me, putting her hand on my bicep. "My son Greg is in her grade. Greg Bryant?"

She says this name like it's something I'd register, like I see my daughter all the time and catch up on her day, her friends, her life. Like my daughter is more than the three-year-old framed picture on my desk at work. I shrug to brush her hand away and half listen to her gab about her kid's academic acumen.

"Mr. Michaels, the crafts teacher, says Greggie has great potential in woodworking," she gushes, bouncing up and down with enthusiasm, as if we're having cocktails on a first date. "He made this box out of popsicle sticks that is simply di-viiiiiinnnneeee."

I politely smile and nod in what I hope is a convincing manner, like I think her son's popsicle box means he's obviously destined to open up his own handcrafted furniture store.

The large clock at the end of the pool ticks loudly over the sound of the restless parents and their kids. I can hear it counting the seconds down, the ticks echoing around my anxiety-riddled brain. Here I sit, waiting for my execution.

"Don'tcha think?"

Shit. I haven't heard a single word.

"Er, sorry, what?"

"I just think being involved in our kids' lives is the most important thing," she says, with her crazy stiff smile. "It's so great of you to come out in support of Gracie, even with your . . . well, pardon me, but with your history with LeeAnn."

Corrine feigns embarrassment over bringing up such an unsavory topic, slightly shifting her eyes away from me, but I can tell she's loving every second of it.

"Putting your kid first, that's what's important," she agrees with herself.

I stare at my hands. I shouldn't have come here.

✦ 3 ✦

Gracie

"MAMA, WE'RE GONNA BE laaaate," I whine.

Mama looks flustered like I'm stressing her out. She keeps moving her hands around the steering wheel and squeezing it really tight.

"We're almost there," she insists. "Just relax. You've got your goggles, right?"

"Yes, Mama." I roll my eyes the way Becky does sometimes. "I forgot my goggles one time, and you always talk about it."

"I just want to make sure, sweet pea," she says, turning into the school parking lot. "I don't want you to miss your meet. Or give those other women an excuse to crucify me," she mumbles.

"What does 'crucify' mean?" I ask her.

"Oh, um, it means give me a really hard time," she explains, looking surprised that I heard her even though she's just in the front seat, and I'm right behind her. Grown-ups never think kids can hear them.

We pull into a parking space, and I've already unclicked my seat belt and grabbed my swim cap and goggles. I push the door open and hop out.

"Gracie Lynn, I told you no getting out of the car until I say it's okay!" Mama nags.

I take a step back to the car obediently. I forgot the rule.

"Come on, let's go now," she says, guiding me forward by my shoulder. "I was just saying, sometimes the car isn't turned off completely, and it's not safe for you to just go bounding out."

I follow Mama to the pool, walking very quickly because I'm worried I'll be late and that Coach Grant will be angry. We walk up to the table to sign in, and I see Becky's mama at the booth. She has a cute orange cat on her shirt. I like cats.

"Hello, Mrs. McGovern." I smile politely.

"Hey there, Gracie!" she says, smiling too. "You ready for the meet today?"

"Yes, ma'am," I reply, holding up my goggles so she doesn't think I've forgotten them like I did that one time.

"Great, you can head on over to your group," she says, and then she turns to Mama. "Hey, LeeAnn, do you have a second?"

"Sure, Paula, what's up?"

I ignore them and speed walk over to Coach Grant and Becky and the rest of my team because you're not supposed to run next to the pool.

"Am I late?" I pant as I reach them.

"Just in time, Gracie," Coach Grant says. "Go ahead and hop on in and start your warm-ups."

I gingerly dip my toes in the water, quickly but still one at a time the way I always do before I get into any pool. I don't like any surprises when it comes to the temperature. Then I sit down and put my legs in. The side of the pool is so hot I worry it'll burn my bottom, so I hop in the water faster than normal.

"Hey, Becky," I say, paddling over to her.

Becky smiles. Her hair's already wet, so she must've been practicing her flip turns. I'm jealous because she's better at flips than me even though I'm a faster swimmer.

"Hey, Gracie," she says. "You didn't miss anything, except Greg cannonballed into the pool and got Coach Grant wet and he got mad. But it was funny."

I'm surprised that Greg did that. I'd be too scared of making Coach Grant mad to ever cannonball in the water, even if it was funny. Coach Grant has us practice our flips and finishes; Becky's still better than me even though I'm improving. Then we dive off of blocks a couple of times, just to get the feel of it. Then it's my favorite part—the practice laps. Since we are swimming the butterfly and breaststroke today, it takes a little bit longer than freestyle, but I don't care because the butterfly's my favorite stroke in swimming. I close my eyes and picture myself fluttering down the lane. If only I had my shimmery purple swimsuit with the cool silver squiggles instead of the boring plain blue one I have to wear. Then I could look like a pretty butterfly while I swim the butterfly.

I swim two practice laps and am faster than all of the people on our team—Becky tells me good job and Coach Grant says I can go last in the meet to help the team make up for any lost time. I'm very proud and look around for Mama to see if she saw me. But she's not in her usual seat.

It's really hot out so maybe she's sitting in the shade somewhere—but there's not much shade in the bleachers. I keep looking, and then I see her back. She's standing in front of some people and she's hunched over. I can't see who they are, but Mama seems tense, like when she's having a grown-up discussion with Grandfather and makes me sit in the chairs by the front desk at the home. I hoist myself up on the side of the pool to get a better look, but I can't see, and Coach Grant calls me back in the water.

"Okay, guys, line up in your order, meet's about to start!" he shouts.

I practice one more flip before pulling myself out of the pool and taking my place in line.

◆ 4 ◆

LeeAnn

"WHAT EXACTLY ARE YOU doing here?"

It isn't meant to be an accusation, but it comes out that way. Just when I was lulled into the safety of forgetting Dan existed thanks to the busyness of my routine, there he is, sitting in the stands at Gracie's swim meet with Corrine "it's Bryant now" Carter practically on his lap. It feels like a bomb has gone off.

The instant we arrived, late as usual, Paula pulled me aside. "Dan's here," she whispered, and everything around me came crashing to a halt. I couldn't meet her eye or the eyes of the other moms there; they all knew the hurt those words caused me.

Panicked, I rushed toward the bleachers, scanning the crowd for those broad shoulders, that dimple. And now here he is, hunched over, embarrassed, looking like he wishes he could curl into a ball. Not this time. This is my turf. He has to go.

Standing in these bleachers with Dan so near is giving me extreme déjà vu. When we were in high school, I used to cheer him on from the bleachers as he ran onto the field. He'd look out into the crowd and brush his thumb against his nose twice, our signal that he was thinking about me. It gave me a glow. So much about Dan made me feel light and warm and special, until it didn't. Until it made me feel just the opposite.

"I'm here to watch Gracie's swim meet," he says now in a voice filled with fake confidence.

"Like hell," I spit back.

"Now, LeeAnn," Corrine interjects, giving me a saccharine smile and reminding me that she is perfectly sausaged in the middle of our domestic drama. "Dan has every right to see his daughter compete." She places her hands on his arms and gives him a compassionate squeeze. I feel like I'm about to vomit.

"Why don't you mind your own business?" I snap at her as more heads start to turn. I can feel the heat rising from the concrete, up through the bleachers, and all the way up my neck. My whole life is spent trying to avoid spectacles like these, trying to make it through, to survive unscathed. I glance at the pool, relieved to see Gracie is facing away from us.

I turn back to see Corrine purse her lips and give several parents knowing looks. *There goes that bitter, shrill hag who drove her husband into another woman's arms.*

"How did you even find out about this?" I ask him, ignoring her hand on my husband's arm.

"I saw it on the school's website," he says quietly.

"It's not on there, Dan," I hiss back. "Why don't you tell the truth for once?"

"Okay, fine, I signed up for the emails," he mutters. "Is that such a crime?"

"I can't believe you would come here," I whisper back, furious, but desperate not to let the other parents hear me. "We haven't seen you in months. Today is supposed to be about Gracie, and you've once again found a way to disrupt her life and make everything about you."

Corrine leans forward, insistent on inserting herself. "He is her fa-theeer," she cries out like she's Nancy Grace, clinging to Dan and causing even more of a spectacle.

Dan wiggles away from her grasp, ducking his head away from me as he stands up.

"No, she's right." He averts his gaze. "I shouldn't have come. I'll go now."

He pushes his way past a shocked Corrine, whose mouth is literally hanging open, as I try to keep my cool.

"I'm sorry," he mumbles, still unable to meet my eyes. "This was a bad idea."

He rushes down the steps and past the crowd of curious parents, all watching us.

"Well, I hope you're happy." Corrine loudly tuts her clear disapproval at me, her oversized teeth glinting in the sunlight.

I ignore her, turning back to the pool. Gracie is flipping around with Becky, giggling. Relief sweeps over me. I may have made a fool of myself in public, but at least she didn't have to deal with seeing Dan right before her big meet.

Once again, I saved my daughter.

Gracie

THE TRICK IS TO have more strawberry yogurt than Reese's Puffs. You scoop your spoon through the strawberry yogurt—if you're lucky you'll get a strawberry chunk—and then you pick up about three or four Reese's Puffs and you place them into the middle of scoop of yogurt. Then you open your mouth very wide and put the entire spoon inside. This is my favorite thing to eat for my snack after swim meets.

Sometimes if I ask really nicely, Mama will even let me have it for breakfast. It takes a bit more time to eat than a normal bowl of cereal, but normal bowls of cereal are boring. I call it Strawberry Surprise because the surprise is the sweet, crunchy Reese's Puffs. Mama says Strawberry Surprise is gross and not very healthy, but she still lets me eat it a few times a week. I think it also helps that I know how to make Strawberry Surprise myself, so Mama doesn't have to cook anything like the grit, even though I liked the grit. Mama doesn't like to cook because she says it's never "as good." I don't know what she's comparing it to, but Mama seems certain, so I guess she must be right.

I crunch my Strawberry Surprise and hold up my first-place ribbon that I got for swimming the butterfly in my meet. I can't wait to show Grandfather.

"Mama, can I bring my ribbon to the home tomorrow?" I ask, putting down my spoon and wiping my mouth off. I need to make sure we're going to the home because tomorrow is the day I want to tell Grandfather about my plan and go on our adventure.

"If we go to the home, then sure, sweetheart," she says, distracted.

At least she's not saying no. Grandfather says that no "no" is as good as a yes, which is kind of confusing, but I get it.

"Can you pin it to my backpack?" I ask, waving it through the air to get her attention.

"Give Mama just a second, sweet pea," she says.

I sit quietly for a moment. Mama is looking at her computer, and she looks upset.

"What are you looking at, Mama?" I ask.

She closes her computer and shakes her head. "Um, nothing, baby girl. Just preparing for work," she says, and presses her hands against her skirt like she's trying to get out the wrinkles. Her eyes have purple circles under them and she forgot to wear earrings again, but she's still beautiful. Mama has to go in to work today for a few hours, even though it's a Saturday. But I get to go to Becky's house, so it's okay.

Mama seems to be worried most days—worried about my unruly hair, worried about Daddy, worried about Grandfather. Not only does she have purple circles under her eyes, but they are also starting to get little lines around them that crinkle when she's upset. When I look at the lines, I imagine cracks in paint.

Once, when I was five, I helped Mama paint my room. I got to pick the color out myself—Luscious Lavender, like one of my favorite flowers. We painted over cracks in the paint, and I asked Mama what caused them.

"Time, Gracie," she said. "Over time all of our cracks start to show."

That scared me. I looked at my arm, to see if there were cracks. I thought I saw some, but Mama said those are just veins and they have blood in them. It's weird that there's blood in my arm. I can't feel it. Once I got a bloody nose, and I could feel the blood then. And that's not what my arm feels like.

I want to get older so that I'll finally be old enough, but I don't want the cracks to show. I'm scared that when I'm old enough my cracks will be showing and I may break apart. Grandfather says I can't let fear run my life, but sometimes it feels like fear is hugging me. Fear is probably a girl because when I feel fear I feel other things too, things that come out of fear's belly. When I feel fear, I feel panic and I feel pain because when I am afraid I bite my bottom lip.

"Don't bite your lip," Mama commands.

"I can't help it," I say. "It's the pain that comes from fear's belly."

Mama looks confused, but she doesn't say that I'm wrong.

"Mama, who were you talking to at my swim meet?" I ask, suddenly remembering that I saw her in the bleachers.

Mama's back is to me, but I see her go stiff again. She picks up a Ziploc bag and puts in some leftover Reese's Puffs from my Strawberry Surprise carefully.

"Hmmm, what do you mean?" she asks in a funny voice.

"I saw you in the bleachers today," I tell her. "You weren't in your usual seat."

Mama keeps her back to me and her voice still sounds funny, but she says, "Oh, I was just talking to some parents. They were deciding who is bringing snacks to the other meets this summer."

What Mama's saying seems normal, but she doesn't sound normal. I can't tell if she's necessary lying or not. I make a reminder to write this down in my espionage notebook after Becky's house.

But I'm not really worried about Mama. It's Grandfather I'm worried about. Tomorrow's a big day, and if my plan goes right, we can have an adventure and defeat the worm. I just hope Mama will be okay without me. I hate to leave her behind, but I have to save Grandfather, so it's what I'll have to do.

I look at my new swimming ribbon. It looks good on my yellow backpack. I'm glad I got in one more meet before our adventure.

♦ 6 ♦

LeeAnn

I ONLY ALLOW MYSELF ten minutes a day. Ten minutes of online self-hate. I usually wait until I've clocked a good three or four hours of work and then I get my ten minutes. I long for it, an emotional cutter, wanting to feel the hurt just one more time. Linda always takes her lunch break later, and that's when I normally seize my opportunity. But today she's not here at all. After this morning's meet run-in, I'm jonesing for my social media fix more than ever.

"You have a smart, beautiful little girl, LeeAnn," she'd say if she were here. "Why do you need to remind yourself of that bastard?"

But I can't help it. Dan P.L. (post-LeeAnn) fascinates me more than he ever did before he left. Not that I remember much of our life together before that post-LeeAnn time. Were we ever a unit like they are now?

I still can't believe that woman has the nerve not to set her account to private. You'd think when you stole some-one's husband and impregnated yourself with his baby that you'd at least have the decency to keep his estranged wife from seeing your selfies. At the same time, I don't know what I'd do without my ten minutes on their pages, scrolling for signs of their life together like an addict looking for just one more hit.

Today I'm in for a special treat. She's posted an entire album of photos: "Summer Beach Antics." *What "antics" will these crazy kids get up to next? They're so silly.*

It's like she's taking some sick pleasure in proving that she won. And she did. If social media is the barometer of success—which these days it truly is—then she's had nothing but sunshine with a high of seventy-five for the past two years.

Beach pictures seem particularly cruel since we never took Gracie there. In one photo, Dan is building a sand castle with a little boy who has my daughter's dimple—Dan's dimple. He's laughing as Dan pokes his nose. My husband used to do that with my Gracie, our Gracie. Sometimes I have to remind myself that technically she's his too. He looks just as tanned and fit as he did today in the bleachers. But instead of curling down on himself, like he seems to do whenever he's within five feet of me, he's sitting tall. I guess she really does bring out the best in him. Good for her.

I don't post pictures of Gracie or write statuses or share links. I only use my account to find Dan and hate stalk her. What would my status even read? *Daddy needs adult diapers now and my daughter can't stop wetting the bed either. Hopefully there's a two-for-one sale!*

The thought almost makes me smile—almost. But Dan's picture-perfect family keeps me from cracking through my fog of self-loathing.

"ABERNATHY!"

Mike's piercing voice causes me to jump so high I almost need adult diapers myself. His pointy chin comes around the corner before the rest of his pinched face. He's dressed in a full baggy suit and polka dotted tie, which seems a bit much for the head of a bathroom supply company's data management department. He locks eyes on me, as he makes a beeline for my desk. I close out of the tab.

"We were overstocked on lemon soaps by almost a thousand units last month," he declares, glaring at me as if I personally persuaded customers not to like the smell of lemon. "We simply can't afford to have another miscalculation of that proportion."

I nod, trying to make it seem like I too think the fate of hand soap on this Saturday afternoon is as important as the work of Doctors Without Borders.

"See that this doesn't happen again," he says, leaning closer to my face than anyone with Mike's breath ever should. "It's good you came in today for some extra hours. We're going to need some extra man time if these mistakes continue."

He peers down at me, accusatory, waiting for my apology as the one in charge of ordering cleaning products. I refuse to cave. One thing I'm pretty good at is never admitting wrongdoing, except when I'm confronted with my parenting skills at 2 AM, covered in sweat.

I obediently nod without offering up any culpability and present a mild grimace that seems to satisfy his blame game. As much as I hate working at Beyond Baths, I need this job. Forget the fact that the name is totally a rip-off of a national chain or that Mike sincerely believes he can change a person's life with the proper shower heads and curtain rods; this paycheck is the only way I can keep my shaky existence from crumbling entirely. The worst part about working here is that I have Dan to thank for landing me the job in the first place.

When I graduated from high school, I worked a merry-go-round of menial jobs in Reading, shuttling back and forth to see Dan in Columbia on the weekends, listening to him wax poetic about our future and brushing aside my feelings of inadequacy over the fact that he'd gotten out and gone to college while I was still here, figuring my life out.

"As long as we're together, what does it matter?" Dan had asked me, and I'd agreed. My future felt so tied to Dan's that retail and waitressing work felt like a means to an end. And then I got pregnant. Dan left USC and finished up the last year of his degree at the community college in Reading. I know he was sad to leave Columbia, but we agreed to put Gracie first. Or at least I thought we had. We had a civil ceremony at the courthouse the week before Gracie was born, and I regret every day that I didn't ask Mama to come. I'd just assumed we'd do a bigger service once Gracie was here; the courthouse was just a formality. But that second service never happened.

The day Gracie was born still elicits the most conflicting feelings of joy and devastation. I took three years off from work after her birth just as Dan's career was starting. I needed that time to recover, to come to grips with everything that had happened—the good and the terrible. There I was, not able to legally order a drink yet, but holding a tiny baby in my arms, responsible for her very existence. I hadn't accounted for the level of change my life would be subjected to in one brief week—a marriage, a birth, and the greatest loss I'd ever experienced. The weight of it all felt enormous, unbearable.

But after a few years of surviving on Dan's entry-level marketing paycheck, it soon became clear that I'd need to chip in too. He didn't like the idea of me salting fries or wearing that cheerless blue vest while I was still tied to him, so he reached out to a friend from college and got me a part-time gig in the Beyond Baths data management department. That's a fancy way of saying I sit in a cubicle and plug in forecasts for toilet seat covers, faucets, and hand towels. It's truly the Lord's work.

After Dan left, the importance of the job was greater than ever. So I upped my hours and pretended to be just as passionate about the different shapes of sinks as Mike wanted us to be. Every day when I walk in, I'm reminded that it's because of Dan that I even have a job—yet another thing I owe the man I have made it my mission to despise. Thankfully, Daddy's house is paid off and I'm still on Dan's health insurance plan since we're not officially divorced, so for now, I'm making ends meet, but just barely.

My phone starts buzzing just as Mike saunters off with the swagger of a multi-million-dollar CEO. I make sure he's completely closed the door to his office before picking up.

"Hi, Susan," I whisper.

"Hey, Lee," Susan says in my ear. "How you doing?"

"I'm fine," I say, not wanting to continue the conversation but knowing it's my duty to do so. "How's he doing today?"

"He's real good, LeeAnn," she says soothingly. "Very lucid. Ate his full breakfast and lunch today, which is pretty rare. But they've been monitoring him closely ever since the hospital and, well, last week's incident too."

I exhale, letting the air I'd been holding in spill out of me. It still feels so strange to get daily progress reports on "Big John" Abernathy—more a myth than a man. He used to command crowds with his legendary stories and far-off tales. He rubbed elbows with local politicians and had

friends on the police force. Now I know every detail about
the regularity of his bowel movements.

But as part of the home's policy, resident suicide attempts
mean daily check-ins and progress reports for at least a
month. I dread the calls from Susan, not knowing what I'm
actually hoping to hear. Do I want him to get better? Or do
I want this to be over? Those silent questions fill me with
shame, but not enough that they disappear completely.
When it comes to me and Big John, my emotions have
always been tangled.

I sift through my mental tally of the days as a blur of
appointments and incidents swirl through my exhaustion. It's been almost two weeks now since the nurses
found Daddy lying on the floor with a jagged cut across
his right wrist, blood staining the beige carpet in his
room. He'd used a pocket knife he kept in his old hunt-
ing boots. I had forgotten it was even there, tucked away
in a hidden pouch. But though Daddy can't remember to
put socks on most days, he somehow remembered that
knife.

They'd rushed him to the hospital where he made up
some pathetic excuse about slipping while holding the knife
he wasn't allowed to have in the first place.

"Honest to goodness, Lee, I just lost my god dern balance," he'd said angrily. But he couldn't meet my gaze. Not
that I wanted him to. I could barely stand to look at him.

Even the home's staff, who were usually charmed by his
tales, found this one hard to believe. Susan had waited until
we were out of his earshot to tell me that she'd be conduct-
ing daily check-ins to give me updates. She'd said this with
a reassuring smile, as if these calls would offer me comfort.
They didn't.

A few days after he left the hospital, Gracie and I visited him at the home. I'd done my best to explain to her that her grandfather wasn't feeling well, using my tried and true excuse of "the worm" in his brain. I don't know where I first came up with the analogy; it just came out of my mouth one day. Now Gracie constantly asks me about the worm: Where is it? What does it eat? Is there only one?

My lie has gotten so far out of control that I don't know how to reel it back in. Gracie took the worm and ran with it, using her brilliant mind to craft a web I'll never be able to get myself out of. So it shouldn't have been a surprise to me that she'd one day present the idea of the worm to Daddy.

It happened so innocently and swiftly that there was no one to blame but myself.

"Did the worm chew on your wrist, Grandfather?"

The tiny question shattered my heart into so many pieces that I didn't have the capacity to jump in, to stop her from telling him.

"The what now?" he asked her, wrinkling his nose.

"The worm that's in your brain making you sick," she said. "Did it go down through your body and hurt your wrist too?"

Vague recognition had spread across his features as he realized exactly what Gracie was saying, and he rounded on me. Any softness in his face that was reserved for Gracie had vanished.

"What the hell kinda lies have you been filling her head with, LeeAnn?" he screamed at me as I practically shoved Gracie out of the room, ordering her to go down the hall and sit in the chairs at the front desk.

"Well, I had to tell her something, Daddy. I had to explain that you're not always yourself," I replied, trying to keep my voice calm the way the nurses had told me to. They'd said he'd have these outbursts from time to time and that I shouldn't react, but it's hard not to react when the man who's supposed to protect you stops protecting himself. There were a lot of ways we had to adapt to deal with Big John growing up, but taking care of him had never been necessary. The man could slither his way out of any scrape and come out without a scratch, making you wonder why you'd been worried in the first place.

"The hell I'm not," he barked back. "I'm a grown-ass man, no matter how much you try to strip that away from me. And I don't need you bad-mouthing me to Gracie, dammit. I know you don't want to spend a second in my company, but she does. And the more lies you spread, the less she will. Is that what you want? You want to take everything away from me?"

He towered over me like he'd done all my life, except now his once muscular body hunched over like a shepherd's staff, bringing our faces almost parallel. Though he could certainly still intimidate, the memory of him in his prime diminished his current ability to subdue me.

"Daddy, I'm doing everything I possibly can to make sure you're as happy as you can be," I replied, my voice shaking with anger, thinking of the daily sacrifices I make for him. "We're here every other day. I answer every call, fight every battle, make sure every bill is paid. Who else is here? Sarah? I don't think so."

"You don't come see me alone unless you think I'm close to death," he shouted, and I shuddered slightly because I knew he was right. "You use that poor little girl as a shield to defend yourself against me."

The truth and injustice of his words hit me hard, and I could no longer contain my anger.

I looked straight into his eyes and shouted right in his face. I'd never done that before—in fact, the moment was so rare that I almost wonder if I imagined it completely now. "Are you kidding me?" I shouted, feeling years of pent-up frustrations bubbling over. "When was the last time you addressed me when you weren't being spiteful? You blame me for putting you in here and you favor her because she's nothing like me. But you never even got to know me, Daddy. It's not like you raised me or ever even asked a damn question about my life. You were never there."

He looked stunned, like he'd never expected me to yell or even to talk back. He fell backward into his wheelchair, which he rarely allowed anyone to see him sitting in. The moment filled me with a shameful dark joy. Even then, seeing him sitting there looking so frail and fragile, I didn't pity him. The colossal magnitude of just how self-centered he truly was had never been more apparent, and I refused to give him a single inch of ground to stand on.

We haven't spoken about the fight since then, but if it's possible, he's been even icier toward me lately.

And then, last week, there was the incident. I can't bring myself to call it what it was because the mere thought of it brings up bile in my throat.

"Do you think he's ready to see Gracie again?" I ask Susan now, praying she'll say no.

"I think so, sweetie," she replies. "He hasn't mentioned the other night once. And he keeps asking about her. I honestly don't think he remembers it at all. These episodes do happen, and unfortunately they'll probably start to happen more often. But he loves that little girl of yours, and I don't think there's anything wrong with him seeing her. It could help him, even."

"Do you think it's time to move him to B wing?" I ask, picturing the sedated zombies in the B wing, shuffling with their walkers down the hall. I can practically hear Sarah complaining about the increased residency fees all the way from Columbia.

"Not yet, darling," she says gently. "He's still very self-sufficient. The other day he was trying to get Charity to do the foxtrot with him in the dining room. Quite the southern gentleman, your father."

I roll my eyes, glad Susan can't see my dubious expression.

"Oh yes, he sure is," I say, trying to keep the deepest levels of disdain out of my tone.

"So will I see the two of you tomorrow then?" she asks.

"Yes, I guess so," I say, resigning myself to my fate. "Thanks for calling, Susan."

"You bet, Lee," she replies. "Talk soon!"

I click off my phone and set it on the desk, rolling my shoulders back to relieve the tension. The last thing I want to do is to go see that man, to put my daughter into any kind of harm's way. But she loves him and Mama loved him, though their reasoning eludes me. As much as I'd prefer to write him off the way Sarah has, I can't desert him, even if he deserves it. Gracie would never let me, and even the idea of Mama's disappointment in me is enough to bring me to my knees.

The office echoes with Mike's aggressive typing in the other room. I hate being here without Linda, but I need the overtime money this month. Gracie's swim gear isn't cheap, especially the name-brand suits they insist the kids wear. I don't want her to be the only one out there not wearing the right uniform. She's already the girl without a dad. Or the girl with a frazzled mom, depending upon who's relaying the information.

Linda is my only friend who isn't six. I used to have more. But apart from Gracie, these days I only have my weekly inconveniences—like meeting with the home's staff and filling out Daddy's tax forms—to keep me company. As annoying as they are, I don't know what I would do without them.

My life didn't used to be this monotonous. Mama would make me dinner every Tuesday when Daddy had a veterans' meetup. Dan would schedule happy hour drinks with his coworkers to give Mama and me some solo time together. He knew that Daddy always made gatherings more difficult because if the focus wasn't on him, there was no point to a gathering in the first place. Red beans and rice, seafood gumbo, chicken and rice casserole, Lake Murray stew, there was no end to what Mama could create from scratch. We'd play cards and talk about my friends from high school and which flowers had been in my prom corsage and what Hallmark movies we wanted to DVR that week.

"You're going to do great things, Lee Lee," she'd tell me with her all-knowing look. "And I'm not pressurin' or anything, but I can't wait to see you as a mama."

On my worst days, I picture what life will be like when Gracie leaves home, and I am stuck in this cubicle with nothing to look forward to but the occasional phone call. Mama and Dan are already long gone in their own ways. Truthfully, Sarah's been gone for a while. And now it seems that Daddy's on his way out too. But when Gracie's gone, what will happen to me?

I click back into the secret tab, allowing myself a few minutes more. It's not like my mood can get much worse. I stare at the screen and try to remember what life with Dan used to be like.

"What'd I ever do to deserve a girl like you?" he'd ask me, kissing me slowly and softly. When I close my eyes and concentrate very hard, I can still feel his lips on mine. It seems insane to long for a man who did to me what Dan did, but I do, almost every night. Or maybe I long for how I used to feel when he was mine, back before Gracie, when Mama was still here and the world made sense.

♦ 7 ♦

Gracie

I DID IT! I got an exceeds expectations on my report card. It came in the mail tonight, and Mrs. Hoyt gave me an extra gold sticker because I read the most books of anyone in the class. Becky got the second most, she told me on the phone, but I don't think she was mad about losing. She never gets jealous. That's why she's my best friend.

Because I got an exceeds expectations on my report card, Mama says we can visit Grandfather in the home tomorrow, just like I planned. I'm so excited I can barely sleep. But I know I'll need my rest for tomorrow. I've already packed my backpack with my most important things—my favorite *Magic Tree House* books, my favorite purple sweater in case we go somewhere cold like Iceland, and three lollipops I stole from the bowl on Miss Susan's desk the last time I was in the home. I wanted to eat them really bad, but I saved them for our adventure. Normally I'm a good girl, but these days I'm a bandit, an outlaw, like John Wayne. Grandfather loves John Wayne and sometimes I watch his movies with him. John Wayne normally is a good guy, but he likes adventure, just like me and Grandfather. I wish we could ride horses like John Wayne on our adventure, but I haven't seen any horses around here, so the car seems like a better plan. I asked Mama if we could ride in Grandfather's old car tomorrow—that way, when he and I leave, she will still have her car.

Mrs. Hoyt says I have good attention to detail, and I think this is a good example of that.

The last thing I pack is my secret letter from Daddy. Grandfather is the only other person who has read my letter, and I know he never told Mama about it because then she'd want to read it. Grandfather's a really good secret keeper, that's why I know he'll like my plan.

I've written down my entire plan in my espionage notebook to leave for Mama—to help her understand. I even drew in a few pictures to help, in case Mama's imagination isn't as overactive as mine. I wish I'd had time to solve some of my other mysteries, but maybe Grandfather can help me with that when we're on our adventure.

Mama comes in to kiss me good night. She pulls up my covers to just under my chin and tucks them under my sides until I feel like I'm in a caterpillar's cocoon.

"You're so jumpy tonight," Mama says. "Like you're full of beans!"

I giggle. Mama is always saying crazy things like that. Grandfather too.

"I'm just excited to see Grandfather tomorrow," I tell her, hoping she doesn't figure out my plan.

She smiles a small smile and kisses the top of my head.

Mama is in a better mood than she was when she came to pick me up at Becky's house tonight. When she came in she was on the phone with Aunt Sarah and she was very upset. Becky's mama let her go talk to Aunt Sarah in the other room while we were coloring, but I heard some of it.

"I'm doing everything I can, Sarah," I heard Mama tell Aunt Sarah. Her voice was squeaky, and I could tell she was crying again. "I'm there every other day, but there is only so much I can do with Gracie and work."

Becky was coloring a giant blue whale in a giant blue ocean. I was jealous because Becky's very good at coloring and I'm not so good. I always go outside the lines by accident. She was using my second favorite crayon color, cerulean, but I let her because Becky is my best friend.

"What would you like me to do?" Mama asked and her voice sounded so small I had to strain to hear it. "You're never here. You've just left me to handle him on my own." There was a pause and Mama let out a rattly breath. "Yes, I got the money. That's not the point . . . Well, not all of us could marry lawyers, Sarah . . . Okay, I understand. I'll figure it out." I think Mama hung up the phone then because I heard her mumble, "Congratulations on your perfect frogging life."

Only Mama didn't say "frogging." But she told me to replace the bad word with that word in my memory anytime I heard it. I always try to listen to Mama. I wasn't sure if I should tell Becky to replace the word because she doesn't know our house rule, but she didn't seem to notice.

After bath time, I ask Mama about Aunt Sarah.

"Why doesn't she want to visit Grandfather?" I wonder aloud. "I love to visit Grandfather."

"I know you do, Gracie, and I love you for that," Mama tells me, smiling and squeezing my hand. "But sometimes fathers and daughters have different relationships than grandfathers and granddaughters. Grandfather is very sweet to you, but he wasn't always that way to me and Sarah."

"Why not?" I ask. "Were you bad?"

"No, baby," she says. "It's just a different relationship."

I don't ask any more questions about Aunt Sarah because I don't want Mama to cry again. But there is someone I do want to ask her about tonight. Before it's too late.

"Mama, how come I never talk to Daddy anymore?"

The question comes out small, like a whisper, but I know Mama hears me. Mama doesn't like it when I bring up Daddy, but this may be my last time to ask her before my adventure. And maybe I can solve one of my mysteries. Mama's face falls a bit, her smile turning down.

"Because Daddy went far away," she says.

"Why did he leave us behind?" I ask.

"Because your daddy was . . . confused about what he wanted," she replies, not looking into my eyes.

Suddenly I have a scary thought.

"Does Daddy have a worm in his brain like Grandfather?"

She pauses like she's thinking about it, but then says, "No, he doesn't, baby girl. Sometimes people make big mistakes, and your daddy made the biggest one of them all. Sometimes mamas and daddies are just people too."

I always thought mamas and daddies had learned all of their lessons and never made mistakes. It seems weird that Daddy has made such a big mistake even though I don't really know Daddy that well. But I do know Mama.

"I'm sorry, Mama," I say. "But I don't think you're just people."

"What does that mean, sweet pea?" she asks me, looking surprised.

"Maybe Daddy's just people, but you aren't."

Mama doesn't say anything else, and I think I see a tiny teardrop in the corner of her eye. I hope I didn't make her sad. Mama gets sad a lot these days. She squeezes my hand and turns off the light. I will probably have to count sheep to go to sleep tonight, or maybe I'll count evil worms. Tomorrow's the start of my adventure, and I have to be ready.

♦ 8 ♦

LeeAnn

I'M NOT ONE TO pray, but I say a silent one as I pull into a parking spot outside of the home. Gracie is practically levitating off of her seat with excitement. She couldn't even eat breakfast this morning. She's wearing her best dress with the daisies on the collar and keeps smoothing it out, as if she's heading to prom. It floors me that she'd ever want to come back here after last week. I know I don't. I've stopped by a few times, dropping off supplies for Daddy at the front desk with Susan, but never going back to his room. I could barely stand to be in the room with him before it happened, never mind after.

Big John was always in search of an audience. When I was little, I happily obliged, but the more I grew, the more I did my best to avoid him. I didn't want to be another faceless member of his congregation, my worth only measured in my reactions. Sometimes I wanted him to listen to *me*, to care about my stories, my life. But that never happened.

Sarah and I used to play a drinking game with our sodas every time he said, "Did I ever tell you the one about . . . ?"

I went through three cans in an hour once when he was on a particularly animated streak. He scaled the pyramids to help a distant princess retrieve her veil. He worked with the mechanics who serviced the clock face outside of Big Ben when it stopped turning one day. He saved an entire bus of elementary school kids from an icy death after the driver had had a seizure and crashed into a lake in January.

Daddy and his stories. I don't know which version of him I want to see now, the larger-than-life performer or the shriveled old man from last week who haunted my dreams.

I grab Gracie's backpack and hand it to her. It feels particularly heavy today. She must have had trouble deciding which book to read again. Though I rarely take a minute to appreciate my life, I can't stop glowing over how well she's doing in school. Despite Dan and Daddy and me, that little girl has managed to do such a good job that her teacher called me personally to rave. I could have sat on that phone call for hours but eventually Mike came out of his office and tapped his watch as if my phone time was putting the nail-biting fate of the lemon soaps up in the air yet again.

Gracie sprints through the lobby, giving Susan a wave and rushing down the hallway. I quicken my pace, flash Susan a sympathetic smile, and try to beat Gracie into the room. I'm not sure what to expect when we open the door, but I'm relieved to see Daddy sitting on the sofa, fully dressed and looking like his normal self. Well, as relieved as I ever am to be in my father's presence.

"Grandfather, Grandfather!" Gracie cries, rushing over to him and flinging her arms around his neck. Again, her lack of caution astounds me.

Dad coughs in surprise before lighting up.

"Why, Gracie Lynn, could that possibly be you?" he asks, not bothering to look over at me. I stand awkwardly in the doorway as if I need an invitation for their special moment.

"Yes, Grandfather, it's me!" she says. "I wanted to come sooner, but . . ."

"We've been really busy," I cut in, and Daddy's weathered, tan face falls slightly at the sight of me. "Sorry, Dad."

"Well, you're here now," he says, turning his attention back toward Gracie, his do-over daughter. "I was just thinking about you the other day because there was a program on about one of your favorite places."

I briefly wonder if my dad would have been able to name one of my "favorite places" growing up.

"Italy?" Gracie asks breathlessly as Daddy nods. "But I've never been there. I've never been anywhere."

I feel a slight pang of guilt, knowing my inadequate parenting and meager bank account are responsible for not giving my daughter any true life experiences. This mixes with my ever-present resentment toward my father for filling Gracie's head with these out-of-reach expectations.

"You haven't been there *yet*," Daddy says, and I shoot him a warning look that he ignores. He's always telling Gracie about his travels when he was in the army and convincing her that any day they'll be on a plane across the Atlantic. Somehow he always leaves out the part where he doesn't have a cent to his name because he spent my entire childhood wasting all of our money on his get-rich-quick schemes and "big picture" plans. He fails to mention the countless Saturdays Mama drove us from town to town, searching for yard sales and new thrift shops so she could afford clothes for us, pinching every penny while our father extravagantly tipped cashiers at fast food chains and the guys running the auto car wash place. It was all about appearances for Big John. If there was one thing he wouldn't stand for, it was someone calling him on his BS. I know this because I watched Sarah try several times.

I've begged him endlessly to stop bringing up international travel because it only leads to more and more questions from Gracie about when she'll get to go, but surprise, surprise, he keeps doing it. I would blame that on the worm too, but Daddy has *never* respected a boundary his daughters have set—worm or no worm.

"Can you tell me about Italy again, Grandfather?" she asks, eagerly plopping herself next to him on the worn leather couch that used to sit in our living room.

"Why, of course I can, m'lady," he replies, tipping his fake hat to her with a flourish. She grins and turns to face him, readying herself for his tale. I could literally dissolve into the floor and neither of them would notice.

"Did I ever tell you about the time I went to Florence at the personal invitation of the pope?" he begins.

Gracie shakes her head fervently. I don't even think she knows who the pope is. I'm also pretty sure the pope resides in Rome, but I've learned to hold my tongue when it comes to fact-checking these things.

"Well, Florence is a maze of red rooftops and cobblestone streets," he tells her, his gnarled hands gesturing passionately in the air like he's throwing pixie dust to create a shimmery image before her. "You get lost down one and find yourself in another world. The Duomo lies at its heart, like a beacon pulling lost travelers in with its beauty."

Gracie is rapt with attention, glued to him like he's broadcasting Saturday morning cartoons through his eyes.

Daddy moves his hands through the air, accentuating his points, like a conductor leading a soprano through a stunning aria. I literally cannot picture a time when he gave me even a fourth of this attention growing up. I was never as worthy an audience as Gracie.

"The walls of the Duomo aren't just boring whites and browns. They're made up of a beautiful pink and green marble, so the closer you get, the more breathtaking it is," he says. "And you can climb to the very top of the dome and look out over the city."

"Is it very high up, Grandfather?" Gracie asks, mesmerized.

"It's five hundred steps!" Daddy half shouts, flinging his arms up as Gracie jumps in surprise and wonder. "That old pope asked me to climb to the top because there was one stair that was extremely squeaky, and he knew I could put it right. Now, every step you take up, you get closer to the ceiling of the dome, which is covered in the most detailed mural—that's a painting—I've ever seen in my entire life."

His mustache moves up and down with excitement as he tells his story. I study it and the lines in his face like I always do when he talks.

"Did you fix the stair?" Gracie asks.

"'Course I did!" he answers, slapping his knee for effect. "When the pope asks a favor, you follow through. All it took was a few turns of my screwdriver and the thing popped right back into place like it was its sacred duty. Then I got to spend the rest of the weekend in Florence where the best of life is at your fingertips."

"What kind of foods do they eat in Italy?" Gracie asks, even though I know she knows.

"You name it—pizza, pasta, ice cream!" Daddy proclaims as her eyes get wide again.

"Those are all of my favorite foods!" she says with a slight bounce on the couch.

"In Italy the ice cream is called 'gel-ah-toe,'" Daddy pronounces, with an exaggerated accent. "And when you're living la dolce vita, it's a rule that you must have two gelatos a day."

"Mama says I only get one ice cream a week, and I normally save that for Sundays," she whispers conspiratorially. I'm the half-witted villain who's always ruining their superhero fun.

"Well, it's wise of you to save your one ice cream until the end of the week, but you won't have to in Italy," Dad says, again ignoring my warning glances.

"Mmmm, that sounds marvelous," she says, borrowing Big John's favorite word. Suddenly Gracie turns to me and asks, "Mama, I know I can't have ice cream, but could you maybe go to the kitchen and see if they have any hash browns left? The grumble in my tummy won't go away."

"Of course, sweet pea," I reply. Honestly, I'm relieved to have an excuse to leave the room. Even with my Gracie buffer, being near Daddy drains me. Without a second thought, I go out the door and down the hall.

9

Gracie

"GRANDFATHER?" I SAY QUICKLY and quietly because I don't know how far Mama has gone down the hall. The kitchen is on the other side of the home, but I know I still have to be fast.

Grandfather turns and tilts his head to listen. He can tell I have my espionage voice on.

"I just told Mama a necessary lie," I tell him.

"Oh, really?" Grandfather says, and he gives me a little grin. He has his mischievous voice on. Mischievous was a big word I asked Mama to look up from one of my chapter books. It means when you're being sneaky and secretive. Grandfather is an excellent secret keeper and therefore has a very good mischievous voice.

"Yes, but I had to," I say. "Remember the worm in your brain that I told you about?"

Grandfather's face gets angry, like I knew it would. I told Grandfather about the worm in his brain after he was sick for a few days and Mama wouldn't let me come visit him. That was after she got the mystery phone call about the blood. When we came to visit him, his wrist was wrapped up in a bandage, and I thought that maybe the worm had hurt him and that's why there was all that blood. I wasn't supposed to tell Grandfather about the worm, but I thought he had the right to know. The worm is in his brain, after all. But after I told him, Grandfather and Mama got into a big fight and they were shouting, which I could hear even though Mama made me go down the hall. And Grandfather said some bad words and so did Mama, and when she left, her eyes had black lines running down from them, so I know she had been crying. I feel bad bringing up the worm again, but it's important that Grandfather understands the plan.

"Now, Gracie, about that, I . . ."

"The worm is there," I say firmly. I know it is rude to interrupt, but I don't have time to not be rude. And I have rehearsed this in my head so many times. I have to finish. "He goes to sleep when the sun is up and he wakes up at nighttime, and he makes you confused."

I can't tell what Grandfather is thinking, but he doesn't say anything else, so I keep going.

"Mama told me that the Earth is a ball," I explain, getting more excited now because I've been waiting to tell him my plan for so long. I'm very proud of my plan. "The ball is constantly turning around the sun. So if you're traveling or on an adventure, you can be in a place where the sun is awake there when it's asleep here."

"That's true . . . ," Grandfather agrees slowly, but I can tell that he is confused. I thought he would understand my plan sooner. Grandfather has a great imagination just like me. The worm must be really messing with his brain.

"So we need to leave the home," I say. "We can finally go on an adventure. We'll chase the sun so that it will always be daytime and the worm will always be asleep."

I take a breath and try to see Grandfather's reaction. He seems to be understanding more. He doesn't have that little frown that he does when he's confused. But I don't know if he'll agree with my plan because he's not saying anything.

"I had Mama drive your old car here today," I tell him, hoping that if I give him more details he'll agree. "The keys are in her purse right there. Also she has twenty dollars in her purse, which she said is for emergencies. I think saving you from the worm is an emergency. And I have ten dollars from allowance money, which makes thirty dollars."

"That's very good math, Gracie Lynn," Grandfather says. I smile because I'm the worst at math, but I figured out that addition in my head. It's pretty easy addition. "But, sweetheart, I can't leave the home. Much as I'd like to go, I'm here for the rest of my days."

I really hate that he said that.

"No, Grandfather," I insist. "That's what they want you to believe, but I know better. Mama doesn't think we can get the worm out of your brain, but I know we can. We can trick the worm and you will get better."

Grandfather is shaking his head no. I don't like this. I thought he'd like my plan. I thought he'd want to get out of the home and get rid of the worm and get better. Tear bubbles form in my eyes, which makes me mad because I don't want Grandfather to think I'm a baby. No one wants to go on an adventure with a baby.

"Gracie, sweetheart, please don't cry," Grandfather tries to soothe me. "I love you for thinking of me and coming up with this idea, but I just can't do it."

Now my bottom lip is wobbling, and I'm worried I'm going to cry my loud tears.

"P—please don't give up, Grandfather," I beg him. I am keeping my voice very quiet so I don't let out a sob. "Everyone gives up. Daddy gave up, Mama gave up, and I need you not to give up."

It is silent in the room now. Mama would say "You could hear a pin drop," but I don't really know what that means because when a pen falls off Mrs. Hoyt's desk I can almost always hear it.

"Nobody's giving up, Gracie," Grandfather assures me, but his words don't match. His voice sounds defeated. Everyone around me always sounds defeated. I hate it. I have to do something. I have to make him understand why this is so important. So I decide to tell him. Mama told me not to, but I don't have any other choices. I have to tell Grandfather about "the incident."

"Grandfather," I say slowly, keeping my eyes away from his face. "The worm made you hit me."

I say this last bit very quietly because I'm afraid of what Grandfather will do. I hold my own hands and push the nails into my palms to distract myself from Grandfather.

After a minute he says, "What?"

His voice is very quiet too and scratchy, but it sounds very serious.

"Last Thursday when Mama and I came to see you, the worm was awake and it made you hit me," I tell him. "It happened right here." I point to the carpet in the spot where I fell. I haven't looked at that spot all morning.

Grandfather looks around as if he's searching for something.

"Thursday?" he asks, and for a moment I'm worried the worm is awake because he looks very confused. "I didn't see you Thursday. I haven't seen you for weeks."

I know we were there on Thursday of last week. I know because Mama picked me up at Becky's house after swimming practice, and my swimsuit was still wet. The sun was setting and Mama said we had to be quick, so I walked really fast into the home, so fast my flip-flops were slippy and I almost tripped.

Grandfather's room was dark when we got there, and I remember wishing Mama had turned on the light so things wouldn't be so spooky. He was slumped over in his wheelchair and I walked over to him to give him a quick goodnight kiss like Mama told me to. But when I called out to him, something hit me hard across my face and made me fall down. I didn't believe it was Grandfather at first, but then his nurse Miss Charity came in and turned on the light and I saw him try to hit her. It was a really scary night, but I was mostly scared for Grandfather.

"We came to see you, but you probably don't remember," I explain, trying not to sound too upset. I don't want Grandfather to feel bad. "Mama says the worm makes you forget. That's why we have to get you out of here and trick it into staying asleep."

"Oh God," Grandfather groans, and I'm very scared now because his voice is crackly like it was that night. I've never seen Grandfather cry before, but it looks like he's about to now. I'm scared and also I can't look away. "Gracie, I don't know what to say. I am so very sorry."

He puts his face in his big pizza pie–sized hands.

I feel bad that he seems so sad. The hit didn't hurt that much. It just scared me, and it really upset Mama. But I only feel bad for Grandfather. It's like he gets this blindfold over his eyes, and he's no longer himself. That is scarier than anything that's ever happened to me. And I went to a really spooky haunted house once.

"Grandfather, that's why we have to go," I tell him, trying to be patient. "We have to trick the worm. We have to go on an adventure. Otherwise, it might be too late."

Grandfather's shoulders slump; he looks like a round raisin with all of his wrinkles and frown lines. I remember his face the night of the incident. It was completely blank—not a trace of Grandfather in sight. The worm made Grandfather disappear while he was sitting right here. We have to stop it.

I don't want to be rude, but I don't want Mama to come back before he decides.

"Will you please do this for me?" I ask again.

Grandfather looks at me and his face is filled with sadness. He never looks at me with sadness. It's making me uncomfortable. But at least I know that's him in there.

"Gracie, we can do whatever you want," he says.

10

LeeAnn

I STUDY A PAINTING in the hall of two men playing jazz. This one happens to be my favorite in the home, mostly because it's the only one that's not of a country landscape but also because Mama used to play jazz when she was in a good mood.

"Beauty lies in chaos, Lee Lee," she'd tell me.

Finding beauty in my current chaos is hard, but perhaps it's time to start appreciating the little things, like having a moment to myself. It's been a while since that's happened. At home I'm tidying up or making sure Gracie's okay, at *the* home I'm tiptoeing on eggshells around Daddy, at work I'm counting down the minutes and avoiding Mike's pointed stares, and in the car I'm making endless lists in my head of things to do.

But Daddy seemed back to his normal Gracie-loving, storytelling self, perfectly lucid and without even a whiff of the monster he seemed to be last week. Plus, the two of them are so content without me there. So I'm going to stand here and stare at this painting for a minute. And if it helps me avoid time with Big John, all the more reason. The brushstrokes seem as loose and as free as the jazz music I grew up listening to. The colors blend together, going far outside the lines of the artist's original concept. It would be nice to step outside the lines sometime. It feels like the lines have surrounded me my entire life. *Wouldn't it feel great to smear some paint?*

Daddy brought home a painting once. I was about Gracie's age, and he walked in the front door with a big smile on his face. His mustache tipped up so much it almost curled.

"Whatcha got there, John?" Mama asked him. Her face lit up like the angel on top of the Christmas tree, every ounce of her enthusiasm genuine. The image is seared in my mind.

"This is an original Walter Max," Daddy said, holding up the painting for us to examine. We all crowded around it, Sarah included, and it's one of the few times I can remember her willingly listening to him with any kind of attention. It was one of the most normal family moments of my childhood.

"I met this guy in the army training camp," Daddy said. "He was recruited with me, and he was the artsy type. Used to draw little scenes on the assignment sheets for the day. We'd gather around each morning to see what he'd come up with. Bit of a bright spot for all of us, truth be told. I'd heard a fire broke out at the munitions depot on his base and there were more casualties than we ever saw in combat, but I never could find a list of the dead. I didn't know if he made it or not, but this painting was made seven years ago, so he musta got out!"

"Oh, John, how wonderful," Mama said. Daddy didn't talk about his time in the army much, apart from describing the places he'd visited. There was always some outlandish detail that alerted you to the fact that you were dealing more

with fiction than truth. He never mentioned any army buddies or anyone getting hurt. I had always thought of his
army days as one endless plane ticket from country to country, wild story after wild story. I never thought of him as
being in combat or losing a friend. It was more like he was
on an all-expenses-paid vacation around the world. One I'd
never get to experience myself.

I remember the painting looked alive. The brushstrokes
were so three-dimensional that I could see them coming off
the canvas. It was a seascape painting, and it was the first
time I felt I'd really seen the ocean, not like in a movie or a
photo, but truly *felt* the waves that had never, in reality,
touched my skin. I'd always been more familiar with rivers,
having one practically in my backyard that served as Daddy's
second home and my unwanted hangout. But seeing that
painting, I knew I needed to be by the sea.

It was nothing like the painting in the hall of the home,
which in reality is just a print. Now I have to close my eyes
to picture the original Walter Max. Daddy sold it when I
was a teenager after he lost his job selling dictionaries and
his plans for a local museum dedicated to a lesser-known
Revolutionary War battle inevitably failed. I watched it
leave the house with tears in my eyes—one of the few happy
memories of my father going with it.

I wonder what childhood memories Gracie will have
when she's my age. I hope they'll be everything mine were
not. That she will hold onto the sweet moments like her
swim meets and her Grandfather's praise. Not the other
stuff.

I'd better get those hash browns for her. Lord knows
once my daughter gets an idea in her head, it's impossible to
get out.

♦ 11 ♦

Gracie

GRANDFATHER SAYS WE HAVE to be sneaky to get out of the home. He takes the emergency $20, grabs one of his combs, and takes out a long, thin tube from his closet. I don't know what the tube is for, but if Grandfather thinks we'll need it, then I trust him.

He also calls Mama's cell phone, which she left in the room, and leaves her a message. I'm not sure it's such a good idea, but he insists. He says I'm Mama's whole world, and it would be mean to let her think that something bad had happened to me. He's probably right, but I want lots of time for us to follow the sun, and if he gives her too many details she might stop us. Plus, I don't want to get in trouble for being the one to come up with the plan. Grandfather promises me that I won't be in trouble.

"I'll take the heat, Gracie Lynn," he says, giving me a wink, even though I'm not sure what that means. "Been in hot water all my life."

I've officially decided to leave my notebook for Mama to find so she can put the clues together and understand why we had to leave. I think it's nice of me because I love writing in my notebook, and I'll be sad to leave it. But I love Mama more.

I've never seen Grandfather so excited. It feels like there's a buzz in the room, like he is humming with happiness. It has been a very long time since he went on an adventure. There is pink in his cheeks, and he keeps patting his hair down in the mirror.

"Okay, Gracie Lynn," he says like he's out of breath. "You ready? You think we can pull this off?"

I nod and smile, handing Grandfather the car keys and looking around the room one last time to make sure I'm not forgetting anything. I want to take Brown Bear, but Mama might need him in case she misses me when I'm gone, so I leave him on the couch next to my notebook.

"Here's what we're gonna do, Gracie," Grandfather declares, moving his hands around wildly. "You're going to go sit in the armchairs by the front desk like you do sometimes. I'm going to follow you, but I'll stay out of sight down the hallway. When you see Susan leave her desk, whistle and I'll come running."

"But Grandfather, I don't know how to whistle," I tell him, suddenly worried. "It just comes out in spits."

Grandfather looks shocked. "I never taught you how ta whistle? Well, I am so sorry, Gracie Lynn, that is bad grandparenting!"

I feel like the whole plan is ruined, but Grandfather still has his mischievous voice on, so maybe it's not so bad.

"How about you cry 'caw-caw' like a raven?" he asks.

I have never seen a real raven, but I think that I can caw-caw like one. I practice it and Grandfather says I've done a good job, but to not make it too loud or it might make Miss

Susan suspicious and then she'd come back to the front desk. He puts his comb, the emergency $20, and the car keys in his pockets, fumbling to fit them all inside. And he tucks the tube under his right arm.

"Contraband," he says, patting the tube and grinning. I don't know what that means, but it sounds fun.

As we leave the room, Grandfather does not look back once.

I can't stop jiggling my leg while I'm sitting in the armchair next to the front desk. I want Miss Susan to get up and go do something so badly, but I can't tell her this, so I just have to sit patiently and hope that Mama doesn't come back and see me.

"Would you like a sucker?" Miss Susan asks. Miss Susan calls lollipops suckers. She doesn't know that I have a lot of her lollipops in my backpack, so I take one to keep her from getting suspicious.

"How's your grandfather doing today?" she asks, and suddenly I'm scared that she knows my plan.

"He's very well, thank you," I reply carefully in my most polite voice. Polite people aren't as suspicious.

"You know that he didn't mean to hit you the other day, right, Miss Gracie?" Miss Susan asks, looking very seriously into my eyes.

Miss Susan always calls me Miss Gracie, even though I told her she can just call me Gracie. It makes me feel more grown up. But I don't want to talk about the night that Grandfather confused hit me. I don't want to be distracted from the plan. But I also don't want Miss Susan to think I'm rude or up to something.

"Yes, ma'am, I know," I say, looking away. "He's better now."

"You're a very brave girl for coming back here and so sweet wanting to see your grandfather," she says.

Even though I'm very focused on the plan, this makes me mad.

"He wants to see me too," I protest, feeling my eyebrows making a frown. "I don't know why everyone says I'm so sweet for visiting Grandfather. He is the most interesting person I know."

Miss Susan looks surprised, but it's annoying how everyone is telling me I'm so great for spending time with Grandfather. It doesn't make sense. Just because Grandfather has a worm in his brain and lives in the home doesn't mean that he's not an interesting person that I'd like to visit.

"You know what, Miss Gracie," Miss Susan says kindly. "You're absolutely right. It makes sense that you'd want to see your grandfather. I wish more granddaughters felt that way."

"Thank you, Miss Susan," I mumble quietly, because now I'm a little shy after getting upset.

She smiles at me and then stands up. My heart shoots up in my throat, and I look away so Miss Susan doesn't know that I'm about to jump off my seat and caw-caw down the hall.

"I'm going to go speak to the nurse on call in B wing, will you be okay here by yourself, Miss Gracie?" she asks.

"Yes, ma'am," I say, and my voice sounds a little trembly. Thankfully, I don't think Miss Susan notices, and instead she picks up some papers and goes down the hall. I count to five the way Grandfather told me to and then I caw-caw quietly down the hall. I see Grandfather's head pop out from around the corner, and suddenly I'm very excited and very scared all at once. My tummy feels like there are fifty frogs jumping up and down inside it, which doesn't really feel that great.

He walks as fast as he can, which is not that fast since he insisted on leaving behind his cane, which is a big stick that sometimes helps him walk. When he reaches the front desk, Grandfather rummages in his pockets and grabs the keys to the old Chevy. We walk through the front doors and Grandfather lets out a "whoop!" I'm afraid that someone will hear and come running, but I can tell that Grandfather has been waiting to go on an adventure for a long time, so I let him whoop.

The Chevy is parked in the far right corner of the parking lot under a giant weeping willow tree. I think weeping willow trees are very beautiful, but it makes me sad to think that the tree is named after someone crying. I try not to think about it as Grandfather opens the front door of the Chevy for me. Normally I have to sit in the back seat because Mama says it's safer, but Grandfather is older, so I think he knows more. And maybe I'm old enough to sit in the front seat because I'm almost seven now.

After I get inside, Grandfather eases himself into the driver's seat very slowly and lets out a "harrumph" when he finally sits down. I don't know why he can't just sit down normally. His shaking hands place the keys into the car and twist. The Chevy bursts to life, humming and grumbling with the same jittery excitement I feel now.

"Alright, Gracie Lynn, you ready?" he asks. Mama always checks to make sure I have my seat belt on, but Grandfather doesn't ask. I guess he thinks I'm old enough and that bandits don't have to check other bandits' seat belts for them. I put it on anyway because I know Mama would want me to. Grandfather doesn't put his on, but I don't want to correct him because that would be rude.

"I'm ready, Grandfather," I reply. But I don't know if that is true. He pops down the stick in between us that I'm always too afraid to touch, and the Chevy screeches out of the parking lot.

LeeAnn

AN ANCIENT WOMAN WITH '50s-style kitten glasses that turn up at the end shuffles her walker near me. She has a cardigan wrapped around her shoulders with the top button clasped across her collarbone. I've noticed her here before, mostly because she looks like an older version of Mama.

"Betty?" The woman looks at me like she recognizes me too, but clearly she's confused.

"No, ma'am, I'm sorry," I say. "I'm not Betty."

"Well, I know that," she replies. "I'm not loopy."

I laugh. It comes out creaky and unsteady, like a water spigot you have to force on after months of disuse.

"I've been looking for Betty," the woman says. "Do you know where she is?"

"Is Betty a nurse?" I ask.

"No, she's my daughter."

"No, I'm sorry," I say. "I haven't seen a Betty."

"Not your fault, darlin'," she brushes away my apology. "No one else seems to know either. Would you like to sit and have a cup of coffee with me?"

"Oh, I'm sorry," I say. "My daughter is upstairs with my father, and I need to get her some breakfast. Some other time?"

"Of course," the woman replies, ignoring my excuses. "I'm Doris, by the way. Doris Day."

"Nice to meet you," I reply, extending my hand and knowing that can't be her real name. "I'm LeeAnn."

Her icicle fingers send a shiver up my arm, even as a bead of sweat forms on my upper lip from the enveloping humidity.

"If you see Betty, can you tell her that her mama's lookin' for her?" she asks, and I politely nod. I gently drop her hand, avoid her intense gaze, and head toward the kitchen.

The gritty truth of humanity sits unapologetic within these walls. The décor is reminiscent of a gaudy parlor in a saloon from a movie western. The stained seat cushions cause a wave of nausea to wash over me. There are a handful of residents sitting at tables, drinking weak coffee and staring into space. They look like me at the office.

The air smells faintly of piss, and you can feel the resignation smothering you from all sides. This is where people come to die. This is where the journey ends.

I've wasted enough time down here. I have to get back to Gracie with her hash browns even if it means facing Daddy and his eternal disappointment. I squirt some ketchup on the plate because I know Gracie won't eat the fried patties without it, and head back upstairs.

"Everything okay in there, LeeAnn?" Susan stops me as I pass the front desk.

"Yeah, things seem much better today," I tell her.

"Oh good, I was a little worried when I saw Gracie earlier," she says. "I didn't know if he was in a mood or something."

That was a weird way to phrase it. But I'm sure Susan's just being a good friend. It's a relief to have people like that looking out for you. I smile at her, hold up the plate of hash browns as an explanation, and roll my eyes in faux annoyance as I head back toward Daddy's room.

The monotony of my walk down the hall is almost as dull as updating my inventory spreadsheets at work—one turn left at the bingo room, one turn right at the generic watercolor of a vase of flowers, the same route I've taken every other day for the last two years.

I take a calming breath before entering, readying myself for another disapproving look or comment. My sandals scuff against scratchy gray carpet that covers his floor as the door swings open, gently hitting the back wall.

Stillness surrounds me.

My first instinct is not fear but confusion. Dad's wheelchair is sitting in the middle of the floor with the brakes off, and Gracie's notebook is open on the sofa next to her teddy bear. It feels like they just stepped out. I can sense their presence, can practically see their outlines, but they aren't visible. They're just out of my reach. For one thrilling second I wonder if they've gone on a *Magic Tree House* adventure through time the way Gracie has always wanted, but then I snap back to reality. I peek into Daddy's bedroom and see his untouched bed, the sheets pulled stiffly up with military-style corners. I check the bathroom and find it empty. It feels like they're playing a joke on me.

Come out, come out, wherever you are!

There are only so many places they can be. It's not like this room is a suite at the Ritz. They could have gone down the hall to the reading room or maybe somehow I missed them on my way back from the kitchens. But Daddy never wants to the leave this room—at least, not when I ask him. I feel like a moron, unable to comprehend their obvious joke.

I absent-mindedly set the plate of microwaved hash browns down on the bed—an act I'd never allow Gracie to do—and pace around the room. The air around me is dry and filled with dust. I've always hated being inside the tomb-like darkness that fills Daddy's room. But whenever I suggest we go outside for a walk, he brushes me off with some disparaging comment. The black-and-white photographs on the wall bleed into a muted gray. I'm about to head back down the hall when my phone lights up with a text from Linda.

Do you remember the SKU number for Rainforest shower nozzles?

I can't believe he made her work on a Sunday after I had to come in on Saturday. I almost laugh, picturing her nodding obediently to Mike while secretly rolling her eyes behind his back. I'm on the verge of writing her back, when I see the notification underneath her text. One I'd missed when I was out of the room. It's a voicemail.

I know that number. It's the only other phone in this room. I don't want to check it. I don't want to hear whatever it says because that means I'll no longer be living in the time before I listened to the message and knew something was wrong. I stand there, rooted to the spot and shaking like a leaf, willing myself not to panic just yet.

Finally, I sit down right next to the hash browns, almost squashing them in the process, and press the button to listen to the message.

◆ 13 ◆

LeeAnn

IT'S SILENT FOR A few seconds and my entire body leans forward, trying to hear any signs of Gracie. But it's Daddy's voice that comes through, hushed and urgent.

"Hey, Lee," he starts, and already I'm on edge because he seldom uses my nickname.

"I know this is gonna seem harebrained and irresponsible to you, but I had to go." Once again I force my eardrums to pick up any sign of Gracie. I don't care where he's gone; I only care about where she is.

"Gracie has this silly scheme that she thinks is gonna help me. And after she told me what I did to her, I wasn't really in the mood to argue. I'd rather be dead than stay here and hurt the people who love me. Being in here is killing me faster than being out there will. I promise you that."

His voice is steadying, like he's trying to comfort me into accepting his death. He clearly doesn't understand that I don't need that acceptance, haven't needed it for a long time. He was never the parent whose death mattered.

"Look, I know things have been complicated with us," he adds.

And for the first time I'm really listening to him, surprised by his candor and his sudden understanding. I don't see the man at the podium. I see the one hunched over in the wheelchair.

"I guess I didn't know how to be a father to you," he says, and I'm stunned. "But when Martha died and Gracie was born, I did my best to be a grandfather to her. That part wasn't hard. Now I just need this one last day with her, outside of this place, to say goodbye."

Goodbye. The word sends fresh waves of panic through me.

"You deserve more than this message. You deserve more than me, but that's all I can give you now. Goodbye, Lee-Ann. Take care of our girl."

His gravelly voice goes dead, and I think I hear Gracie call out just as he hangs up the phone. I play the message two more times. The words don't really register more than they did the first time.

He's taken Gracie. They took the car. He's saying goodbye. A man with dementia who can barely button his own pants has my daughter—my world—and he's driving her around in an old pile of junk. This man is my father. But that title means less to me than it does to most.

I want to scream, to vomit, to do something, but I feel paralyzed, frozen in time. Instead, I sit down on the sofa and Gracie's notebook slides over, tapping my side. I pick it up, this journal she's had glued to her hand for weeks. It's covered in stickers and doodles. They mock me with their cheerfulness. I flip it open to the last page. Her giant sloppy letters unevenly fill the page.

The werld is a ball, it goes arownd the son. Grandfather's werm stays awake win the son is out. We will chace the son.

Now I really do feel sick. I'm the one who told her the Earth is round. I'm the one who told her about the worm. And I am the reason my daughter is currently at risk of God knows what.

As the terror begins to well up inside me, Charity walks in for her inspection. She looks perplexed as she surveys the room, looking for Daddy and seeing my dismay.

"Charity," I manage to croak. "You need to call someone right now."

◆ 14 ◆

Gracie

"I KNOW WE'RE MEANT to be heading on an adventure, but would you mind if we stopped by the house first?" Grandfather asks me. "I've been dreaming of it for months."

We're rumbling down the road in the old Chevy, and my seat is bouncing up and down. The sunshine is bright yellow. Maybe the worm is allergic to yellow and that's why he stays away when the sun is shining. After this adventure, I will always keep my backpack on me and only wear bright yellow from now on. Well, maybe a little purple too.

Grandfather said we should take the back road so that the police won't catch us, but I think he really just wants to drive on the dirt. He looks so happy, holding onto the steering wheel as we hit the holes in the road. Mama calls those "potholes," but I don't understand that phrase because I've never seen a hole in a pot and there are no pots in the holes on the road. He keeps turning around in his seat and looking behind us for "the fuzz," which makes us hit even more holes in the road.

"I'd like that, Grandfather," I reply. "I've been wanting to show you the garden where I'm growing flowers."

"It's settled then!"

Maybe this sounds weird, but the Grandfather I'm looking at now is the Grandfather I always see in my mind when Mama talks about him or when I think about him. He's the same person as the Grandfather in the home, but he looks very different. The Grandfather I see in my mind and the Grandfather in the car with me now has skin that has seen the sun. He's always excited and ready to try a new adventure. He's not old, even though he has gray hairs, and he's joyful.

I like that word, *joyful*. I feel joyful when I'm swimming the butterfly or when I get a new *Magic Tree House* book. I think that people can be alive but not joyful, and if you're not joyful while you're alive, what's the point? That's why I hate to miss my visits with Grandfather because I know that deep down there's that joyful person and I want to find him again.

Grandfather's whistling to a song on the radio that I don't know. Maybe he'll teach me to whistle today. I look at his face, and I know my plan was a good idea. Grandfather needed this and I needed Grandfather. And I think Mama needed a break.

"These are my freesias." I point, showing Grandfather the purple flowers. "They're my favorites."

When we got to the house, I immediately dragged Grandfather to the backyard where my garden is. I know he wants to see the rest of the house, but I've been waiting to show him my garden for so long that I couldn't wait one more second.

"They're beautiful, baby girl," he tells me, and I see him study the flowers carefully. I'm glad Grandfather is taking my garden so seriously. I have spent a lot of time on it. Mama has helped, but she says I've done the majority of the work, so I should take the credit.

"And over here are the cornflowers," I explain. "I don't know why they're called cornflowers since they're purple and not yellow like corn, but that's their name."

"So all of your flowers are purple?" Grandfather questions me after surveying the whole patch.

"Yes!" I exclaim. I'm happy Grandfather has noticed. I spent a lot of time finding the best purple flowers. "Purple is my favorite color, so I wanted an all-purple garden, except for the daisies, which Mama says are basically weeds. It's my own little corner," I add, smiling.

I learned about "my own little corner" from the Cinderella movie that Mama showed me once. It was not a cartoon movie, and Mama said it was very old and "out of date." I thought it was a little strange because the girl who played Cinderella had brown hair like me but she is supposed to have blonde hair. Cinderella always has blonde hair, except in this out of date movie. Maybe that's what out of date means, when the main character has a different color hair.

But in the old movie Cinderella sings a song called "In My Own Little Corner," and it's all about how she has a hard life because her stepmother makes her clean the house a lot and her stepsisters are mean and don't share their dresses with her. But even though she has a hard life, she still has her own little corner where she goes to daydream and use her "overactive imagination," as Mrs. Hoyt would say.

When Cinderella's in her own little corner, she imagines that she's whatever she wants to be and she's never alone. I like that song. Sometimes when I feel alone, I come to the garden and I imagine all sorts of things. I'm so glad that

Grandfather likes my garden. I bet Jack and Annie from the *Magic Tree House* books would like it too, even though they're not real people.

"Well, you've done a beautiful job, Gracie," he says.

I know Grandfather's not necessary lying because my garden really is beautiful. I feel so proud, and I'm very happy he got to see it. I want Grandfather to know I'm taking good care of his house so he won't worry.

"Did I ever tell you about the time I grew a squash that was bigger than a baby?" Grandfather asks me, and I shake my head. I'm excited because I haven't heard this one before, and I love Grandfather's stories.

"When I was a boy, we had this neighbor named Mrs. Wilkins who was always having babies," he says, reaching up to shade his eyes and stare at me, the thrill of the story dancing across his face. "By the time I was your age, she had twelve babies and was pregnant with another one."

"That's a lot of babies," I say, because it is. I don't think I've ever even seen twelve babies together at once.

"It sure is," Grandfather agreed. "And the crazy thing about these babies is that when they came out, they were already really strong. Most of them were sitting up by one week and walking by one month. So our neighborhood was overrun with their little legs, stomping through yards and the fields. Mrs. Wilkins's babies would crush everything I tried to plant that year—carrots and corn and cucumbers—all destroyed. My mama had her heart set on cooking up a squash soup she made every fall, but she thought there was no chance because of Mrs. Wilkins's babies. So I decided to do something about it. I gathered some trellises and built a border around the squash patch so that Mrs. Wilkins's babies couldn't get in there. I built it so high that I had to use a ladder to reach the top."

Grandfather puts one hand on his lower back and points up in the air with the other hand, unfurling the curve of his spine. He arched backward, reaching up, and I can picture that squash growing its vines up to the sky like Jack's beanstalk.

"I tended to that patch every day and guarded it every night because sometimes Mrs. Wilkins's babies would sneak out of their cribs and come searching for food to eat. And because I did, the squash grew and grew. Until one day I decided that the next morning I would harvest the squash for Martha's soup."

"Was Martha your mama's name?" I ask him.

"No?" he replies, looking confused. I feel bad because the question caught him off guard and stopped the story. I know Grandfather doesn't like it when his stories are interrupted.

I stay quiet, and Grandfather's face relaxes again, and he keeps telling his story.

"So I'm standing guard at the squash patch, but I fall asleep this time," he continues. "And when I wake up, I see Mrs. Wilkins standing on my ladder looking down into the squash patch below."

"What did you say?" I ask him, reaching up to shade my own eyes so I can see Grandfather better.

"I didn't say a word," he tells me, his tone hushed. "I pretended to be asleep and stayed quiet watching her. Then she reached into the pocket of her housecoat and pulled out some glittery powder I'd never seen before. She lifted her arm over the top of the trellises and sprinkled the powder down into the squash patch. I squeezed my eyes closed, leaving just a thin sliver open until I could barely see her. But I saw her climb down the ladder and rush home. I fell back asleep and when I woke up and moved the trellises aside, I saw the most massive squash I'd ever seen in my life. One of Mrs. Wilkins's babies came over and walked right up to that squash and kicked it, and it was so big that it didn't even budge. It towered over that baby. You see, Mrs. Wilkins had always been good at growing things—babies mostly—so it made sense that she could help grow squash too."

"What was the special powder she sprinkled?" I ask.

"Exactly what I wondered!" Grandfather answers, putting a finger to his nose. "I went back and searched the squash patch, but I saw no sign of it. Almost like it had vanished into thin air. And when I tried to ask Mrs. Wilkins about it, she acted like she had no idea what I was talking about. But I know what I saw that night and what came next. That squash was so big that Lee made her soup for a month."

"Mama did?" I ask, confused again.

"Yes, my mama did," Grandfather says firmly as if I'm being silly. I start to try to ask him again, but I decide not to. It's getting very hot out here in the yard, and I don't want to make Grandfather too tired. He slowly walks up to the screened-in back porch, and I help him over the step up because he's shaking a little. He leans on me, and my knees buckle a little bit as I try to get him inside. I wish we'd brought his wheelchair for him to sit in or his cane to help him walk when he gets tired. It's the first detail I have forgotten.

We walk into the kitchen, and Grandfather looks around. I don't think we've changed much, except some of my drawings are on the fridge. But Grandfather doesn't say anything about those, which makes me kind of sad. But I already bragged about my garden, so I don't say anything. He shuffles

over to the countertop and leans his elbows against it, looking out the window. I don't like silence, but I try not to say
anything because I can tell Grandfather is daydreaming, just
like Cinderella. I know he does not have his blindfold on
because he is smiling, even if it looks like a sad smile. Finally,
I can't hold it in anymore, and I have to say something.

"What are you thinking about, Grandfather?" I blurt
out.

"Oh, you know, moments from a past life," he says as he
reaches out to touch the yellow curtain.

That confuses me because I didn't know Grandfather
had a past life.

"Are they good moments?" I ask.

"The best." Grandfather nods. "But I didn't always
appreciate them at the time. I wish I had now."

"How do you know you are having a good moment you
should appreciate?" I ask.

Grandfather grins. "Well now, that's the question, ain't
it?"

"Maybe *this* is a good moment we should be appreciating," I say.

"You know what, Gracie Lynn, I bet you're right,"
Grandfather agrees. "How 'bout we make some sweet tea
real quick before we hit the road?"

I smile. I love Grandfather's sweet tea.

♦ 15 ♦

LeeAnn

I STUMBLE DOWN THE hallway in a haze, like a drunk trying to cling to something stable. Thank God there are hand-rails. The pale yellow walls in this place sicken me. It looks like a dog has lifted its leg and relieved itself in this dank corner of the world. If I weren't in such a blind panic right now and didn't resent my father for his role, or lack thereof, in my life, I might feel sorry for him being in here. Human beings aren't supposed to be in places like this.

Charity rushed away somewhere, hopefully to get help, and I was able to drag myself to the front desk. Susan isn't behind it, though I just saw her here a minute ago. Or was it an hour? *How much time has passed?*

I try to slam my hand on the bell, but it just makes a soft clang that barely reaches past my own ears. I slap it again, this time with more force. It makes a bang like I've dropped a boiling pot. *Why is no one here?*

My gaze unblurs slightly as I look out the front doors and see the spot where I parked Daddy's old Chevy is empty. Gracie was the one who asked if we could bring it. She said she liked the way it smelled. I feel a pang of betrayal, knowing she did this on purpose. She kept secrets from me . . . for him. Gracie normally tells me everything. *Doesn't she?*

"Lee?"

Susan's walking back toward the desk. Her habitual smile falters slightly when she sees my face. I must look like a mental patient.

"He took Gracie," I whisper, willing my voice to convey urgency.

"What'd you say, darling?" she asks quietly, like she's appeasing a toddler.

"My father took Gracie and the car," I moan. "They're gone."

Susan looks much more alert now. She whips her head around, as if double-checking my facts. Like I would make this up. Then she rushes behind the desk and picks up the intercom phone.

"Andrew to the front, Andrew to the front, we have a code blue."

The announcement reverberates through the home's speakers and jolts a new wave of nerves through me. This is serious. This is happening.

A portly man with a mustache as thick and gray as Daddy's comes jogging over to the desk, raising his eyebrow to Susan.

"Charity just told me what's up," he says. "Details?"

"John Abernathy, room 158," she tells him. "Has his little granddaughter Gracie with him. They are in his car. It's a . . ."

She looks to me for clarification, but my mind is an empty wasteland. I'm still trying to understand how all of this could have happened.

After what feels like another decade, I blurt, "It's a brown '85 Chevy Impala."

Andrew smiles at me as if to say, *Good job, darlin', you did it!* and rushes outside to the home's van. I watch him hop in the front seat and pull out of the lot.

"Wait," I abruptly call out, and Susan turns to me alarmed. "That's it? Shouldn't we phone the police? Shouldn't I have gone with him? What am I doing?"

I know my voice is reaching a level of hysteria that's not socially acceptable, but I can't help it. This all feels wrong. How can some random man in a van find my manipulative, scheming, fantastical father and my brainy daughter without any information other than the car they're driving in?

"Lee, sweetie, they probably haven't gotten very far," Susan says, once again trying to lull me into calm with her silky voice. "They've probably just gone for ice cream or something. And technically that's not against the home's policy. He's allowed to leave with his family. He even has a valid driver's license if I remember correctly."

I feel another wave of shame at my error in judgment. Daddy had pleaded with me to let him keep his license.

"I'm not gonna use it, Lee," he had insisted. "I just like having it. Makes me feel like a man."

Yeah, you're a big, strong man, asshole.

"But, Susan, you know he's not stable," I continue, practically pleading with her now. "What if he has another episode in the car? What if they crash?"

Susan looks appropriately concerned, but I'm not encouraged by the way she remains seated in her chair.

"You gotta trust the system, sweetie," she says. "We'll find him."

I don't give a shit if you find him. Find HER.

I shove myself away from the desk. I don't know where I'm going, but I have to do something. Gone are any manners or respect Mama tried to instill in me, because if Susan's not going to help me, then I'm not going to waste any more of my time here.

I stomp down the Lysol-scented halls of the B wing, trying to think of someone who will drive me around town to search for my daughter. Linda's still under Mike's tyrannical orders for the next few hours. That severely limits my options. I don't want to call Paula and tell her I have lost my daughter. She already has to watch Gracie all the time, now she'll never let me return the favor and watch Becky.

It's time to phone one of the last people I'd ever want to ask for help. But desperate times call for even the most desperate of measures. I take two deep breaths before dialing her number. The rings echo in my rattled brain.

"What is it, LeeAnn? I'm getting started on lunch."

Hello to you too, sis.

"Sarah." My voice comes out choked and hollow at the same time. I wish this was the Sarah I played Barbies with and who taught me how to drive, not the grown-up Sarah who only talks about money and who looks down on me for staying in Reading.

"What's wrong? Is it Dad?" she asks with the smallest whisper of something resembling concern.

"He's taken my little girl," I cry, and the sob grows in my throat, finally coming out.

"What?" she asks, measurably more alert now. "Who's taken Gracie? What is happening? Is it Dan?"

"Daddy has taken Gracie," I tell her, not able to form the words to properly explain myself.

"Oh," she replies, now sounding significantly less concerned. I wish I could just tell her that I need her to feel the same terror I feel. I need someone to take this seriously. But I didn't tell her that Daddy hit Gracie, and I couched his hospital visit as an accident, trying to make it seem less serious. She, like Susan, thinks this isn't that big of a deal.

"Well, where'd they go?" she asks in a bored tone that implies that I'm a moron who lost her car keys. "Why didn't you go with them?"

"G—Gracie asked me to get her hash browns, and when I came back to the room, she was gone," I blubber, leaving out the part where I took my sweet time because I would rather stare at a painting in a hallway and have idle chitchat with a confused geriatric than be around our father.

"Wait, so he just walked out of the home?" she asks, confused. "Is he even allowed to do that?"

"I don't know," I tell her. "Susan sent out a man in a van to search for them, but, Sarah, I'm really scared. Daddy's been getting worse and worse."

"I'm sure it's fine," she says, the tone in her voice returning to normal, the threat gone. "It's Big John. He goes where he wants, and he's always running late. Don't freak out."

"Sarah," I plead, trying to find a way to convey the urgency of the situation.

"LeeAnn, seriously, I don't have time for this," she replies, exasperated. "You give Daddy way too much of your time. Plus, I promised Phil I'd get to work on packing for our golfing trip this weekend and the kids haven't even—"

"Daddy tried to kill himself two weeks ago. That's why he was in the hospital," I cut through her monologue of excuses. "He says it was an accident, but nobody believes him. And last week, he smacked Gracie."

It's strange to hear those words come out of my mouth. I hadn't said them aloud yet. Charity had been in the room when it happened and reported the incident so I didn't have to. With the darkness that was wrapped around us at the time, I barely knew if it was true myself. Daddy is hot tempered, but never physically violent, especially not with Gracie.

"What?" Her voice is razor sharp. Finally, I've struck a nerve.

"We came by the home too late one night, and he was having an episode, and he smacked Gracie so hard that she fell to the floor," I say, trying to sound believable, because right now it feels like I'm almost making it up. "And two weeks ago, he sliced his wrist open with a pocket knife, and they found him bleeding out on the floor."

I look at the carpet that runs through the home, picturing my daughter strewn across it, her sprawling outline stiff with surprise, then I picture the blood stain I know they've covered with another rug.

"Oh my God," Sarah murmurs, and the concern in her voice sounds sincere.

"It's been getting worse and worse for months, Sarah," I say, the words spilling out. "I've been trying to tell you, but I didn't know how. He's not the same man he was even two months ago. He can't take care of himself, his episodes are more and more frequent, and he has my daughter."

I can hear a dog barking on the other end of the line, but even that noise grows muffled as my fear envelops me. I need her to understand. I need her here. I need someone, anyone.

"I'm on my way," she says.

I'm too terrified to thank her for the first kind gesture she's made to me in years.

16

Gracie

I TAKE A DEEP breath. It's been a long time since I have had Grandfather's sweet tea, and I want to savor it. Mama always says she wants to savor something when she eats it really slow—normally it's a dessert. Now I want to savor Grandfather's sweet tea because I don't know when I'll have it again. The old wooden spoon clanks against the pitcher as he stirs in the sugar. I had forgotten how much I used to hear that sound in Grandfather's kitchen before he went in the home.

Sometimes I wish I could record forgotten sounds so that I will never forget them. I wish I could have a place for all of my memories so they would never go away. But I guess then they wouldn't be memories anymore because memories are for when something is over.

"Are ya gonna stare at it all day or drink it?" Grandfather teases me. He's already had half of his cup. He is letting me drink out of the fancy glass cups, not my normal plastic one with Mickey on it. He says it's a "special occasion."

I smile and take a sip, feeling the sugar hit my tongue. The taste of the tea is a memory. Now I understand what Grandfather means by a past life. The sweet tea is from a past life, before Daddy went away and Grandfather moved to the home and Mama got so worried all the time. It's a life I miss very much.

"Sweet tea is my favorite drink," I confidently declare.

"Mine too, unless you count whiskey," he replies and lets out a booming laugh. I'm not quite sure why that's funny. I think he should just pick a favorite drink. I'm always picking my favorite things—favorite flowers, favorite color, favorite drink. I want to be sure I know them myself in case someone ever asks me. It would be embarrassing not to know one of your favorite things when someone asked you about it. It would be like not knowing yourself, and that's silly.

We sit there for a minute longer and it's very quiet, but a nice quiet, like when Mama is brushing my hair in the mornings.

"There may be nothing wrong with you, but I can plainly see, exactly what is wrong with me," Grandfather begins. I love it when Grandfather recites his poetry. It's always very sudden, like the idea just popped into his head. He never does it around Mama, so I know it's our special thing.

"It isn't that I'm indolent or dodging duty by intent. I work as hard as anyone, and yet I get so little done. I nibble this, I nibble that, but never seem to finish where I'm at. I'd do so much, you'd be surprised, if I could just get organized."

I giggle and clap as Grandfather grins a toothy grin and takes a little bow.

"Grandfather, that was *marvelous*," I say, stealing his word. "Did you write that yourself?"

"You bet I did," he says firmly with a nod. "I got about a dozen of them poems I've written. Read one to Nancy Reagan once, damn near brought her to tears. And one of these days I'ma get them published."

I don't know who Nancy Reagan is, but she sounds important since Grandfather is using both of her names.

"Like in a real book?" I ask him.

"Darn tootin'," he says, ruffling my hair. "And I'll dedicate it to my granddaughter, the Incomparable Gracie Lynn Abernathy!"

This makes me so happy because I love books, and now my name will be in one. Grandfather kisses the top of my head with his tickly mustache, and I take another long drink. This has been a great adventure already. But I know we have to get moving.

"So where would you like to go today, Grandfather?" I ask. "We don't have too much time to hang around the house. We have to make sure the sun doesn't go to sleep."

"Hmmm," Grandfather ponders. He looks very thoughtful like he hadn't considered this before. I guess it's not fair to assume he would've planned our adventure. After all, I'm the one who came up with the plan, and I've had more time to think about it. I thought that being in the home would make him daydream about all of the places he would like to go on adventures. But I think being in the home has made Grandfather less joyful, so he doesn't daydream anymore.

"Maybe Italy?" I suggest hopefully. "I haven't used my once-a-week ice cream yet this week so we could get some gelato."

Grandfather chuckles. A chuckle is a deep laugh that old men make. I can't make a chuckle, but I like Grandfather's.

"Italy might be a bit far for us to reach today," he says. "Maybe let's start by going to the river."

Grandfather's never taken me to the river before. Mama says he used to practically live on the river when she was growing up. She says she didn't like the river because it was stinky and there were snakes and Grandfather always made her get up early to go fishing. She did not like any of those things, so she didn't like the river. I'm not sure that I'll like it either, but that's where Grandfather wants to go, and this is his adventure, so I'll give it a try.

"I'd like to go to the river with you," I tell him, which isn't even a necessary lie because I would like to see the river with Grandfather to see why he likes it so much. Maybe the river is his own little corner.

"Marvelous," Grandfather claps his hands together, and I can tell again that he's happy. "Let me go grab your mama's old rod and reel, and we'll hit the road."

I don't know what a real rod and reel look like because I've only seen them in cartoons, but Grandfather goes to the shed and comes back with another thin tube like the one in the car and a medium-sized blue box.

"Today I'm gonna teach you a thing or two about fishin'," Grandfather tells me.

"Like a lesson?" I ask, suddenly excited.

"Exactly," he says.

Grandfather seems to be moving around better than he was this morning. He hasn't needed my help to walk since we've come inside, and I feel better about forgetting to bring his wheelchair for when he is tired. Maybe he won't need it.

Maybe the worm is already looking for a new brain to bother, because Grandfather is standing up tall again.

We get in the car and Grandfather turns left, away from the house and the home. The dust is swirling around in the air behind us. It makes pretty shapes as I watch it in the mirror. Driving on dirt roads is prettier than driving on the pavement.

17

LeeAnn
45 Minutes Gone

I ANXIOUSLY TAP MY foot on the pavement outside the home waiting for Sarah to arrive. She used to be such a constant presence in my life, and now she's a virtual stranger. Mama would make sure we were always together—the three amigos, Musketeers, the three Abernathy women. Then Mama was gone, followed by Sarah . . . or was it Sarah was gone, followed by Mama? It's been so long now that sometimes it feels like I've imagined our time together entirely.

Whenever I think back to what life was like when it was the three of us, one memory stands out above the rest. It was this one day in the middle of July when I was about twelve or thirteen. That morning, Mama set down her spatula, wiped her brow, and declared, "That's it, we're going to the beach!"

She loaded me and Sarah into the Chevy, threw in a pile of towels, a bottle of sunscreen, and three magazines, and we hit the road. I had a swimsuit, but it was just the boring old one-piece I wore underneath my shorts to go to the river whenever Daddy needed someone to hold his lures and extra fishing line. The only thing I knew about the beach was that it was "too damn far" and "filled with trashy tourists," according to Daddy.

"Rivers connect places, oceans push them apart," he'd always tell us. "'Course I swam halfway across the Atlantic when I was doing my military training. Drill sergeant told us to swim until we were tired, and I never stopped. Had to send the Coast Guard out to bring me back in."

I had no interest in involving the Coast Guard or setting any records, but ever since the original Walter Max painting, I had wanted to see the ocean for myself.

I still remember Sarah's fuchsia pink bikini with neon green stripes. She looked like the coolest girl in the world to me. She was only three years older, but somehow I knew she was a proper teenager while I was still a little girl. I wouldn't slim down and fill out in all the right spots for another four years.

The car was humid so Mama rolled down the windows and let the breeze blow in. I can still feel it tickling the corners of my face. As we approached the beach, the wind whipped harder and smelled of salt water. At one point a seagull flew next to my car window, and I screamed because I'd never seen one before.

"Lee Lee, that's the official bird of the ocean!" Mama informed me. "He belongs here as much as we do."

I loved the thought that we belonged at the beach.

Sarah rolled her eyes, lazily flipping through her magazine. The salty air nosed its way into the back seat and tickled my hair, flicking it behind my ears. The fresh wind whipped around us, making the car feel light and breezy— the opposite of the smelly river water that Daddy always seemed so obsessed with.

As we drove up, we passed candy-colored homes three times the size of our house. I craned my neck up as if they were New York skyscrapers. Each house had a special name and a sign out front.

Murphy's Marsh
Daisy's Dockside
Cali-Fornia Dreamin'
Gator's Grotto
Remy's Ranch on the Rocks
Kya-Bungalow
Hakuna Matata

"What would you name your house, Sarah?" Mama asked.

"Well," Sarah considered, finally looking up from her magazine. "It would be pink, obviously."

"Ahb-vious-lee," Mama agreed in a joking tone.

"I'd line starfish along the border and have French door windows that I could open every morning to look out at the sea," she mused, giving in to Mama's game of make-believe. "A dreamy place like that would have to be called something like Juliet's Hideaway."

Mama gave Sarah a warm smile, turning to face her, her eyes dancing.

"Sounds perfect, Sarah Bell," she told her, giving me a slight pang of jealousy. Nothing was more gratifying than Mama's approval.

Sarah, of course, had been cast as Juliet in our high school's production of *Romeo and Juliet* the year before. She'd beat out seniors for the part, captivating everyone with her beauty and undeniable stage presence. Mama had sat front row at all five performances. Daddy had been out of town.

"What about you, Lee?" Mama turned to me now, expertly able to shift her focus in a way that made me feel just as important as Sarah to her. I paused, trying to think of an answer to rival Sarah's.

"Mine would be blue," I told her finally, picturing the yellow curtains in the window as bright as the petals of sunflower. "And I would call it 'The Beach Shack,' which would be funny because it would actually be a mansion."

"Why would you call a mansion a shack?" Sarah asked, and wrinkled her nose the way she did when she thought I was being stupid.

"Because it's ironic," I mumbled, suddenly embarrassed.

"Whatever," Sarah replied and resumed flipping through her magazine.

Mama reached back and squeezed my knee, which she did sometimes when she knew just how I was feeling. It was our special language. That squeeze told me she understood.

We parked on the sand-covered asphalt and grabbed our towels from the trunk. Then Mama led us, climbing up the stairs and scrambling down the wooden walkway and onto the beach. As we reached the top of the stairs, the water slowly spread out before me, like a blue picnic blanket being laid across the sand.

It stretched as far as I could see from side to side. I had never seen anything so massive before. Sarah kept going, but I stopped and stared for a minute. Mama came up and put her arm around my shoulders.

"You like?" she asked.

"Mama, it's the most beautiful thing I've ever seen," I said in awe. "I want to take a picture, but I don't think it would capture it."

"Let's just try," Mama said, and pulled a disposable camera out of her bag. Mama loved to take pictures with disposable cameras. Sarah tried to get her interested in her tiny digital Canon, but Mama would say, "Now where's the fun in that? Takes the surprise right out of it."

Mama knelt down and held the camera facing us and snapped the shot, cranking the wheel back so it would be ready for the next photo.

The picture later developed only to reveal that she'd cut out the beach entirely and focused on our smiling faces. It still sits on top of my wardrobe at home.

"Are you guys coming?" Sarah called from the bottom of the walkway, her toes already in the sand.

"We'd better go get her before she runs off with a lifeguard from a warring family," Mama teased, mussing up my hair.

Studying Mama closely, I could see that the beach breeze and the warm sun were already bringing her even more to life than usual. Her cheeks had a healthy pink hue to them and were raised up in an almost permanent smile. Far away from the kitchen and the chores, her true magnificence was finally captured. Everyone said it was Big John who had the charisma and who could command a room. But I only had eyes for Mama. She was the hidden star, the kind so special she didn't need to shout it to make it known.

I slipped off my shoes as we reached the edge between the sand and the walkway and jumped into the tan grooves. The texture felt funny and I wriggled my toes hard, soaking it in. The sand wrapped around my feet, covering them with a warm blanket.

"First thoughts?" Mama asked.

"I think we should replace the floors at home with sand," I declared.

"Hmm, might get a little messy, but I'll look into it," Mama said, winking at me.

Sarah had already walked away and was fanning her towel out on a free, sunny patch. Once she had it straight, she eased herself down, lying on her stomach and sunning her back as if she did this every weekend. Everything came so naturally to her.

"Don't get too crispy, sweet pea," Mama told her.

"It's fine, Mom," she replied in an exasperated tone. "I'll know when I'm burning."

Mama pulled out her sunscreen, and I turned so she could dab it on my back without objection. It felt ice cold against my skin and I jumped.

"Alright, jitterbug," she said. "It'll be over in a minute."

Mama's worn hands rubbed circles of lotion across my back and arms as I itched to explore the beach and leap head-first into the water. I couldn't understand why Sarah would want to simply lie out on a towel, but it was also my lifelong ambition to be her, so it felt like something might be wrong with me instead.

"Mama, can we go in the ocean now?" I begged, once I was covered head to toe in the oily lotion that smelled so strongly it was starting to give me a headache.

"Sarah Bell, you gonna be okay?" Mama asked Sarah.

"Sure, Mom, I'm fine," Sarah replied, barely paying attention.

"Then let's blow this popsicle stand!" Mama shouted, grabbing my hand and sprinting toward the waves.

While I'd been ready to plunge into the water, I hadn't been expecting to be practically flung into the surf. With Mama in charge of our direction and speed, there was not a moment's hesitation. The proximity to the ocean had ignited a thrill in my mother I'd never witnessed. In unison, we went head first, diving into waves and popping back up, laughing and spitting out bits of the ocean that had found their way into our mouths. The waves crashed so hard they knocked me off my feet, but I wasn't afraid with Mama by my side.

Her curly hair glinted in the sunlight and shone about as brightly as the look on her face. The freckles across her cheeks mesmerized me. Mama showed me how to take a giant breath and plunge myself underwater, doing a front flip and resurfacing with a flourish. She also demonstrated how to lift my body up and lie back, floating over the rolling water as I said silent prayers another wave wouldn't catch me off guard. I'd learned to swim at the community pool when I was six, but my measly lessons were no match for the violence of the sea.

"There's no better place than the sea, Lee Lee," Mama said. "I could lie here forever watching the clouds go by."

"Then why have we never come before?" I whined, floating on my back. "I want to be here always."

She was quiet for a moment, before saying, "Sometimes life gets in the way, Lee. With both of you girls to look after and your father so busy with work, I've got my hands full, missy."

The sound of the moving water eased me into a comfortable state, but I couldn't shake Mama's words.

"Mama?"

"Yes, Lee?"

"Why do you stay with Daddy?"

I said the words very quietly, keeping my gaze on the sky, because the mere idea of questioning my parents' marriage was horrifying to me.

"LeeAnn." Mama's voice didn't sound angry, but it was firm, like she wanted to make something clear. "Your Daddy and I have lived a lot of life together. We have seen each other at our best and at our worst. He blessed me with two beautiful girls and provides a roof over our heads and food for us to eat. He is my family. You'll understand one day just how special that is."

"But he's never home, Mama," I reasoned. "He's always away, and we never know what he's doing."

"I know enough," Mama said, cutting me off slightly. "Your father has big dreams, just like you. But they have never quite panned out for him. He's working hard, and he's looking for the next dream."

"You mean like his stupid museum plan and that travel agency?" I asked.

"Lee, it's not stupid if it's something your father believes in," she said in a disapproving tone.

"But the travel agency never happened, and he's been talking about that museum for years!" I exclaimed. "He spends all this time working on things that will never happen. He could have been here at the beach with us."

"I know, Lee Lee," Mama said, sighing. "But you can't be too hard on him."

"I just thought dads were supposed to be around more," I complained. "You know, take their kids to baseball games and stuff. The only thing Daddy's ever done was drag me out on that smelly river."

"Listen, you know how I tell you every day that you are a special girl who will grow up to do special things?" Mama stopped me.

"Yes."

"Well, your Daddy heard the same things from his mama. He heard that every day, and then when he grew up, his plans never seemed to work out."

I pushed up from the bottom of the ocean to jump over a medium-sized wave.

"Can you imagine how disappointing it would be if you'd been told your entire life that you were destined for greatness, but you never achieved it?" Mama asked.

"I guess so." In all honesty, I thought that Mama constantly praising me was just something that parents did. I never assumed it meant I would actually do great things. If anyone was destined for greatness, it was probably Sarah. She was more sure of herself than I ever felt.

"It's hard to explain," Mama said. "You still have so much life ahead of you. You still have big dreams and plans and life hasn't brought you down. None of your illusions have been shattered. Unfortunately, it happens to all of us at some point."

A seagull loudly cried out, perched atop a nearby buoy. Its throaty call muddled my thoughts.

"Which of your illusions have been shattered, Mama?" I asked her.

She smiled a sad smile, and for once her freckles didn't sparkle as brightly.

"To me, that stuff doesn't matter, baby girl," she said. "I'm looking right at my dream."

She grinned and winked at me, splashing a little water in my direction.

The water's rhythm rocked us in tandem. Though Mama was in a playful mood, this was the most honest, upfront conversation we'd ever had, and I was afraid to break the spell.

"I hope that me and Sarah are enough for you," I said, suddenly feeling guilty and inexplicably sad.

"Oh, sweetheart, you're everything to me," Mama said. She reached over and kissed the top of my head just as a wave collided with us. We burst up out of the water, giggling and gasping for air as we floated closer to the shore.

"Sarah, sweetie, come on in!" Mama called to Sarah on the beach.

I looked back at my sister on the sand. She stood at the water's edge, cautiously dipping her toe into the foamy remnants of a wave. Then she shook her glossy hair and turned back to her towel. Her sun-drenched outline standing on the shore, tossing her curls away from us, is seared in my thoughts as I watch her car pull up to the home's front door.

18

Gracie

MAMA SAYS I'M NOT supposed to swim in the pool until it's been thirty minutes since I've eaten or had anything to drink. I don't know if these rules apply to the river. I also don't know if I'm supposed to be wearing arm floaties. I don't wear arm floaties when I'm swimming in the pool anymore, but the river has a current. A current means that the water moves really fast. I don't know why it moves in the river and not in the pool. Maybe the fishes swimming in the river push the water around. Once I went in a Jacuzzi and the water moved in there and made bubbles like I do sometimes in my chocolate milk. The river makes bubbles too, but Grandfather says that's the fish eating.

"When you see lots of those bubbles, you know you got yourself a hole," he tells me.

Grandfather has opened up the tubes and is sitting on a log, fiddling with his fishing pole. That's what was inside the "contraband": fishing poles. He attaches the reel to the rod. They are made of shiny silver metal in real life. In *SpongeBob* they are normally just purple lines and circles. At the end of the fishing line, Grandfather puts a hook and on the hook he puts on "bait."

One time on *SpongeBob*, Patrick used himself as bait to attract the jellyfish when he and SpongeBob were jellyfishing. That's what Grandfather's bait is doing too. It wriggles like a worm, and the fish think that it's their food, and they bite the worm. I like these plastic worms much more than the evil invisible worm in Grandfather's brain. I feel bad that we are using them as bait because they're so pretty that it seems a shame to put a hook in them.

Grandfather has taken the fishing line and put it on my rod. My rod is smaller than Grandfather's, and it's bright red. It looks more like the rods you see on *SpongeBob*. I wish it was purple, but I don't complain. I hope the fish won't see the red and know that I'm tricking them with bait. Grandfather says I can pick whatever bait I want, so I pick the purple one that has sparkles in it. His is brown like mud and has an orange tail. He says it's his favorite and is called "pumpkin seed."

"These suckers brought me to the ultimate victory on May 27, 1992," he says, holding one up in the air and waving its squirmy body around.

"What happened on that day?" I ask.

"On that day, I caught 104 fish on this stretch of river and set a record for the county," he tells me proudly. "And all after having to fend off a hungry alligator."

My eyes get real big because I can barely believe Grandfather. But it seems like a strange necessary lie to tell, so it must be true.

"An *alligator*?" I ask, looking to the left and right, suddenly afraid.

"The meanest alligator you ever saw," he tells me. "It had teeth the size of a butcher's knife, and it was gunning for me.

That gator decided that I was the sorry sucker who was gonna be his meal that day. But it didn't count on ol' Big John. It didn't know that I had trained with the toughest fighters this side of the Mississippi, and that even with all those teeth and all of its brute strength, I could still take 'em."

The insects hum loudly around us, but I can only hear grandfather.

"Well, that thing whipped its tail at me and lunged, but I was quick on account of my days running from enemy fire. I leaped up on a rock and jumped right on its back like I was riding a steer at the county fair."

"You *rode* on the alligator, Grandfather?" I ask him now, because I never in a million years could imagine doing something so scary.

"Bet your bottom dollar, I did!" he tells me, and his eyebrows go high up into his hair. "And it tried to flip me under and drown me, but I wouldn't let him. I dug my heel into the side of that gator and rode him on down the river until it split off to the sea—fifteen miles, it was! But I couldn't stand the thought of that thing coming for someone less equipped than myself. So I rode him out, and leaped off right as it entered the ocean. I landed on the bank with my rod still in my hand. And I made my way back up the river, fishing the whole way. The fish were so grateful that I'd gotten rid of that no-good gator that they happily bit onto my hook, and I took all 104 of those beauties home, and we had ourselves a feast that night."

"You ate the fish?" I ask.

"Sure did, Gracie Lynn," he says. "I'd earned it, after all!"

I wasn't expecting this. I didn't know that fishing means you eat the fish too.

"That seems mean," I say, thinking about the fish in *Finding Dory*, which Mama let me watch on TV.

"That's the circle of life, Gracie," he says. "We go through this life hoping to make the best of it, to contribute as much as we can. And eventually we go back into the earth."

"Is that when we die?" I ask. I know that Mama's mama died, but I'm not sure what that means really. Mama says her mama is not coming back, and that is scary to me. But it doesn't seem scary to Mama. She just seems sad.

"Yes, everyone dies at some point," he says. "That's why you've got to make sure you're making every day count."

I think about it. I don't know that I'm making every day count. I don't go on adventures. I don't leave the town. All I do is swim and read *Magic Tree House* books. What if I'm not living right and then I die when I'm not making it count? I used to think that only old people died, but Mama says that we can die at any time, which is also scary. But she says not to think about it too much.

"Are you making every day count?" I ask Grandfather.

He's quiet for a minute and looks sad.

"I'm making today count," he says finally. "Thanks to you."

The reeds around the river rustle. The water's calm now, but I'm still afraid to leave the bank because I don't want the current to drag me away. Grandfather says I'll be fine, but I also don't like the idea of the river water touching my church dress. I know that Mama wouldn't be happy about that. Plus, there are weird things touching my feet that feel pretty gross.

Grandfather says it's just algae that builds up on the river's bottom, but I don't like it. It squishes when I step on it, and it feels like I've stepped on a frog and made its guts spill out. It's not a pleasant thing to think when you can't see what's underneath your foot. I'm starting to understand why Mama never liked the river the way Grandfather does.

Grandfather has waved his rod back and forth several times. He calls this "casting." I duck down low to avoid the rod and my dress almost touches the water because I'm afraid that the fishing line and the hook are going to hit me. He chuckles.

"Come on, chicken liver!" he taunts. "I ain't gonna get-cha! You forget your Grandpa has done this a time or two."

One or two times doesn't seem like that many times, but Grandfather's having fun, so I try not to duck again the next time he is casting. I'm happy that Grandfather is making today count. Today is our first adventure together in a long time. I used to think that to go on an adventure you had to get on an airplane, but now I know that adventures can happen wherever you are as long as you are with other people who like adventures.

Grandfather's fishing line makes a jerky movement, and he jumps. His rod curves into a giant arch and starts shifting from one side of him to another. I'm scared that the rod is going to pull him into the river, so I throw my rod into the tall grass on the bank and grab Grandfather's arm.

My dress is definitely in the water now, but there's nothing I can do to stop that. Grandfather keeps shouting "Yee haw!" very loudly and is turning the handle on his reel very fast. But it seems like it's harder to do than it was before, like something is pulling on the fishing line.

"We got ourselves a live one, Gracie Lynn!" Grandfather cries out. "Just gotta reel 'er in."

I don't know how Grandfather knows the fish is a girl. Maybe she has something in her belly. I'm excited and scared at the same time. I've never seen a real fish up close that was alive.

Grandfather's twisting all around, pulling on the rod. He's letting out big puffs of air and looks tired. I'm worried again about not bringing his wheelchair.

"Grandfather, maybe you should stop," I shout to him. "Is this too much?"

"You want me to just hand over my rod to this fish?" he hollers back. "We do not surrender in this house!"

We're not in a house, but I'm guessing he means in our family. I've seen that word before: "surrender." I saw it in *The Magic Tree House: The Knight at Dawn*. Mama told me it means to give up or to be defeated, so that doesn't necessarily seem accurate. Daddy was my family, and Daddy surrendered. And sometimes Mama seems like she has surrendered too. But maybe Grandfather is just talking about fishing.

Now he's wriggling so much I'm worried he's having a seizure. I saw a little boy have a seizure at the art store one time. He fell down on the floor and started wriggling and spit up white stuff out of his mouth. It was very scary. But the ambulance came, which was cool because it had a siren, and they took the boy to the hospital. Mama told me he was okay, but I don't know how she knew that.

But Grandfather doesn't have any white stuff coming out of his mouth, so I don't think he is having a seizure. But he keeps pulling the handle of his reel around and around.

Then I gasp because I see the fish pop out of the river very quickly.

"Grandfather! You caught her, you caught her!" I squeal. "I saw her come out of the water for one second."

He smiles but doesn't respond. His face is red with concentration as he twists the reel harder and harder. Finally he lets out a giant rattly breath and looks over at me.

"I don't think I can finish the job, Gracie," Grandfather says, and he sounds tired. "What if you bring 'er in for us?"

"Me?" I ask, suddenly scared.

I've never had to reel in a fish before. Grandfather's strong and he couldn't even do it. But we are bandits, in this together, so I have to try.

"Okay, Grandfather," I tell him. "But can you please hold onto my shoulders so I don't fall in the river and get caught in the current?"

"Of course, Gracie Lynn," Grandfather says as he hands me the rod and reel. He places my fingers around the handle of the reel and shows me how to crank it back, then he holds on tight to my shoulders, and I feel safer. The fish is pulling really hard against me, but I plant my feet very firmly into the squishy ground, even though I have to touch the algae with my bare toes.

"Come on, Gracie," Grandfather says, but his voice sounds crumbly and rough. "You've got this, baby girl!"

I pull with all of my might and lose my balance, knocking into Grandfather, who lets out a surprised cry and stumbles backward. His foot slips on the algae-covered rock and as he falls into the water, I scream out. Grandfather starts splashing and shouting, "Frogging rock, piece of frogging shit!" Mama didn't teach me a substitute word for shit, but I know it's a bad word to use because Greg Bryant got in trouble for using it at swim practice.

"Grandfather, I'm sorry. I'm so sorry!" I call out, trying to reach down to help him stand up. But our hands slip since his are all covered with river water.

"God dern it, frogging shit!" he bellows, and I feel tears in my eyes. I'm still clutching onto the rod and reel with one hand and trying to help Grandfather with my other. He pushes my hand away roughly and grabs onto the rock, pulling himself up very slowly. I'm biting my lip and trying not to cry too hard, but Grandfather's never screamed at me like that before. He's done it to Mama, but never to me. It feels horrible.

Grandfather is dripping wet and his hands look like they're vibrating down by his sides. There's a dark red bruise on his arm that I can see getting larger and larger from where he hit it into the rocky bed. He turns to look at me, and I want to hide behind the rocks. But his eyes change when he sees me, and they don't look so angry anymore.

"Gracie, don't cry," he tells me and reaches out to pat my arm. "I'm sorry, I shouldn'ta yelled at you like that."

I'm shaking and crying and everything feels blurry. Then we both see the fish pop her head out of the river again, so close to us we can practically reach out and grab her. Her body is hiding in the water, but her head is larger than my hand.

"Grandfather, did you see that?" I say, startling myself from my tears.

"That fish was the size of a Buick!" Grandfather says, clapping his hands together, any signs of anger vanished. "And you've got 'er by the 'nads, Gracie girl. Come on!"

I'm too excited to understand what Grandfather's saying. The sun is beating down on the top of my head. I take a deep breath, and I do my best to be a big girl. I want

Grandfather to be proud of me again. I'm cranking the wheel of the reel, and Grandfather is cheering in a cloud above my head. I can barely hear him I'm focusing so hard.

The fish pops out of the water, but this time she doesn't go back under. I keep pulling, and Grandfather is shouting something. He sounds very happy, but I can only pay attention to the fish. She skims across the surface of the water, until she finally lifts up into the air and swings on the line. Her tail is flipping, and it slaps my tummy. I squeal with both fear and delight.

Since she's not in the water, she's not pulling on me anymore, and now the fish is even heavier than before. She's twitching and thrashing in the air, left and right. I never knew something so little could have so much strength.

Grandfather reaches around me and holds the fish in his hand. She's flopping around, but Grandfather smooths back her spiky fins and keeps her still.

"Well done, Gracie Lynn," he congratulates me, patting me hard on the back, and his voice is back to a normal volume now that my bubble of focus is gone. "I am so proud of you."

I smile. I bet Becky has never reeled in a fish before. I can't wait to tell her all about it. I have sweat on my upper lip and my dress is very dirty now, but I don't care. Grandfather is still dripping wet, but I can tell that the sun is already drying out his clothes. He doesn't look angry anymore, and I feel relieved. For a minute there, when he pushed me, I was afraid that the worm had come out. But maybe he didn't see my hand and was just trying to stand up.

Grandfather holds the fish out to me.

"Grab 'er by the lower lip, and I'll jimmy the hook out," he instructs me.

I look at the fish's open mouth. She has rows of tiny little teeth. My fingers could fit all the way inside that fish's mouth. She could chomp down on me with her sharp baby teeth.

"No, thank you, Grandfather," I say. "I think I've done all of my fishing for today."

"No, ma'am, Miss Gracie Lynn," he commands. "It's time for you to finish what you've started!"

"But Grandfather, what if she bites my fingers?" I ask nervously.

"You've got a few more," he teases. "Catfish once tried to take off my whole thumb, but I wrestled it out. And this is just a smallmouth bass. It's right there in the name—*small mouth*."

Fear is hugging me, and this time it's also giving me a buzzing feeling in my stomach. I know I'll hold up the fish by her mouth. I know I'll do it because Grandfather asked me to and because I secretly want to. I bite my lower lip anxiously and reach out my hand very cautiously, placing my thumb in the fish's mouth. I make a little squeal sound like a piglet because it helps me get out some of my nerves. I can feel every single one of the fish's teeth pushing into my finger. It hurts a little, but I know that she won't bite my finger off. Grandfather holds the fish for a moment longer, and then he moves his hand and it's just me, pinching the fish's mouth between my thumb and my fist. It's still flopping a little bit and I'm scared to drop her, but I'm also scared that if Grandfather can't get the hook out soon she will die. So I stand very still like a statue and hold on very tight.

Grandfather's hands are shaking a little bit, and I think that's funny because mine are so steady, and he's the grown-up and I'm the kid. He jiggles the hook that's in her right cheek. I bet that's very painful. It seems kind of mean that we did that to the fish. It's not the fish's fault that we tricked her with bait.

He jiggles and jiggles, and I see her cheek ripping and now I'm crying again.

"Grandfather, please hurry, you're hurting her!" I beg him.

I hear Grandfather take a calming breath, the kind Mama takes when I ask too many questions. He gives the hook one last yank, and it finally comes out. I stand there for a minute, not sure of what to do, and then I let go and the fish plops into the water. She floats at my feet, stunned for a minute, and then she swims off as if nothing ever happened. I'm shocked. I thought for sure that she would die and that I would be a fish killer in addition to being a bandit. But the fish is alive, and now I'm laughing because I'm so relieved and so happy.

"What'd I tell ya, Gracie?" Grandfather says in a booming voice as he pats my shoulder. "We caught her, and we set her free."

"Do you think she'll be okay, Grandfather?" I ask, remembering the fish's cheek rip.

"Okay? Why, she's going back to all of her fish friends to tell them about Queen Gracie—River Warrior and Slayer of Fish!" Grandfather declares, throwing one arm up in the arm and pumping his fist in victory.

I giggle because Grandfather is being silly, and I haven't seen him being silly in a long time. I wish I had a camera so I could take a picture of Grandfather being silly to show Mama. But I don't, so I'll have to take a brain picture instead so I can tell her about it later. I blink and make a small click in my mind, being careful to remember Grandfather exactly as he is now, with the hot sun shining down on him and the lines on his face turned upward in a smile.

The sticky heat isn't so bad while we're standing in the river. I'm happy it's helping to dry out Grandfather's clothes. I don't even mind the algae on my toes anymore. I think I like it here.

"Grandfather, I'm really sorry I made you fall in the river," I tell him, looking down at the current.

"Not the first time and not the last, God willing," he tells me, putting his arm around me to give me a squeeze. "You didn't drop the rod, that's the important bit. You did me proud, Gracie Lynn."

I look up at him and smile because I know he's not necessary lying. His face is bright and stretched wide in a grin.

Grandfather reaches down into the water, rinsing some muddy dirt off his arms. That large spot is still there and now it's closer to black.

"Old man skin," he says, pointing to the spot, which looks like paint splatter.

He picks up a rock and puts it in his pocket, then he reaches down again and picks up a second rock and hands it to me.

"So you'll always remember the day we made it count," he says.

I wrap my fingers around the rock and squeeze it tight.

♦ 19 ♦

LeeAnn
1 Hour Gone

SARAH PULLS UP IN an SUV I've never seen before. I'm almost too worried to resent her for it. Almost. She opens the door and I see her strawberry blonde curls first. They surround her perfectly made-up face. Sarah got Mama's curls, though I know that she dyes them to make them even brighter.

My lank brown hair hangs limp at my shoulders as I stand outside the home trying to look both pretty and pathetic at the same time so that Sarah won't change her mind and leave. The click-clack of her stilettos make their way up the drive to the entrance as her white blouse clings to her every curve and her jeans stretch perfectly across her sloping hips. For a fleeting moment I imagine her cooking lunch in such a ridiculous outfit, dodging the grease stains and blobs of mystery sauce. It's the kind of thing I'd have worn on a blind date had anyone ever thought to set me up on one. She must have a full-body apron to keep herself free of peanut butter and jelly splatter. But I know that peanut butter and jelly splatter doesn't dare touch women like Sarah.

"You ready?" she asks me without a hug or even a small smile. She doesn't act like we haven't seen each other in seven months. Instead, she sounds more like an annoyed parent picking up their misbehaving child from camp. I flash to riding in Mama's car with the windows down when we were kids, belting out the Spice Girls from the cassette tape Sarah got for Christmas. I was always Baby and she was always Posh. It feels like the same roles still apply, but the band broke up decades ago, and Posh no longer wants to be involved.

"I think so," I murmur, still intimidated by her all these years later.

"Do you have any idea where they might have gone?" she asks.

"A few," I say vaguely, "but we should probably start at the house just in case. That guy who went out looking from the home didn't even ask for our address."

I slide into the car and smell what I assume is "new car smell," though I've never personally experienced it before.

"This is nice," I half-heartedly offer, motioning around the giant beige interior and trying to sound casual. "Is it new?"

Sarah perks up.

"Yes! We got it last month," she gushes. "A little early anniversary present from Phil."

"It's nice," I repeat lamely, thinking about the cheap gifts Dan used to buy me back when we were young and had even less money—tarnished trinkets and thrift store jewelry that I used to treasure, but I'm sure won't cut it with his new girlfriend. Maybe she's getting a new beige car for Christmas this year. I'm sure I'll see the photos if she does.

I clasp my hands back and forth in my lap. I've always had my mother's hands. Sarah got Mama's curls, but I got her hands, short and stubby, with no real fingernails to speak of. I still remember the day I realized it, studying the backs of my hands out of boredom at work. Gracie hadn't been sleeping through the night, and I was dead tired. Then I saw the lines around my knuckles crisscrossed like the pattern of a patchwork quilt. It's the same pattern I'd blankly gaze at while Mama sang me lullabies as a child. The moment felt like a sign, like Mama was there, nudging me to keep going. I wish she was here now to hold me close, to say all the right things I've never known how to say. Her palms were always smooth, but mine are slick with nerves and trepidation.

Sarah is drumming her manicured fingernails on the steering wheel as she waits for the light to change. I'm hypnotized by her movements, allowing them to distract me from the terrifying reality that's threatening to crush me where I sit.

She stays quiet as we drive down the road with some horrible pop song on the radio. I steady myself by hugging my arms around my middle, occasionally pinching my sides to stay in the moment—a nervous tic I've developed in recent years. It feels good to be taking some sort of action, but the combination of my panic over Gracie and my anxiety over being around my sister again is too much to handle. The dilapidated buildings of the old downtown section with their '90s advertisements, boarded-up windows, and peeling paint rush past the windows of Sarah's new ride. I'm almost embarrassed for Reading, like I should apologize for its appearance to Sarah even though she grew up here too.

"So you were gone for how long before you noticed they were missing?" she asks, snapping me back into the car.

It's the question I've been dreading.

"It was maybe twenty or thirty minutes," I reply, continuing to look out the window as the AC blasts me in the face. Standing in the heat I had longed for AC, but now it feels like I'm in a frozen tundra. "I had to go to the other building and then I got sort of held up in the kitchens."

Sarah doesn't respond, but I see her nod her immaculately coiffed head in mild recognition out of the corner of my eye. After a few minutes, we roll onto our street like we're in a military tank invading the area. As the SUV pulls into the driveway, I frantically scan the yard for any sign that they've been here.

The Chevy isn't anywhere in sight, and I can't tell if there are any lights on inside with the sun blaring down on the windows. I slip out of the SUV anyway, my flip-flops hitting the ground hard, desperate for some clues. If only I had my daughter's espionage skills.

I try not to be too self-conscious as I watch Sarah surveying the faded wood paneling on the side of the house. I remember when Daddy got that installed the year he did well at the bank. He was so proud to have the polished wood lining our home. Now it looks rotten and filled with holes. I'm sure there's some sort of upkeep treatment that I should be doing, but Sarah, thankfully, stays quiet.

Kneeling down, my hand grazes the circular paver next to our doormat. It's stamped with a four-year-old Gracie's tiny handprint at the center of the concrete slab. I run my fingers against the ridges, remembering the feel of her tiny palm in mine. Pushing the paver and my panic aside, I grab the spare key hidden underneath and stand up on shaky legs.

My hand trembles as I put the key in the lock, so hopeful that I'll open the door and my little girl will come bounding into my arms. The green door swings open, cutting through the nothingness that awaits me.

"Gracie?" My pointless, mangled cry echoes down the empty halls.

I don't even have to go inside to know that Gracie isn't there. But I do anyway. Sarah follows close behind, looking around as if for the first time while I scour the counters, searching desperately for clues.

"You certainly haven't changed much in here," she casually notes. Out of habit, I wonder briefly if she means to sound so judgmental, but thoughts of Gracie force out those questions I've been asking myself since childhood.

I briefly survey the room, noticing it for the first time in years. She's right. The kitchen still has the same appliances and accessories that Mama put up during her redecorating kick in the late '90s. They're all outdated now, but at the time, they'd been cutting edge. The moth-eaten yellow curtains Mama made before I was born are practically threadbare. It's as if someone took a dimmer and dulled all of the colors, sucking the saturation and life out of the room, and threw in a few cobwebs for good measure. The big cushy armchair in the adjoining living room has little pilled pieces all over it that I pick at when I'm anxious. All of the photographs on the mantel and around the room are at least seven years old, with the exception of a few of Gracie's school photos and drawings. Without the lights on, this place looks like a mausoleum, a somber shrine to our childhood, to a life that once included Mama. I feel particularly aware of this having Sarah in there, knowing she remembers the house's former glory, how it used to shine in Mama's care.

"Yeah, well, my home décor budget hasn't exactly been high lately," I reply, sounding more bitter and defensive than I intended.

She doesn't respond, and I know I'm tiptoeing a dangerous line. If I piss her off too much, she'll leave, and I'll be alone yet again. And I can't be alone. Not now. I need help—help to find Gracie, to murder Daddy, all of it.

I pull back the cabinet doors and everything seems to be in place. Then I open the fridge and notice something new—a pitcher of Daddy's sweet tea.

"Sarah, they were here!" I cry out in a strangled voice. I try calming my breathing. Sarah walks up and rubs her hand lightly against my back. It's not a familiar gesture for her.

"That's a good thing, Lee," she assures me. "It means Dad's probably in his right mind. Take a breath for just a second."

The kindness of her words soothes me. As Sarah edges closer to the familiarity I've wished for all these years, it feels completely foreign. There's always been so much unsaid between us. Sarah left home the first chance she got, and it always felt like her perfectly polished head couldn't be bothered to look back. I, on the other hand, could never force myself to leave the past behind me. Hell, this entire home is like a faded postcard of our former life. This room especially is filled with memories too precious for me to surrender—of Mama cooking us huge breakfasts, the smell of sizzling sausages, baking biscuits, scrambled eggs, and her favorite apricot jam wafting through my mind, a tempting tease of happier, easier days. We would sit at the kitchen counter in our pajamas with our feet dangling off the barstools, filling our stomachs with as much as we could physically handle, long before we knew to be self-conscious about our waistlines.

"Lee?"

Sarah's sharp voice breaks the memory. She's standing farther down the hall, staring into Gracie's open room.

"What?" At first I think she's seen something, but instead she turns to face me, her expression serious.

"Have you called Dan?"

His name has the immediate tendency to make me feel sick to my stomach. The image of him cowering in front of me at the swim meet swirls into my thoughts. *Why should I call Dan? What could he possibly do to help?*

"I don't think we need to get him involved," I say, my voice stony.

"Lee, that's his daughter," Sarah says, gently reminding me of the fact I'd like to reject and making me flash to Corrine Carter's taunting voice crying, "He's her fa-theeer," at the swim meet.

"Sure, in blood, but Gracie hasn't seen him for months," I protest. I don't add that I saw Dan yesterday, or that Gracie asked me who I was talking to at the meet. Did she see her father? Does she want to go see him in person? Would Big John appease this request? Daddy and Dan had never really had much of a relationship other than that of polite strangers. But though he'd never said anything directly, I'd always felt like Daddy sympathized with Dan after our split, which did nothing to help my relationship with him.

"What if Gracie went to go see him?" Sarah presses.

"Why would she?" I try to sound incredulous, as if Sarah's idea is thoroughly ludicrous.

"Well, I don't know, but kids tend to stick with what they know," Sarah says.

"She doesn't even know where he lives," I insist, though I suddenly can't remember if that's true. "We haven't seen him since Christmastime. He brought some gifts over for her. You know, checked off his dad duty."

I leave out the part where he'd been asking to see her for months prior to that, and I'd blown him off every time.

"Yeah, but with Daddy behind the wheel, you never know where they could be going," Sarah says. "You've got a great kid, but Big John's a bad influence with a knack for the extreme. We both know it."

Her words have gotten under my skin. As much as I don't want to call him, it now seems negligent not to. I won't be the bitter ex-spouse who refused to check every possible option when looking for her missing daughter. Things are always better when Dan is the clear villain of the story.

"Fine," I say roughly, not meeting Sarah's eye.

I do one last pitiful scan of the shabby kitchen and look out into the backyard where Gracie's beautiful garden sits. Her patch of cornflowers wilts slightly in the hot sun.

I pick up the phone and dial my husband's number.

20

Dan

"**D**AN! I NEED YOU in here."

Ashley's voice carries from upstairs, and I set down the newspaper and rush up to Jack's nursery to join her. Her auburn hair is pulled into a bunch on the top of her head, and she has a muslin cloth draped over her shoulder. On the changing pad, my little boy is giggling and kicking his legs as a fountain of urine arches over him and onto the top of the dresser. His once tiny baby legs with their thick, doughy rolls have gotten stronger and leaner as he's transitioned into toddlerhood, but he's still short and squat like a little tank. Ashley is tossing diapers aside, looking for something with an acute sense of urgency, one hand placed on our son's stomach to keep him from flipping off the changing pad. I quickly pluck the muslin from her shoulder and place it at the source of the urine stream, to stifle the flow.

"Oh, duh!" Ashley laughs with the slightest hint of self-consciousness in her tone, absent-mindedly patting her shoulder where the cloth was as if she was just now remembering it was there. "The Diaper Whiz Kid had quite the blowout just now and decided to pull a two for one special right after I cleaned him up."

"Whiz Kid, very funny, m'lady. Is this true, young Master Clarmont?" I turn to face my son's broad face, giggling wildly on the changing pad.

Ashley surveys the scene, looking beat. I scoop up Jack, and zoom him through the air to the bathroom, placing him in the bathtub while I use the shower nozzle to spray his legs down. He laughs and splashes the water, getting it all down the front of my shirt. I can't help but picture Gracie in the pool yesterday, and a familiar pang of guilt hits me. I try to brush it off, grinning at my little boy, snapping myself back into the moment.

I feel a hand on my arm—Ashley, coming in the room to watch our little family. It feels very picture perfect, even though I know it's not. Not quite.

When someone cheats, people always focus on the sex. Obviously, there was some of that before there should have been. But the moment I actually cheated on LeeAnn happened long before the sex. It's a moment that I both treasure and regret.

Ashley and I were coworkers who always got along but never so much as held a lingering glance, until one night when we stayed late to meet a project deadline for an ad campaign we had coming up. I often volunteered to work late to avoid going home. We were eating crappy Chinese food and going over a slideshow, when she made some silly joke and I laughed.

"There it is," she said. "I've been waiting months just to see you smile."

There was no aggression in her voice. She wasn't trying to make me stray. Ashley genuinely wanted me to be happy.

No one had wanted that from me for a long time. No one had wanted anything from me for a while, except to be quiet and to stay out of the way. And in that moment, my already dwindling loyalties to LeeAnn vanished.

Ashley quickly became the best part of my day. I would rush out of my house, brushing off the disappointment I brought to my wife, anxious to walk toward the light and eager to feel some sort of joy. I was like an addict, needing my next hit of Ashley's praise, her laugh, the way her nose would twitch when there was a problem she couldn't work out.

It became easy to forget about LeeAnn and the cloud of toxic negativity that followed her, to pretend like my ties to her didn't exist. Few people ever ask dads about their kids. For every mom in the office, there were constant discussions about daycares and the sharing of photos, but I could hide my parental shame without anyone knowing. I was a stranger to my own child, but that didn't matter because I was *just* a dad. I'd tried for years to do the right thing when it came to LeeAnn and Gracie, to find the right words, but it never worked. She had to do it all on her own. She made it clear time and time again that I was just in the way, that they didn't need me. By the time Ashley came along, the disappointments had piled up so high I couldn't see to the other side.

"Thanks," she says now, sounding relieved. "It was turning into a war zone in there."

"Of course," I reply, more than happy to help. Happy to feel like I know what I'm doing for once in my life. Happy she trusts me to do it.

"Alright, Master Clarmont, let's get you dried and dressed, mister," I jovially command, sweeping my son high into the air and swinging him back and forth to get the excess water droplets off as he squeals.

I set the not-so-little guy down on the changing table, which is decorated with tiny blue whales. He squirms, but I hold him steady with one hand, searching for wipes and a new diaper with the other. At first, I treated him with kid gloves, terrified to touch him, to accidentally bring him any harm. But after a few months with Ashley by my side in the trenches of it, it got more natural, the way it never had with Gracie.

"We're not the enemy, he's the enemy," Ashley used to jokingly tease any time we started to get irritated with one another.

LeeAnn let me change Gracie's diaper once, when she had the stomach flu and literally couldn't get up from the toilet for a few hours. It was the only time she let me help. Those first few months were brutal; I felt like an outsider in my own home, watching LeeAnn fight back tears as she tried to get our newborn to latch, and I stood by useless.

"Just give us some privacy, please," she used to say through gritted teeth as she tried to cover up from me, her husband. As if I hadn't seen every part of her. As if I hadn't held her hand while she delivered our daughter. She refused to pump or use formula, and I was too afraid to question the determination in her eyes, so I never even got to feed Gracie.

The first few days, she let me hold Gracie to see if I could get her to settle, but her tiny, squishy form had wailed and thrashed in my arms. I tried to hold her in different ways, always covered in sweat while under the critical gaze of my wife, terrified of doing anything wrong. After what felt like milliseconds, LeeAnn would always snatch Gracie back, briskly saying "Never mind, I've got it" or "You're just making it worse," as if I were a nuisance she didn't have time for. Eventually she stopped letting me try at all, and I stopped offering.

For months, she would carry Gracie around in this wrap thing, literally strapping our daughter to her body like a suicide vest. "It's the only way she'll sleep," LeeAnn always insisted, though I rarely asked. I'm not sure if LeeAnn got more than two or three hours of sleep a day for those first few months. My coworkers would occasionally ask things in those early weeks like, "How much sleep ya getting?" And I'd shamefully make up some half truth, like, "Doing the best I can!" never letting on that I was sleeping a full eight hours each night while LeeAnn lay on the floor of Gracie's room refusing to leave her side.

Meanwhile, I kept retreating further and further into my shell. I used to creep around my house quietly, like an intruder not wanting to disturb the inhabitants. I spoke so softly or not at all on the weekends that come Monday my voice developed a hoarseness I had to battle at work.

That time felt like a storm we had to weather, those tricky newborn months, and then we'd make it through and be a family again—or for the first time. But when I finally looked up one day, a year had gone by, and my daughter and wife were strangers to me. We were like roommates, forced together and no one pleased with the living arrangements. I started working later, mostly because work was the only time I felt appreciated, like anyone saw me. LeeAnn never noticed, or if she did, she never seemed to object.

"I like that outfit," Ashley says, admiring the dinosaur-printed pants with claws on the feet that I picked out for Jack.

When she told me she was pregnant, a wave of terror spread down my arms and through my fingertips. It felt like watching a building being demolished—one moment standing tall, the next every inch of sturdy concrete crumbling. The fear wasn't just because I was still married and hadn't left LeeAnn yet, but the idea of screwing up again with another kid felt like even more of a colossal misstep than it had the first time around. I looked into Ashley's eyes and saw the same fear that resided in mine. But it wasn't like what I went through with LeeAnn. Ashley wanted to share that fear. She wanted us to be in this together. She wanted a partner, not a place holder. She didn't hesitate to ask for help. One day, weeks after the baby had come and months after my life with LeeAnn and Gracie had imploded, I came into the living room to find Ashley on YouTube.

"Can you try on this wrap thing?" she asked me, holding the pools of fabric up. "I can't figure it out."

I blinked back joyful tears as I scooped up our son, gently tucking him into the folds of the fabric, and feeling his warm body against mine, his heart beating in time to his tiny rhythmic breaths. I knew I would never let anything happen to him, to us. Not like before. It was like I had never known how much I wanted to be a father until I wasn't allowed to be one.

It made me ache for a chance to try again with Gracie, to do things right. But that chance feels gone now. It certainly felt gone yesterday in those bleachers. Before LeeAnn had approached me, I'd gotten one glimpse of Gracie, rushing to her friends in the water. She's so grown up now. I don't even know if she'd recognize my face. Apart from the brief drop-off of Christmas gifts Ashley had suggested and LeeAnn had grudgingly allowed, I can't remember the last time she's seen me for more than an hour. I am a stranger to her. She's never been to this house, she doesn't even know she has a brother. LeeAnn balked when I brought up the idea of telling her. I thought she might vomit just from hearing the word leave my lips.

I've seen how quickly things change for Jack, week to week, day to day. Gracie's life now is nothing like it was when she lived with me. I don't even think I knew what it was like back then, if I'm being honest.

I smooth the neckline of my son's shirt so the wrinkled edges don't irritate him. As I do so, my phone rings in the other room. Ashley goes to grab it.

"Umm, it's for you," she cautiously shouts. By her tone I know who it is. Ashley typically doesn't hesitate to answer my phone for me, except when it comes to one person—my wife. I know Ashley wants us to move forward with the divorce, but LeeAnn has refused to even broach the subject because of our joint health insurance and her unwillingness to be in a room with me for more than ten minutes, and truthfully, I'm afraid to bring it up. I barely ever get to see my daughter as it is.

Ashley has to remind me frequently that Gracie is my daughter too. For so long she seemed to be just LeeAnn's. We share a dimple and that's about it. Jack has it too—that tiny indent is the one thing the three of us share.

I meet Ashley in the living room, handing our son to her and taking the phone. The familiar heat of my shame crosses my cheeks as I answer. "LeeAnn?" Anytime she calls, I wonder if it's an accidental butt dial. Why would she ever voluntarily speak to me again after what I did? Dan Clarmont—the cheater, the fake. But today I'm scared she's calling to yell at me more about my disastrous swim meet cameo.

LeeAnn's voice is hurried and strained. Her words come out as if she's holding her breath. "Is Gracie with you?"

The words are English, but they muddle in my mind. Why wouldn't LeeAnn know where Gracie was? Why would she ever think she'd be with me?

"What?" I reply dumbly. Did we have some alternate reality plan that I forgot about in a moment of amnesia?

"Gracie and Daddy have . . . well . . . they've gone out, and we thought they might have gone to see you," LeeAnn says, sounding less and less convincing.

"Gone out?" I ask. "Do you mean they're *missing*?"

"Look, it's a long story," LeeAnn says, exasperated. "Can I take that as a no?"

"Umm, yeah . . . I mean, no, they aren't here," I say, slowly comprehending what she's saying to me. "So Gracie and John have run away?"

Ashley's eyes widen as she bounces Jack on her knee, trying to distract him as he lunges for some glass bowls on our coffee table.

"No!" LeeAnn practically shouts, reprimanding me in a tone I know all too well. "Gracie has *not* run away. They have simply gone out together, and we don't know where they are. Those two come up with these crazy schemes and stories, and I think this time it just got out of hand. I'm sure it's fine. We just haven't been able to track them down, so I thought I'd check."

I can tell by her tone that it is not fine and that she doesn't want me to know just how bad it is.

"Okay," I reply slowly, not wanting to anger her again. "What can I do to help?"

"Nothing," she snaps, clearly regretting the decision to call me in the first place. "I've got to go."

"Lee?" I ask. I hear her sharp intake of breath on the other end of the line. "Will you please just text me when you hear something?"

"Sure."

She's already hung up the phone, and I just sit there, stunned, wondering if I imagined the whole thing. I feel like a dummy with no ventriloquist, unmoving, unfeeling. My daughter is missing. I have a daughter. And she's missing. I still picture her as the round, giggly baby with her pudgy arms and long eyelashes. But she's so much bigger now. She's a full walking, talking little human. And she's missing.

"Dan?" Ashley's curious eyes meet mine. She seems more concerned than I am, probably because to me this isn't real. "What's going on with Gracie?"

Ashley's never met Gracie. I doubt she ever will, unless I die and they both attend the funeral, but even then, it's a slim chance. But she's never tried to diminish Gracie's importance, even though I'm barely a father to her. In fact, I think my lack of involvement in Gracie's life bothers Ashley even more than me. She doesn't understand why I'm not more proactive when it comes to my own daughter. Why I can be so confident and assertive in so many aspects of my life except the one where it matters most? But she wasn't in that house—she doesn't know what LeeAnn went through, what we both did. I've already done so much to hurt my wife that every decision I make involving Gracie feels like another twist of the knife deeper into LeeAnn's back.

"LeeAnn said she's gone out," I reply lamely, repeating the awkward phrasing.

"And she thought she came here?" Ashley's surprise slightly hurts my feelings, even though I had the same reaction.

"She's with John, and LeeAnn thought they might have tried to come visit me," I say. "Though that man was never particularly fond of me, so I'm not sure why she would think that. Last I'd heard, John had moved into a home."

"So Gracie is missing with a man who needs to be taken care of by nurses in a care facility?" Ashley persists.

"Umm, yeah, I guess so," I say, embarrassed by my lack of information, by my unwillingness to get more from LeeAnn.

"Dan, that sounds pretty serious," Ashley says.

I don't reply, not sure of what to say. It *does* sound pretty serious, but in the same way a devastating earthquake abroad sounds serious. What can you do besides feel sorry it happened?

"Well, what are you going to do?" Ashley asks, clearly not under the same impression that I am. If it was Jack who was missing, I'd have already sprung into action. I just never know the right thing when it involves Gracie. I could go to the police, but LeeAnn might see that as me undermining her authority.

"I'll . . . I'll text LeeAnn to suggest that she file a missing person's report, and then, I guess, I'll drive around, try to figure out where they might be," I say, hoping to please Ashley more than anything. She smiles slightly and nods, giving my choice her seal of approval.

I send the text, trying to make it short and unassuming.

Already done, LeeAnn immediately writes back.

But what have *I* done to make sure my daughter is safe?

21

Gracie

"IT SHOULD BE JUST over this way, Gracie Lynn!"
Grandfather is motioning for me to follow him
along the river bank. Now that I caught a fish I feel like I
can do anything. I climb up a little hill moving away from
the river, watching Grandfather's back, which is shaped like
a candy cane. I love candy canes, and I know Grandfather
does too because one time he chipped a tooth biting into
one and he said it was worth it.

"I wanna show you this spot," Grandfather tells me, standing at the top of the little hill with trees all around. His clothes
have completely dried from when he fell in the river thanks to
the heat of the sun that even these woods can't protect us from.
"I used to come here as a boy in the summertime."

As I get closer to him, he puts his hand out, telling me I
should stop.

"Now close your eyes tight, and I'll guide you," he tells
me, reaching out to grab my elbow. I listen to Grandfather
and again I'm reminded of the blindfold he had on the night
of the incident. But I feel more brave now, and Grandfather

seems okay. With my eyes closed I can hear a loud buzzing sound. The buzzing gets louder and louder as Grandfather makes me take step after step on crunchy leaves. Just when I think I'm going to go deaf from how loud the buzzing is, Grandfather shouts, "Now open your eyes!"

I gasp.

All around me—on every leaf and up the trunks of the trees—are so many giant bugs I'd never be able to count them. They have shiny green bodies and large black wings and boy, do they want to talk. They buzz so loud I know they must be telling good stories, just like Grandfather. Some fly through the air like the confetti that came out of the piñata at Becky's birthday party. I don't see a single uncovered patch of woods that doesn't have one on it. I've never seen this many bugs. It's both very cool and very scary.

"What are they, Grandfather?" I ask, unable to take my eyes off them as they swirl around us. They look like the beetles that are in drawings in pharaohs' tombs like in *The Magic Tree House: Mummies in the Morning*—only bigger, and they seem to like to clump on top of each other.

"Cicadas," he tells me. "Amazing creatures if you can get over the creepy crawly factor. Did you know that these critters hide underground for seventeen years sleeping?"

I can't even imagine sleeping for seventeen years. I'm not even seven yet.

"Then Mother Nature just tells them it's time to come out, and they burrow outta those holes in the ground and claim their turf," Grandfather tells me. "I used to come and marvel at them when I was a kid. For some reason, this little glen is a favorite spot of theirs. It's like they want to make their presence known. When you spend all that time away, you want to make your mark."

"It's so beautiful, Grandfather," I say, because even though bugs are sometimes kind of gross, the cicadas are beautiful. They make the forest look like it's sparkling in green.

"Thought you might like it," he says, looking all around just like me. "Never took anyone here before. Wanted to make sure this place wasn't lost. Think you can remember it for me?"

I nod very seriously. If Grandfather is trusting me to remember the cicada spot, I promise I will.

"Good, I know you will, Sarah," Grandfather says, patting my shoulder.

"Sarah? Grandfather, it's me, Gracie." I feel a little prickle of fear in my belly. It's never good when Grandfather doesn't remember my name. That usually means the worm is awake.

Grandfather shakes his head and reaches out a hand to hold onto a tree, knocking some cicadas off, which feels a little mean.

"Gracie, Gracie, yes, of course, sorry darling," he says. "I'm beat, let's go find a less occupied place to sit."

We walk a little ways away from the cicadas, and I try not to get scared. Grandfather probably just mixed up my name. Mrs. Hoyt does it all the time. We find a large tree with many branches. The branches soar up into the air and then rainbow down and almost touch the ground.

They're like weeping willow branches, but I know that this isn't a weeping willow tree, so it must be something else that's making the branches reach low. Maybe the tree is tired like Grandfather. It must be exhausting to have to hold up branches all day. I don't even like carrying my backpack to school even though it has patches and my ribbons on it.

I wish we'd brought some sweet tea with us because after the river and the cicadas, I'm thirsty, and I bet Grandfather is too. This is the second detail I've forgotten.

Grandfather has that look like he's somewhere else. I really hope the worm hasn't taken over his brain. I don't think it has because the sun is out, but it's getting harder to tell these days. Finally his eyes focus, and he looks at me as if he forgot I was there.

"How's your mother doing these days?" he asks.

It seems like a strange question. Grandfather sees Mama as much as he sees me, so he should know how Mama's doing. Maybe I'm not understanding him right.

"You just saw Mama, Grandfather," I say. "Today at the home, remember?"

"I know, but your mama and I don't always talk like you and I do," Grandfather tells me. He pauses a second and looks serious. "Is she happy?"

I think about Grandfather's question. I guess I don't know if Mama's happy. I've never asked her. How can you tell when mamas are happy? Mama cries a lot, and I don't cry when I'm happy so maybe Mama's very sad. Actually, I'm now one hundred percent positive that Mama's sad, and I've done nothing to fix it. I feel the tears on my cheeks before I realize I'm crying.

"What's the matter, darling?"

"I n—never asked Mama if she was happy, and that was selfish, and I don't want to be a mean person," I mumble, wiping away my tears, embarrassed to be crying in front of him, especially after he got so mad at me when he fell in the river.

Grandfather reaches over and gives my shoulder a squeeze. "Gracie Lynn, now you listen to me," he says in a serious voice. "I've never met a less selfish girl than you. Just look at what you've done for me today! I love you more than life itself, and I won't have you talking about my girl like that."

"B—but I should have asked Mama if she was happy because what if she's not happy?" I ask, and I wipe my runny nose on the bottom of my dress that's already dirty.

"It's the parents' job to ask the kids if they are happy," Grandfather says. "The kids shouldn't have to worry about it. Kids just have to worry about being kids. That's why I hate being in the home. I hate having other people take care of me. It's my job to take care of them, not that I've ever been particularly good at it."

I wrinkle my nose and squint my eyes tight, which is what I do when I'm confused and thinking hard. Grandfather has always taken care of me. I don't know why he's always so down on himself. That means when you say mean things about yourself because you're feeling sad. Mama's almost always down on herself too. We should all be up on ourselves and then maybe we'll all be happy. He wipes a tear off my cheek.

"Did I ever tell you the story about the time the Egyptian princess lost her veil at the pyramids?" he asks me.

I shake my head. I think I would have remembered an Egyptian princess. I wonder if Grandfather is thinking about her because the cicadas remind him of beetles too.

"It was the hottest day, smack in the middle of July in the thick Egyptian desert," he says, closing his eyes like he can see it right there. "I was heading through Egypt on the way to visit the military base there when I decided I couldn't go to Egypt and not see the great pyramids. So I went there on my day off with just a few coins in my pocket and my full uniform on. Now when I say it was hot, it was more than 120 degrees outside. You coulda cooked a catfish in two minutes flat on those pyramid steps. But when I got to the base of the pyramid, I saw an Egyptian princess on her knees wailing to the heavens, pointing frantically toward the top of the pyramid. Now, mind you, we didn't speak the same language, but I could see exactly what she was so upset about. Because on the very tip top of the pyramid was a beautiful white veil. She was dressed in a bridal robe and I could tell that she'd lost the veil in the desert wind. Her tears were so endless that they formed a puddle beneath her, even in that scorching sand. So I placed my hand on her shoulder to help her calm down a minute, and then I took off my jacket and made my way up to the top of the pyramid. Now these weren't steps like you'd find in a staircase. They were almost as tall as I was, so I had to hoist myself up each one. The stones burned my hands, but I kept going because I could hear the princess cheering me on. Then the Egyptian police came, because you are not supposed to climb up a pyramid, but when they saw I was doing it for the princess, they let me go. By the time I reached the top it had almost been an hour. I hadn't had any water and my uniform was plastered to my skin. But I grabbed either end of that veil with each of my hands, looked down, and I took a leap of faith. The veil worked as a parachute, floating me down to the crowd that had gathered below. The princess kissed me right on the lips and handed me all the gold coins in her purse. And that day she got married with the veil I had saved from the top of the pyramids. I heard tell she named her first son John after me."

"Is that really true?!" I ask Grandfather, because I have never heard a more amazing story in my entire life.

"Cross my heart, sugar plum," he tells me.

Grandfather takes his hand back off my shoulder, and I see the bandage on his wrist.

"Does your wrist hurt, Grandfather?" I ask him.

He reaches up and roughly grabs his wrist, covering up the bandage with his hand and making a face like it really hurts. He looks away from me and I'm almost afraid to ask him any more questions, but I want to make sure he's okay. Bandits need to make sure their fellow bandits are up for the heist at all times.

"Grandfather, was it the worm that hurt your wrist?" I ask him, knowing he'll probably be mad like he was the last time I brought up the worm.

"It was an accident," he says very sternly, shaking his head. "It was just an accident."

"Mama says accidents happen sometimes. It's okay," I tell him, and reach out to pat his arm, being careful to avoid the purple bruise from where he fell in the river.

His face is kinder now, more like Grandfather.

"Thank you, Gracie," he replies.

"Is that what made you sick a few weeks ago?" I ask. "Mama said you were in the hospital."

Grandfather won't look at me, but he nods.

"I've never been to a hospital before, except when I was born," I tell him. "And I don't remember that time because I was a baby."

"Hospitals aren't fun," he says, still fiddling with his sleeves. "So try to avoid them if you can."

"Okay, I will."

"Unless you find their secret stash of cherry Jell-O that they keep in the vault in the basement," Grandfather says and gives me a special wink. "Then hospitals can be fun."

I smile, picturing a large secret room filled with only cherry Jell-O.

There's a bird chirping down by the stream, but it's so loud that it sounds like it's under the branches of the tree with us. Maybe if it was in the shade with us, it wouldn't chirp so loudly. It's so much better out here than it is in the home. It doesn't smell bad, and there are none of those big rectangle lights that hurt my eyes. Maybe being in the home is what is making the worm be awake more. Maybe that's why Grandfather had an accident. Sometimes I feel sick after I leave there, so it makes sense that Grandfather would feel sick when he's there all the time.

Grandfather has his eyes closed and is swaying a bit where he is sitting on the ground. I'm about to ask him if he is okay when he opens his eyes and begins a new poem.

"I met God in the morning when the day was at its best. And his presence seemed like sunrise, like a glory within my breast. All day this presence lingered, all day it stayed with me. And we sailed in perfect calmness o'er a very troubled sea."

I stay quiet because the poem is so peaceful, even though Grandfather said "breast" and Greg Bryant always giggles when someone says that word even though Mrs. Hoyt says it's not a bad word, but just a body part. I don't want to interrupt Grandfather's words. I don't understand them all, but they sound very sweet to me.

There's a ladybug crawling on my shoe. Mama says to never kill ladybugs because they are secretly God's angels sent down from heaven to keep an eye on us. The ladybug crawls down the side of my shoe and is almost at my foot when I put my finger down for her to climb up. I don't want to kill the ladybug, but I also don't want her crawling on my foot because that would tickle, and I'm very ticklish.

She walks very quickly and then very slowly like she's running sprints. I giggle because it's funny to think about ladybugs running sprints like the kids in my gym class.

"What's so funny, Gracie Lynn?" Grandfather asks.

"This ladybug is running sprints on my hand," I tell him, holding up my hand as proof.

He examines my hand with squinty eyes.

"I dare say that ladybug could win in the ladybug Olympics," Grandfather says. "I was in the Olympics once for climbing, but they canceled the event because no one would compete against me."

I think Grandfather's being silly, but he did climb a pyramid so maybe not. I like it when Grandfather is silly. He should always be silly and never be down on himself.

The ladybug is now running laps around my wrist like she's training for a marathon. I reach my finger down for her to crawl onto my other hand, but I do it too quickly, and she opens her wings and flies away. I wish Mama could see the ladybug fly away like an angel.

"Do you think ladybugs are angels, Grandfather?" I ask him.

He considers my question for a minute, and replies, "Wouldn't that be marvelous?"

"Maybe that ladybug could be Mama's mama," I suggest.

Grandfather is quiet. I forgot that Mama's mama was also Grandfather's wife. He looks very sad, and I'm sorry that I brought it up.

"What a beautiful thought, Gracie," he says finally. "It would be nice to have Martha flying around, watching over us always. I wonder what she'd think of all this."

"Do you think Mama's mama would have liked me, Grandfather?" I ask, a little scared to look at him.

Grandfather clasps his hands together and lets out a big puff of air. "Oh, Gracie! She wouldn't have loved anything in this world more than you."

This makes me feel that warm feeling inside that has nothing to do with the hot day.

"Do you miss her much, Grandfather?" I ask.

"Gracie, I miss that woman more than the wolf does the moon. There's not a person on this Earth that I could miss more than your mother, I mean, your grandmother," he says, fumbling his words slightly. "There are no words that can describe that woman. Martha couldn't be summarized, she had to be experienced."

"That's what Mama says too," I tell him.

He looks surprised, and then smiles.

The sun is high in the sky, and I'm starting to get hungry. I never got my hash browns, and when I checked my backpack to make sure that the secret letter Daddy wrote me didn't get wet in the river, I saw that my lollipops had melted into gross giant blobs. But I didn't pack Mama's cooler bag to keep them from melting. This is another detail I have forgotten. I should have probably packed more for our adventure, but I have never packed for an adventure before, so I didn't know what we'd need.

"How's about we get some lunch, Miss Gracie Lynn?" Grandfather suggests.

"How did you know I was hungry?" I ask, shocked that Grandfather read my mind. Maybe it's a superhero side effect of having the worm in your brain.

"I can hear your tummy rumbling from over here, my little nomad." He laughs.

I don't know what a "little nomad" is, but maybe it's a nickname for people when they are hungry. I like having a nickname.

"Maybe we can pick something up before the sun goes down too much," I say.

"I know just the place," Grandfather replies.

22

LeeAnn
2 Hours Gone

*H*AVE YOU CONTACTED THE *police? I can if not.*
His text mocks me and my obviously subpar parenting. Of course I hadn't done that yet, though it was my initial instinct at the home—just another example of my failings. How dare he choose to be a parent now? I never should have involved him.

"Sarah," I call. My sister is standing in Gracie's garden patch, looking at my daughter's many purple flowers. She had gone outside to give me my privacy. She turns, and for a second I get a chilling glimpse of Mama without any of the glow that used to follow her.

"What's up?" she asks. "What did he say?"

"Nothing. She wasn't there," I say stiffly, trying to convey that it was a ridiculous suggestion to call him in the first place. "But I think we should go to the police. Maybe file a missing person's report or something? I'm starting to feel pretty useless."

I pray she'll tell me I'm overreacting. I pray I am.

"Yeah, you're probably right," she says. "I'll grab the keys, let's go."

The police station sits in the middle of town, which is about two miles from the west side of town, and two miles from the east. It's in a neglected brick building on Blenheim Street with a splintered wooden sign out front in desperate need of a paint job.

Sarah looks like Nicole Kidman walking into a truck stop wearing a ball gown. The incessant tapping of her heels on the linoleum floors sounds like the countdown music in *Jeopardy!* Several heads turn as she walks in. She goes straight to the front desk and loudly calls out, "Can we get some help, please?"

I still marvel at her certainty, her instant authority in every situation.

A man with a too-short haircut and a friendly face walks up. His nametag reads "R. Snow." His eyes linger on Sarah two seconds too long.

"Her daughter—my niece—is missing," Sarah tells him, pointing at me in what feels like an accusatory manner.

"Ma'am?" he says, turning to me as if noticing I'm there for the first time.

"Umm, yes, yes, that's right," I stammer like an idiot. My utter lack of certainty makes it sound like I've made the whole thing up.

He turns back to Sarah as if awaiting instruction.

"We want to file a missing person's report," Sarah tells him assuredly, keeping her tone gentle to placate me but confident enough to grab the officer's attention. "Could you help us?"

"Let's go sit down in here for a second, and then you can tell me what's going on," he says.

He leads us into a depressingly drab room off to the left, and I morbidly wonder how many people have been told that their children are dead in there. Handing me a Dixie cup of water, the officer motions toward the chair, which I promptly drop into.

"Miss?" he begins.

"Abernathy," Sarah supplies before I get the chance to open my mouth.

"Ms. Abernathy, I know it's hard, but I need you to tell me what happened."

I don't want to say the words, especially not to this man. Mama always said that words gave a thing power, and I don't want to give this power.

"Gracie's gone," I finally manage.

"And Gracie's your daughter?" he asks me gently.

I nod. *Yes, I am the parent of the missing child. I am the one that failed her.*

"How old is she?" he asks.

"She'll be seven next week," I say, steadying my voice to keep from crying at the thought of her birthday.

"Oh yeah," Sarah says, and I know she's thinking of another anniversary, one that's not quite as sweet.

I can still see Dan walking toward me as I held my infant daughter in my arms. Her pink newborn smell filled the room as I cradled her perfection close to me. She had just fallen asleep for the first time, and Dan had come back inside looking so serious. I had forgotten he'd left to take a call. I was too enraptured with my daughter.

"What? She's asleep," I said, holding her tiny form up toward him to prove it. Her miniature hat fit perfectly on her newly washed head.

"Lee, it's your mom," he told me. "I don't know how to say this, but she . . . she's gone."

I shake the memory away, wrapping my arms around myself and pinching my sides. I stare at my sister, leaning on her in a way I've been afraid to in the past. But it feels like I have no other choice.

Sarah's curls have lost their bounce in the heat, and a thin layer of sweat is forming across her forehead. She must be miserable outside of her SUV's AC. I'd probably be apologizing to her for the heat I can't control if it weren't for the situation I find myself in.

"Look, Officer, Gracie is with our father. He has escaped from a nursing home and is in the early stages of dementia. Well, I don't know how early. He's a functioning person, but he has episodes, which is why he's in the home in the first place," Sarah explains succinctly.

"He escaped from the nursing home and kidnapped your daughter?" he asks me.

I shake my head. It all makes Daddy sound so intentionally evil. How do you explain a family dynamic you don't always fully understand to a complete stranger?

"It was her idea," I try to explain. "She was trying to help him by sneaking him out."

"How would that help him?" Officer Snow asks patiently.

The idea seems absurd to say and doesn't paint me in the best light, but I know that I owe it to Gracie to tell the truth for once.

"She thinks there is a worm in his brain," I say, looking intently at the floor.

"What?" Sarah asks sharply. "What does that mean—a worm in his brain?"

"I didn't know how to explain to her what was happening to her grandfather, so I told her that there was a worm in his brain that was making him sick. And that when the sun went down the worm woke up," I say, almost in a whisper. "It's called Sundowners Syndrome. It's common with people suffering from dementia. They often get confused and angry after the sun goes down. It was the best way I could think to tell her without actually telling her."

Sarah is quiet. I can't tell how she's reacting because I refuse to look up.

"It seemed like a good idea at the time, but Gracie questions so much, and she thinks that if they drive away, following the sun, the worm will never come out," I finish. The words don't sound as fantastical coming out of my mouth as they seemed in Gracie's espionage notebook. I feel an odd pang of guilt, like I'm not doing her plan justice when I try to explain it. "And Daddy was never the most responsible parent, even before the wo . . . dementia."

I think back to when I was very little, and Daddy convinced Sarah to climb to the top of the apple tree in the backyard. She couldn't have been much older than Gracie is now, but even back then Sarah had a determination, a drive, and a need to prove herself that I've never felt. I've always just accepted whatever version of myself that others see.

"Betcha can't make it to the top, Sarah Bell," Daddy had shouted, cupping his hands to amplify his voice. "You don't have a hair on your chin if you can't touch that top branch with the yellow leaf. I could do that in my sleep."

She'd already made it two-thirds of the way up, but the top branches had some rot, and she was trying to be careful. But with Daddy's taunts, I saw her set her jaw and push up.

Sarah lunged to reach the yellow leaves and the force snapped the branch she was standing on.

Even though I couldn't have been more than four years old, I can still vividly picture Sarah's body flopping down the trunk of the tree, hitting branch after branch like a rag doll as she cried out in pain. When she finally crumpled to the ground on top of a root, I had been sure that my sister was dead. Daddy rushed over and picked her up, taking stock of how bad the damage was. There were cuts across her arms and legs and one on her cheek, but miraculously, she didn't seem to have broken anything. Daddy set her down as she continued crying, her light sobs the scariest part of the whole experience. I'd never heard that sound come out of my big sister before. I wanted to rush over and comfort her, but it felt foreign to me. I was the little sister. I had no idea how to comfort my own idol.

Sarah brushed away her tears, looking up at Daddy, her expression almost pleading.

"Ahh, don't be such a baby," Daddy said. "You've gotta toughen up, Sarah Bell, if you're ever gonna reach the top."

I can still remember the shadow that passed over my sister's face that day. In some ways, I'm not sure it ever left.

The only sound in the station's room now is the buzzing of the vending machine's light. I can hear police officers outside typing away, filing reports about the horrible things that have happened to other people.

"Okay, I think I understand," Officer Snow says slowly. "But how do you know your father has taken your daughter?"

I pull out my phone, place it on speaker, and play Daddy's message. Even without looking at her, I can see Sarah's jaw clench at the sound of his voice. It's worse listening to it a second time because the first time I only registered enough to understand the key points. Now it sounds like a suicide note being read out with a "P.S. I took your daughter with me" at the end. When it's over, there's a loud ringing of silence in the room, and I feel the inexplicable need to apologize for my father yet again.

"That's helpful," Officer Snow says kindly. "I have to ask, ma'am—is there any reason you'd have to think that your father might harm your daughter?"

I pause. The question is crazy. Daddy would never hurt Gracie on purpose. But then I think of him hitting her in the home that night and of Sarah's body as it fell out of the tree.

"He wouldn't intentionally hurt Gracie, no," I reply. "But a couple of weeks ago, there was an incident. Well, actually, there were a couple of incidents."

Officer Snow picks up his pen, poised to take down notes and waiting for me to continue.

"First, he . . . well, he cut his wrist," I say, the words sounding foreign.

Sarah stiffens next to me. Even though I'd already told her this, it's still a blow.

"And you think he was trying to take his own life?" Officer Snow asks calmly.

I pause. Part of me wants to say it was all for attention, but I know the truth.

"Yes," I reply. "He's been very unhappy in the home for some time."

I can still remember the rage I felt when I saw my father lying small and pathetic in that bed. His willingness to leave his granddaughter, to take the coward's way out after everything I'd done for him. Why are all the men in my life such cowards?

"And you mentioned another incident?" Officer Snow presses.

"He slapped Gracie the other night," I say again, this time even more embarrassed, to be telling a police officer I left my child alone with that man after what he did. "He was having an episode, and she walked up to him, and he hit her. He would never dream of doing it in real life, and that's what he's referring to in the message. I'm guessing Gracie told him about it, because he didn't seem to remember it when I saw him, and the home's staff said he hasn't mentioned it since it happened."

Officer Snow nodded as if grandfathers slapping their six-year-old granddaughters is a common occurrence.

"Now, can you tell me what car they are driving?"

"It's a brown '85 Chevy Impala," I say, repeating what feels like a useless piece of information for the second time.

"Plate number?"

I shake my head and pinch my sides, trying not to see my lack of information as yet another failure.

"And what's your father's name?" he asks.

"John Abernathy," I say, unable to hide my disdain.

"He's tall, like six foot two, and has salt and pepper hair, a mustache, and tan skin," Sarah adds, regaining her voice to fill in the obvious blanks I've left behind. "Gracie comes up to just above my hip, and she's got curly brown hair."

Officer Snow pauses. "Wait, are you talking about Big John Abernathy?" he asks, looking oddly excited.

Sarah groans as I nod my head.

"Well, why didn'tchu say so?" he says, as if that should have been the first thing out of our mouths. "Big John is a friend of this station! He once donated sixty bulletproof vests to us out of the goodness of his heart."

Sarah snorts lightly, trying to cover it with a cough. Daddy "donated" those vests after happening upon an overturned truck of stolen goods, he said. He claimed he wrestled the driver to the ground and when the man escaped, he donated the robber's loot to the police department. Odds are he was somehow involved in the original transport of those goods himself, but that was always Daddy's way, find himself in the mud but come out sparkling clean.

"Yes, he's definitely something," Sarah says through gritted teeth. "But lately he's been, shall we say, not his best? So this situation really does need to be taken very seriously, Officer."

Though he seems to still have stars in his eyes at the mention of Daddy, the officer cedes authority to Sarah without hesitation, nodding earnestly.

"How long have they been gone?" he asks, trying to regain a sense of professionalism.

"About two hours," I tell him.

"Does she have a cell phone?" the officer asks. "We could contact the cell phone company and have them ping her phone to track her location."

I sag my head, shaking it back and forth. When the subject was broached at a PTA meeting, I thought the idea of giving an almost seven-year-old a cell phone was laughable, and now it feels like the joke is on me.

"It's okay, ma'am," he tells me. "Usually in the cases of runaway juveniles, they tend to stay near the area where they live. So she's probably very close by."

"She's not a runaway," I spit back, my chagrin gone. "She thought she was helping. She wasn't trying to leave me."

"Lee, I'm sure that's not what he's saying," Sarah says, rubbing my shoulder and turning me slightly away from Officer Snow. "Don't get upset. We're going to find her, right, Officer?"

"We will do everything in our power," Officer Snow responds, and I feel bad for snapping at him. "I'm going to dispatch a lookout advisory and send an officer to the nursing home. They might have gone back there, and if nothing else, the staff should know that not alerting us sooner was a serious mistake."

I feel a small bubble of pride knowing that I wasn't wrong to get upset with Susan, even though she meant well.

"I'll be back in just a few minutes to ask you some more questions," he says. "For now, just take a deep breath and trust our ability to find her. In ninety-five percent of these types of cases, we end up reuniting parents and their children. They may be back in his room already."

I don't ask about the other five percent. I've seen enough *Law & Order* to know the answer. He stands up and quickly leaves the room. I can hear him telling someone else about the make and model of the car and giving them the details that we've just provided. I start to shiver even though it's a warm day. Sarah and I are just sitting there lamely. Maybe if we were different kinds of sisters we'd be talking or hugging or crying. We might even be rolling our eyes at the officer fangirling over Daddy. But we don't.

"If you can just drop me back at the house, I can pick up my car," I tell her. "You don't have to stay here."

She looks at me, and I'm surprised to see she's offended.

"Of course I'm going to stay here," she says. "My niece is missing. Your daughter is missing."

"Yeah, I know," I say, irritated that she thinks I don't understand the gravity of the situation. "I just didn't know if you had other stuff to do. Gracie's my responsibility."

"Would you cut that shit out?" Sarah snaps, causing me to jump slightly. "And why wouldn't you tell me about Daddy cutting himself when it happened? How could you leave that information out?"

I feel chastised like a school kid being rapped on the knuckles by a teacher's ruler.

I shrug. "I didn't think you'd want to know," I mumble. "All you care about when it comes to Daddy is how much it's going to cost."

Sarah looks inexplicably sad when I say this. I'm about to look away when she says, "Lee, I know you think I'm a horrible person."

I'm too stunned to know how to respond. I've never thought of Sarah as horrible. I've idolized her and was jealous of her, but "horrible" was not a word I'd ever use.

"I don't really know what's wrong with me," she says. "My therapist says I cut myself off emotionally out of necessity. I just want you to know that I'm sorry. Maybe Big John deserves some of this, but you don't. I'm sorry I ever made you feel like I wouldn't be here for you. It's just been hard, especially ever since . . ."

She pauses and I know exactly what she's thinking because I'm thinking it too. Once Mama was gone, nothing made sense anymore.

"For the last few years," she finishes finally, not saying the words.

"Umm, thanks, Sarah," I reply, not knowing where to look.

She turns away and I worry I should say more, that I'm ruining a pivotal moment in our relationship, but I don't know how. I try to process this new information. Sarah's working with a therapist. Sarah apologized to me. Sarah doesn't think I deserve any of this. I guess it would be mean if she did, but for a bit there I felt like I deserved some of it. Sarah wants to be here for me. This is all news to me.

I beg myself to say something, but the words don't come. Picking up her compact mirror, Sarah touches up her nose, clearly avoiding any further discussions. The moment has passed.

◆ 23 ◆

Dan
2 Hours Gone

I REMEMBER THIS FEELING now—the all-consuming terror of inadequacy. LeeAnn's contacted the police. LeeAnn's searching all across Reading. LeeAnn's got this covered.

You're not needed here.

Saint LeeAnn, I used to call her in my mind back when I was trying to excuse my behavior to myself. Saint LeeAnn knows everything about Gracie. They share everything, except my dimple. But maybe it doesn't have to be that way. I want to help my daughter. I want to take action, be a man.

I told Ashley I was going to leave in a few minutes to drive around Reading and look for Gracie. LeeAnn would scoff at me.

You don't even know where to begin, do you?

I rack my brain trying to come up with places she might be—her favorite restaurant, her favorite store, her favorite hangout—but even with the limited options in Reading, I'm coming up blank. LeeAnn barely left the house after Gracie was born. I couldn't blame her at the time. The grief that consumed my wife after her mother's death had a tighter hold on her than I ever did.

Jack sits on the floor, picking up toy after toy and shaking them vigorously, letting out the occasional wide-mouthed "ROAR!" Even he is livelier than I am right now.

I jump up, jittery from my nagging impulse to do something. Pacing around the room, I finally decide to sift through the mail on the table in our entryway, delaying my pointless outing—bills, coupons, and a card from Ashley's mom. But underneath that stack is a piece of neon green paper with outlandish lettering on the top.

Swim Team Parents Directory

I pause. I picked this flyer up when I tried to go to Gracie's swim meet, when LeeAnn banished me from the pool. There's a list of all the kids on Gracie's team and their parents.

Gracie Abernathy: LeeAnn Abernathy

I cringe at the last name. LeeAnn couldn't have legally changed it from Clarmont—she'd have needed my consent for that. But I can just see her telling the swim team and the school to "just use Abernathy." As if she can erase my existence completely. Who would question it? It's not like I'm around to dispute it. Something about seeing the name in print makes me even more determined to do something helpful now. I may not have known how to play a part in my daughter's life before, but I sure can now. Maybe if I can find her, things will be different. They'll be better. Not that that's a particularly high bar to set.

I pick up the phone and before I even know what I'm doing, I dial the next name on the list after LeeAnn's—Corrine Bryant. This is what they call going nuclear.

"Hell-ohhh?" The voice at the other end of the line sounds like she's in a commercial for dishwashing detergent. The sugary sweetness is almost enough to make me hang up.

"Umm, hi," I start rather lamely. "It's, umm, Dan Clarmont, Gracie Cla—Abernathy's father."

Even though I know it's true, the words sound like a lie.

"Well, Danny Clarmont!" she exclaims as if I'm her long-lost love come back from the war. "We thought we'd seen the last of you. How *ARE* you?!"

I'm relieved she still seems to feel friendly toward me even after yesterday. Though I barely remember anything after LeeAnn arrived at the meet, I have a vague memory of this woman defending my honor, or lack thereof.

"I'm, um, I'm okay," I say. "Look, I don't know if Lee-Ann has called you yet, but we are having some trouble locating Gracie."

"Oh my goodness!" she practically screams, and I jerk the phone away from my ear.

"I—I don't think it's that serious," I say rather unconvincingly. "I just wanted to reach out to the other parents on the team, just in case anyone has seen her. I know she is close to the kids on the team."

I actually have no idea whether or not Gracie is close with any of her teammates, but I decided to take a wild stab in the dark.

"Well, of course she is!" Corrine declares, blessedly confirming my assumption. "The Reading Raptors are a *fam-ah-lee*! I can't believe LeeAnn hasn't called us yet."

"Oh, um, well, LeeAnn's busy trying to find Gracie," I say, suddenly worried I've broken yet another unspoken rule with my wife. "I said I'd call someone on the team just in case."

"You have absolutely done the right thing," she tells me. "It's just so important to look out for your kids. And that LeeAnn, well, you know, she's always so . . . preoccupied. I don't have to tell you that! The other day I saw her pick up Gracie in her pajamas, poor dear. Some of the other parents and I have been worried about her ever since the two of you split."

I flush at the mention. How does this woman know all of this? Did LeeAnn tell her?

"Oh, well, I know LeeAnn has a lot going on," I reason, trying to sound positive. "I'm just trying to help."

"Well, of course you are! We *MUST* put together a search party!" she insists. "I'll call up the girls, and we'll all meet at the high school. You know, where they have their meets?"

Something about this woman's tone is making me uneasy. She seems far too thrilled that my daughter is missing. Like this search party is her equivalent to an outdoor barbecue. But I started this thing, so I might as well see it through.

"Oh, okay," I say hesitantly. "I can be there in about thirty minutes. I live in Columbia."

"Yes, I know," she says. And again, I have no idea how. "We'll wait until you get there. Should I call LeeAnn and let her know?"

"No!" I practically scream. "I'll call her now, thanks."

"Okay, see you soon! We'll find her, sweetie, don't you worry!"

And with a click I'm left in the silent aftermath of what seems like my biggest mistake yet.

"Who was that?" Ashley asks, coming back in the room and tucking a stray strand of hair behind her ear. Sometimes it's nice just to watch her, so natural, so at ease.

"Corrine Carter . . . err, I guess it's Bryant now," I say, remembering the brash teenager she'd been when I'd known her. "She's a parent of one of the kids on Gracie's swim team. I also went to high school with her. She wants to set up a search party."

Ashley doesn't look impressed. "Well, that's pretty quick," she says. "Have you told LeeAnn?"

"I was, um, just about to," I mumble. Ashley's disapproval, even when it's minor, is worse than anyone else's because she's the only person who believes in me to begin with. She walks over to me, rubbing her hand on my arm comfortingly.

"You're doing all you can, Dan," she says, leaning in to gently kiss my cheek. "Don't stop trying."

The imprint of her lips still gives me a rush. To so many people I will always be *that* guy. But what Ashley and I have is so much more than a brief fling. She was the first person to truly see me, to care about me, in years. Yes, I took the coward's way out and didn't end my marriage first. And now my parents don't call anymore, and I don't get to see my kid. Or maybe I won't get to see my kid ever again. The thought makes me sick to my stomach. Gracie is still out there somewhere with my dimple. I won't stop trying.

"I've got to go," I tell Ashley, giving her one last kiss.

As I leave the room, Jack cries out, "DADDEE!"

◆ 24 ◆

LeeAnn
3 Hours Gone

"**Y**OU WHAT?!"

A blood-red light is blurring my vision. Somehow, out of all the emotions I've experienced in the past few hours, my anger is tunneling past them all, barreling out of my mouth without a filter. The flashes of rage are so intense that I barely register that I'm screaming into the phone from the cavernous interior of Sarah's SUV.

"She wants to help, LeeAnn."

His pathetic explanations do nothing to soothe the ferocity of the animal inside me, longing to burst out and rip him to shreds.

"I was just trying to do something useful."

"Well, no one asked you to suddenly start trying, did they?" I retort, his innocent act infuriating me.

"You called," he grumbles in the dejected voice he used to put on whenever I caught him making a mistake. "And she's my daughter too. I'm just trying to make sure we cover our bases."

"*We? We're* covering our bases?" I shout, barking out a laugh. "There is no 'we,' Dan. 'We' ended a long time ago. Remember back when you got hammered and decided to tell me that you were abandoning your family on our anniversary? Your wife? Your child?"

He doesn't say anything on the other end.

"Well, ever since then, there hasn't been a 'we,'" I continue, too irate to be embarrassed by Sarah sitting next to me, purposefully keeping her eyes front. "So I'd really appreciate it if you stopped trying to pretend like you're suddenly this great family man. I don't have time to worry about Corrine Fucking Carter right now. *My* daughter is missing."

Saying the words aloud again sends an electric shock through me. Suddenly I don't feel so angry anymore. Now I'm just scared.

"*Our* daughter," Dan insists, and I'm surprised to hear a bit of confidence he's rarely displayed before seeping through the phone. "Look, I can just go if you want. You don't have to come. But I don't think it could hurt to have some parents who know Gracie helping to look for her and John. I had to do something, Lee."

I picture him commanding the group of PTA moms as they flutter their eyelashes at him. I need to punch something.

Dan is the villain. Dan is the villain. I mentally repeat the phrase to reassure me of its truth. But I no longer have the energy to fight with him. It's time to stop being stubborn and find Gracie.

"Fine. Where are they meeting?"

Sarah blessedly stays silent as the car bounces down the road to our old high school. She doesn't know any of these women, but I'm sure she knows what to expect. I wonder if Dan even realizes who he's called, the beast he's awakened.

We pull into the hole-riddled parking lot. There are still colorful signs up from the kids' meet yesterday. I see Gracie's name with a purple flower drawn next to it in her sloppy style. My stomach lurches at the sight of this visual memento from my child. Then I see them, descending like locusts upon the car. I'm going to vomit.

Plastered across their overly bronzed faces are the most phony looks of sorrow I've ever seen. Corrine is at the front of the pack, tits out, her bottom lip sticking out like a blubbering infant.

"LeeAnnnnn," she croons as I make my way out of the car. She's wearing a jean miniskirt I'm pretty sure she owned in high school, probably just to show she still fits into it. It feels like tiny creatures are doing a kick line in my stomach. I don't know what to do with my face. I feel a certain level of spite and betrayal from these women, some of whom used to be my friends . . . well, technically. These are the last people I'd ever want to see me like this, but at the same time this crowd has gathered to help me find my missing daughter—again, technically—so it doesn't seem appropriate to express my disgust. If my emotions had their way, I'd crumple to the ground in a heap, have a refreshing cry, and when I came to, someone would present me with my daughter. But it's been hours and no word, no clue, no hope. My throat starts to close, and I fear I won't be able to speak.

To my horror, Corrine and her rock-hard enhanced breasts lunge forward, thrusting themselves at me as she wraps her arms around me in a tight embrace. A fog of booze and candy apple envelops me.

"We are gonna find your little girl," she loudly whispers, tilting her head toward the other moms and squeezing me until I feel like I'm going to explode.

"Yeah, of course we are, but where the hell is Dan?" Sarah interrupts, pushing her body slightly into mine and forcing Corrine to detach. I've never appreciated her more. In her heels, Sarah's a good head taller than Corrine, and I can tell she's enjoying looming over her with a slightly smug smile. If my body weren't bound by paralyzing dread, I'd enjoy it too.

Corrine's faux concern falters slightly as she stumbles backward in her gladiator sandals to get out of my sister's way. Even she is intimidated by Sarah, I notice.

"This is my sister, Sarah," I tell the women with a foreign hint of pride in my voice.

Corrine sizes Sarah up, widely smiling in a way that doesn't reach her eyes.

"Don't worry, Danny will be here any minute," she chirps, clearly pleased that she has more information about my estranged husband's whereabouts than we do.

"Is he bringing that cute little baby with him?" the woman perched by Corrine's left side wearing an "I Sweat Glitter" cami asks her. Looks like I'm not the only one who Facebook stalks.

That's Samantha Summer. She was a year younger than Corrine and me in school, but quickly rose through the PTA ranks thanks to her fitness blog, *Swole Southern Sam*, which is supposed to be for weight loss tips but is more of an excuse for her to post photos of herself in a G-string bikini and spray tan, flexing at body building competitions.

In her last Instagram post, she declared that she was her own #WCW, adding, "For the beautiful woman I am and the imperfect creature I strive to be. I hope my daily devotion to health, home, and happiness will inspire the rest of you."

"Oh, I'm not sure," Corrine replies, her gleaming teeth blinding us. "He called right after my brunch with Jane, so I'll admit, I'm running on mimosa brain!"

The pug-faced woman to Corrine's right, Jane Berk, leers back at the group, pretending to feel guilty for their midday boozefest. Jane has her own Internet business selling contour makeup kits. She posts weekly instructional videos drawing Kardashian-esque lines over her squished face and has been Corrine's faithful sidekick since before I can remember, back when she used to let members of the track team motorboat her behind the bleachers after school.

This unholy trinity stands proudly at the front of the group of other faceless moms. All I can think about is how I don't have time for this. I never even wanted to go to a PTA meeting when my daughter *wasn't* missing, and I certainly have no patience for it now. But my trepidation has rendered me temporarily mute. We're all roasting on the asphalt, but no one moves, as if to suggest getting some shade would be a sign of weakness. I can feel the heat wafting up from the blacktop and through my sandals, but I don't budge an inch. All I can think about is Gracie out here somewhere in this heat. There's no doubt in my mind Daddy won't make her put any sunscreen on. He won't even think to give her some water. Some days he can barely hydrate himself, so there's no telling what my daughter's experiencing. I'm starting to feel an increased sense of panic as I stay rooted to the blacktop in this faux standoff with these women I have to pretend to like. I don't have time for the politics of the PTA. Gracie doesn't have time.

In addition to the heat of the blacktop, I feel even more pressure from their polite glares. I never knew people could politely glare until I became a parent.

I can trace the exact moment I realized I was a social pariah back to one time when I came to pick Gracie up wearing a tank top and no bra a few weeks after Dan moved out. It was about a million degrees outside, similar to today, and I didn't have the energy to wear my blazer over it. When I got home and looked in the mirror, I looked more like a haggard porn star posing as a babysitter than a working mom.

Samantha's littered the web with photos of her half-naked body and Corrine has never worn a turtleneck in her life, but neither of them had their husbands walk out on them during their prime years. My husband left me hot, available, and emotionally vulnerable, therefore I must dress like a nun or suffer the smirks. I'm not sure why they thought I wanted their husbands' shoulders to cry on, but that seemed to be the common fear that rippled among their ranks. It wasn't even because I'm pretty or anything, so I couldn't take it as a backhanded compliment. I'm not the beautiful former pageant queen or even the trendy young mom. If I had a look, it would be "tired chic," but they only saw one thing when they looked at me back then—desperation— and that's the most dangerous look of all.

It wasn't always this way, I think as I scan their curious glances, trying to distract myself and avoid dissolving into a puddle of tears. I would attend Corrine's house parties where she tried to sell off-brand teeth-whitening strips and leggings. I'm pretty sure I still have a pair of chevron-striped blue ones I bought from her somewhere. Jane would host the same get-togethers for her makeup; once I even posed as her model. And Sam tried to get us to all join her CrossFit group, though most of the women bowed out of that one. We would meet up for coffee three times a week, or as often as my part-time hours would allow me back then.

They'd giggle about Mrs. So-And-So who forgot to bring the allergen-free snacks to the kids' lunchtime, and they'd gossip about Mr. What's-His-Name who was caught staring at the teacher's ass at parents' night. I'd sip my coffee and pretend to listen and agree.

When they caught wind that Dan left, their JV gossip about the gluten-free rice snacks and creepy men's perverted thoughts was trumped by my varsity-level news. Instead of the wounded victim, my tattered tank top turned me into the cougar on campus, hungry for their husband's dicks and excited to shatter their illusions of the perfect family. If they had been through what I had, they'd know that a sweaty hookup with a balding middle-aged man was the last thing on my mind. I tried as best I could to get back into their good graces for a few weeks, but eventually I gave up. I had Gracie, so what did I need them for?

Now, here we are, facing off like dueling gunslingers in a B-level western: the Bad Mom vs. the Concerned PTA. I can practically hear that iconic whistle and see the tumbleweed rolling across the gap between us.

Corrine is passing out water bottles to everyone and showing the other moms the latest swim team photo, pointing out Gracie as if they don't remember her out of the ten kids on the team.

"Mama, do you think they'll let me have my backpack in the photo?" I can hear Gracie asking, the haunting echo of her lost voice reverberating in my ears. Suddenly, I wish I'd recorded more videos of her. I pinch my eyes shut, hoping to expel the hair-raising thought from my subconscious.

"Oops, that's not one." Corrine giggles, mercifully breaking up my nightmares by "accidentally" swiping to a split image of herself in a swimsuit, flaunting her post-baby weight loss after she popped out another little boy last year. She already covered the Internet with those photos in the hopes of "encouraging other moms out there." I remember Jane commented, "You're just so brave, C!" My ten minutes of Internet self-hatred aren't always reserved for Dan.

"Now, *I* have already done a thorough search of the high school, including the back locker rooms and under the bleachers by the pool," Corrine announces, as if she's just single-handedly discovered the cure for cancer. "Gracie doesn't seem like much of a hider; we all know that bubbly personality! But I just *had* to double-check. You simply *cannot* give up on your kids!"

A flame of shame shoots across my cheeks. How dare she imply that Gracie is hiding from me or that I'm not doing everything I can?

Sarah takes three steps until she's standing right in front of Corrine, blocking her from the other moms who haven't broken eye contact with her the entire time. They have always been Corrine's mindless followers. I half expect them to walk around Sarah to keep Corrine in their sights—pigeons looking for the crumbs of gossip she drops.

My sister plucks a bottle of water from the plastic bin at Corrine's feet, flipping her salon-perfected curls into my nemesis's face as if by accident.

"I think LeeAnn should probably instruct the group, don't you?" Sarah asks in the same cheery tone, bordering on mocking. "She has a better idea of where to look and all."

Corrine's giant teeth remain clenched together, her smile shining brightly. Only her eyes give away the fact that she loathes Sarah and any chance to not be in charge. But manners win out this time.

"Of course she should!" she cries, reaching over to put her arm around my shoulders in another unwanted embrace. "Now, LeeAnn, I know it's so hard, sweetie. But can you think of where little Gracie might have gone? Did y'all get into a fight?"

The ever-loving nerve of this bitch.

"No," I reply in a tight voice. As much as I appreciate Sarah shutting down Corrine at her own game, I hate that the attention has now been pointed at me. I didn't need another excuse to highlight my insufficient parenting. All of these women stare at me smugly, their children safe. I momentarily register the fact that none of their kids are here because they're all at home with their husbands. Must be nice. "She's with her grandfather. He's . . . well, he's sick, and not very responsible to begin with. She loves spending time with him and thought she was helping him by break-ing him out of his nursing home."

"Her grandfather, do you mean Big John?" Samantha asks and the other moms start whispering excitedly. I forgot Daddy used to come to pickups and drop-offs back before he was in the home when I had work. And he's never had a problem attracting a crowd.

"Oh for the love of God," Sarah mutters now, clearly exasperated.

"We just *love* Big John!" Jane confirms. "We never see him anymore."

"That's because he's in a nursing home with dementia and can't button his own pants," Sarah says a bit harshly as the other moms look taken aback. "So you can see why we're a bit concerned here, no matter how *charming* my father may be."

The other moms look at me skeptically, not willing to question Sarah.

"W—we checked at our house and filed a missing person's report with the police," I stammer, rushing to get out all the information I can think of.

"Is there somewhere you think she might want to go?" Jane asks, her face perpetually turned down in a pouty frown.

"Well, Daddy might like to visit the river back off Mill Creek Road," I tell her. "He used to go fishing there a lot. And he used to go bet on the horse races over in Tuckahoe County. So we could check there, though I know that's a bit far."

"Yes, but what about Gr-AY-cee?" Corrine asks as if I'm in a remedial English class. "Where would she go? Do you have any idea?"

I clench my fists to keep from screaming at her. She doesn't realize that Gracie will go wherever Daddy wants to go. And Daddy always puts his wants first. So I know she's not the one calling the shots.

"Sure, I mean, she loves Baskin-Robbins, and she likes to garden, so she could always be at the nursery over on Peach Street," I reply tersely. "Other than that, it's basically McDonald's and here, at the pool."

"That's it?" Samantha asks, her orange face looking shocked by my daughter's lack of interests or perhaps by my inability to take her outside of a five-mile radius. "McDonald's?" she adds as if I've suggested a brothel.

"It's not like Reading is much bigger than a postage stamp," Sarah interrupts, scoffing. "There aren't any theme parks or even toy stores, so it's not like there's a lot for Gracie to choose from."

Some of the other moms look offended, like they've suddenly developed some inexplicable pride for this decaying town.

"But that's good," Sarah adds quickly, realizing she needs to cater to her audience. "It means there's not many places they can be."

I smile at her, trying to both show my appreciation and also not look too happy that my daughter is missing.

"That is, if they're even in town at all," Corrine chimes in, breaking up the optimism. "I hope Dan's, err, girlfriend is staying at home to keep an eye out in case they go visit him in Columbia."

My mouth literally falls open at her willingness to bring up that woman. I wouldn't have thought she'd have the balls. But apparently those are as big as her cleavage.

As if on cue, Dan's truck pulls into the parking lot. I'm frozen in a swirl of animosity and sudden anxiety at being face to face with him again, and with such an unforgiving and attentive audience to boot.

"There he is!" Corrine cries, as if we don't all see the only moving vehicle in the nearly empty parking lot.

Swinging open the door, Dan grabs his phone and wallet from the cup holder and slides out of the raised driver's seat. He looks good. I hate to admit it, but he does. I'm covered in sweat with pit stains the size of Texas, wearing shorts with a tiny hole in the crotch and flip-flops I've owned since before Gracie was born, and there he is, pristine, well groomed, a country club-bred Southern gentleman.

The last time we were in this parking lot together was our own high school graduation. He hadn't looked so grown up then, but just as handsome and with a charm I didn't find annoying at all.

"This is just the beginning, Lee," he told me then, cupping my face in his hand and giving me a kiss.

The women immediately pivot their attention to my husband, their smiles widening, shoulders rolling ever so slightly back. I feel a mixture of unexpected jealousy and deep-rooted resentment. There he is, the source of all my problems. Well, him and Daddy. How textbook—a girl with Daddy issues and her cheating, no-good husband.

He walks over to the welcoming group. "Hi, ladies," he says with a smooth smile.

What a total moron.

◆ **25** ◆

Dan
4 Hours Gone

THIS IS ONE OF those out-of-body moments you just assume is happening in a dream. Not the good kind of dream where you win the lottery and your favorite baseball team sweeps the World Series, but the kind of dream that involves unwanted people in your life in unusual contexts. Like your least favorite coworker who has convinced you to go skydiving across a rocky overpass.

There's LeeAnn, looking chronically pissed off and extremely uncomfortable. Her body is the only one pointed away from me, like she's determined not to turn and give me the satisfaction of her attention. Next to her is Sarah, ever the glamazon. I haven't seen her in two years, but she's always been at least courteous to me. Now she's got her hand on her popped-out hip and is wearing a pair of ridiculous heels that look painfully pinched at the toes. The juxtaposition between those two has never been more apparent. Something in her stance tells me I'm not going to find much sympathy in her.

"Dannnyyyyy!"

That same irritatingly bright voice from the phone and the swim meet pierces through my discomfort. The unnaturally blonde woman comes rushing forward. Her enormous teeth are nothing compared to her breasts, which fling themselves at me like they're searching for sanctuary.

"Wow, hi, Corrine," I say, keeping my tone pleasant while worrying she'll find it flirtatious.

"Oh, Danny," she bubbles. "We are so relieved you're here. Aren't we, girls?"

The rest of the group, minus LeeAnn and Sarah, graciously nod up and down like bobblehead dolls on a dashboard.

I'm grinning like a doofus, trying to appease her as her grip tightens on my bicep. Already I'm missing my truck's AC as sweat starts to trickle down my face and onto the blacktop.

"Umm, excuse me," Sarah calls out, and I feel Corrine's lock on my arm clamp down even harder. "Aren't we here to look for Gracie?"

Just hearing her name causes me to chance a guilty glance at my wife. She still hasn't spoken. She's barely looked in my direction. The lines under her eyes seem to have grown even deeper than yesterday, when she angrily shouted into my face. She looks rather shell-shocked, though I can't tell if that's from today or if she always looks like that. LeeAnn has always given off the appearance of a wounded and fiercely territorial bird, protecting her nest while trying to heal a broken wing.

I was too busy looking down at my shoes yesterday to really take her in, but now that I'm seeing LeeAnn here, it feels like something's not right. Her collarbone juts out and her cheeks have a sunken quality I don't remember her having before. Despite the heat of this South Carolina summer, she looks pale. I remember Corrine saying she'd seen her pick up Gracie in her pajamas. What she's wearing now doesn't look too far off from pajamas. LeeAnn's always been casual, but some of the clothes she's wearing are so old I remember them from high school. They hang on her slimmed-down frame, accentuating just how thin she is now. I think of Ashley helping me pick out new clothes and asking how my day went. No one's there to ask LeeAnn. Another thing that feels like my fault.

Her features look sleep deprived, like those terrible months after Gracie's birth. I have the urge to walk over to her, to hold her tight, but I don't. I haven't done that in years, and technically, I couldn't if I tried thanks to Corrine's sleeper hold.

"Well, of course we are!" Corrine replies, pivoting herself, and by extension me, toward Sarah and LeeAnn. "But you can't blame a girl for catching up with her high school sweetheart!"

The label makes me internally shudder. If there's anyone who deserves that title, it's LeeAnn, not this woman who I went on one date with back in my junior year.

Sarah lets out a small snort, and turns to whisper something to LeeAnn. Even though it's likely about me, I find myself mildly pleased that those two are almost behaving like normal sisters. LeeAnn could use a real ally for a change.

"Oh, I didn't realize you two dated," a woman with ripped biceps interjects.

Corrine slips her arm through mine, grinning at the woman.

"Yes, Danny and I go way back," she says. "But I never could settle on one guy in high school. Looks like I let one of the good ones go!"

LeeAnn makes a comical choking sound. That's not the way I remember it. I'm pretty sure I took Corrine out for burgers once, and never called her again. About a month later I started dating LeeAnn. She'd made so little impression that I hadn't initially recognized her yesterday, which might also be due to the excessive amount of plastic surgery she seems to have had done since high school.

"Now, Danny, can you think of anywhere that your daughter might have gone?" Corrine asks me, her face filled with something resembling concern.

This time LeeAnn can't control her snort.

"Yeah, Danny," my wife says, breaking her silence and finally picking an emotion to run with—pure hatred. "Any ideas on where *your daughter* might have gone?"

She says "your daughter" as if it's a mere rumor I've been perpetuating all these years, a lie I've concocted to link myself to her. I avert my gaze, too embarrassed to confront her. The smell of the sickly sweet stuff Corrine has on her lips is making me nauseous. That coupled with my wife's venom and these other watchful women is making me want to sprint back to the truck and zoom home to Ashley and Jack.

"Okay, okay," Corrine interjects. "No need to get snippy, LeeAnn. Danny is here to help, like we all are."

She fans her hand out to the other women, who continue to bob their heads in unison. The image is growing increasingly disturbing.

"Now, Danny," she continues, tilting her body away from LeeAnn again. "I was telling the girls that I have done a thorough search of the school and the pool area, and we were trying to decide where to go next. I think Ellen, you, Mary, and Claire should head to the race track in Tuckahoe to see if anyone's seen them, and Sheryl . . ."

"Where do *you* think we should go?" I turn to LeeAnn. She's still tilted away from me, and I can't blame her. I let these vipers out of their cages when she is at her most frantic.

"I'm heading to the river off Mill Creek Road," she replies, her tone like coiled wire that could snap from too much tension. "I think that's the best bet."

"Then that's where I want to go too," I state firmly, hoping to convey my apology for the current situation by standing in solidarity.

She shrugs her rigid shoulders, turning toward the car.

"Great idea, Danny!" Corrine says, as if I'm somehow responsible for the plan my wife clearly just laid out. "June, you and Sheila go check out the nursery and report back. Covering more turf never hurt!"

Her voice is giving me diabetes.

"Danny, could I hitch a ride with you? I was a little naughty and had one too many drinks at brunch." She giggles, pouting her lips like a pornographic school girl.

The last thing I want to do is let that woman into my truck. It'd be like letting a crocodile into a crate of innocent puppies. But I don't really seem to have much of a choice. I nod, stepping toward my truck and finally releasing myself from her grasp while also ensuring that I'll be forced into her company for the next ten minutes.

"Perfection!" she declares, giving a little clap. "Everyone, you know your tasks, please report back if you hear or see *anything*. And don't forget to hydrate! It's a scorcher out here today."

◆ 26 ◆

Gracie

GRANDFATHER SAYS WE HAVE to eat at the Lizard's Thicket, even though I'd rather eat at McDonald's so that I can get my Happy Meal toy. When Mama has her sunshine days, she takes me to McDonald's and lets me get a McFlurry with my Happy Meal and it doesn't even count as my one ice cream a week. I like the M&M McFlurry because when the M&Ms melt they look like a rainbow. When it's a storm cloud day, we eat cereal out of the box and stay home and I can watch whatever cartoons I want. So storm cloud days aren't all that bad.

Mama always tells me that "you can't always get what you want, like the song," but I've never heard that song so I don't know exactly what she means by that. But it's Grand-father's adventure, so I let him pick the place. Plus, *Lizard's Thicket* is a cool name for a restaurant. I hope they have actual lizards, and we can hold them.

He steers the car into the parking lot and rolls over the curb, but it's not scary, and it's actually fun.

"She's a rental!" he shouts, which is weird because I always thought this car was Grandfather's. But he's chuckling and spinning the steering wheel around, so it must be a funny joke.

Rolling over the curb reminds me of when Grandfather taught me how to ride my bike. I still had my training wheels on, but Grandfather said I had to go down the biggest hill in our neighborhood.

"Gotta earn your stripes, Gracie Lynn," he told me.

We got to the top of the hill, and it looked so high up. Grandfather pushed me forward, and I fell halfway down and skinned my knee, and Mama got really mad. But Grandfather said I should do something that scares me every day.

"Keeps you alive!" he said.

I'm definitely doing a lot of stuff that scares me today, like holding the fish and riding over the curb, so I know I'm alive.

"I have had many a piece of pie in here, Gracie Lynn," Grandfather tells me as we walk into the restaurant. He puts his arm around my shoulders and gives me a squeeze.

"Can I have pie?" I ask, suddenly excited, not telling him that Mama doesn't like me to eat dessert more than three times a week because she says the sugar will rot my brain.

"You can have whatever you want, Gracie Lynn," Grandfather says. "There's sweet tea and macaroni and cheese and pie and cobbler, anything your heart desires!"

Really my heart desires a McDonald's Happy Meal toy, but I don't say that because it would probably be rude to Grandfather. When we walk in, I don't see any lizards, but it still looks like a nice restaurant. We get in line to get the food, and it's all lit up on the counter for us to see.

Grandfather was right—there are collard greens and fried okra and mashed potatoes and butter beans and corn bread. I'm not tall enough to see past the other people in line, so I can't even see all of the possibilities. Mama says that my eyes are bigger than my stomach, which means that I always want more food than I can eat. But I think she would understand if she saw the Lizard's Thicket because I want to eat almost everything.

"Why, Big John Abernathy, could that possibly be you?"

A woman from behind the counter is holding up a silver spoon and staring right at Grandfather. I have never seen her before, but Grandfather seems to know her very well. And she knows his full name. If I had my notebook now, I'd be writing down all of these details so I could espionage some answers.

"Cynthia? Well, I'll be! Gracie, this woman before you is a literal saint. She is the Grand Supreme Collard Green Queen of Reading."

I've never met a saint before or a collard green queen. I don't know if I should curtsy or bow. Plus, Grandfather hasn't said her last name so I don't know what to call her. Maybe I can call her Miss Cynthia like Miss Susan. I hope she doesn't think that I'm being rude. It would be bad to be rude to a saint.

"This your granddaughter, Big John?" Miss Cynthia asks.

Grandfather pushes his shoulders back and puffs out his chest as he puts his arm around me and gives my shoulder a little squeeze.

"Sure is! She busted me out of that chop shop they stuck me in for the day, and we just had to come get the best meal in town."

I wonder why Grandfather said "for the day" when we'll be on the road for a long time, chasing the sun. Maybe he doesn't want to tell Miss Cynthia the plan because he wants it to be a secret so we do not get caught. I make a mental note to keep the plan a secret. I'm a very good secret keeper and so is Grandfather.

"We thought you'd forgotten about us," Miss Cynthia says.

"I couldn't if I tried, Cynthia, dear," Grandfather says in his sweet voice, then he turns to me and says, "Gracie, this woman fed me every day for four years and never ran out of my sweet potato pie."

I'm feeling a little bit shy because Miss Cynthia is a stranger to me, and I don't know how to respond when Grandfather is being so friendly and excited. I try to smile at Miss Cynthia, but her eyes are so big that I have to look away. I wish Mama was here to make me feel more comfortable. She always knows when I'm feeling like my shy self.

"Here's a tray, darlin'. Pick out whatever you want," Grandfather says.

I'm relieved because when I'm picking out food I don't have to talk to anyone, and I can be my shy self. There are so many options that I'm overwhelmed. Grandfather goes first and gets chicken fried steak and hushpuppies and green beans with a slice of sweet potato pie and a sweet tea. I get macaroni and cheese and mashed potatoes and some hushpuppies with a sweet tea. I get some fried catfish too, trying not to think about the fish from the river. And for dessert I get pecan pie because it's definitely my favorite pie. Mama wouldn't be pleased that I'm eating so many of what she calls "starches," but Mama's not here and Grandfather doesn't seem to mind, so I don't say anything. I guess starches aren't very good for you, but they sure do taste good.

"When you stopped coming a couple years back, I was worried you'd moved away and we'd never see you again, Big John," Cynthia says to Grandfather.

"You know I wouldn't leave without saying goodbye," Grandfather tells her.

Cynthia smiles and points to Grandfather. "Miss Gracie, did you know this man right here once ate six chicken fried steaks in a row? Saw it with my own two eyes," she tells me. "Earned that 'Big John' title that day."

"Well, Gracie Lynn, the record was four, so I had to beat it and add another for good measure," Grandfather says, patting his belly. "You see, it's not just about the winning, it's about the story you come away with. Plus, Cynthia's cooking is second only to my Martha's, so I can't even pretend like it was a sacrifice."

"We sure do miss Miss Martha around here," Miss Cynthia says, and I know she's talking about Mama's mama.

Grandfather gets real quiet, and he looks away for a second. When he talks again, his voice sounds all funny and cloggy.

"Thank you, Cynthia," he croaks. "I miss her too, so much."

"We liked having you two come in here from time to time," Cynthia says. "Regulars are what makes this place, and you always told the best stories. Had our fry cooks in stitches. I remember that one about the Egyptian princess."

Grandfather smiles a sad smile, and it almost looks like he's crying. I have never seen Grandfather actually cry before, so I wonder if I'm imagining it now. He has come close, but now there are penny-sized teardrops falling down

his face. It's a very strange thing to see, so it might not be
real.

"It's nice to be remembered," he says quietly. "That's the
problem with these old folks homes, no one has any memory anymore. Makes you feel like you don't exist."

Miss Cynthia walks around the counter and puts her
hand on my shoulder. It's warm and suddenly I don't feel so
shy.

"You've got yourself a very sweet grandfather, Miss Gracie," she tells me. "You take good care of him now, ya hear?"

"Yes, ma'am," I say. "I promise I'll do my best."

"Aw, I know you will, sweetheart," Miss Cynthia says
and gives me a wink.

I like it very much at the Lizard's Thicket, and I'm glad
that we did not go to McDonald's, even though I didn't get
my Happy Meal toy and even though there were no real
lizards. Grandfather tries to pay Miss Cynthia with our
emergency money, but she waves him off with a brush of
her hand.

"Forget it, John," she says. "Your money is no good here."

Grandfather rubs his face, and I think he's wiping away
more tears. He stands up very slowly and gives Miss Cynthia
a hug. The hug seems to last forever. They just stand there
hugging, and Grandfather's shoulders are shaking up and
down. Finally, when they break apart, Grandfather is whispering, "Thank you so much, thank you so much," over and
over again. Maybe that's how you are supposed to react to a
literal saint.

A man in the line behind us gives a big sigh and cuts in
front of me. His tray hits me in the back, and it hurts. I smell
a strong smell of dirty socks and something sour as he passes
me.

"Jesus Christ, come on, lady!" I hear him mumble in an angry voice, and he gives Miss Cynthia a mean look.

Cynthia and Grandfather break apart.

"Now just a second there, young man!" Grandfather shouts at him. His voice is no longer sad, but instead he sounds really mad. He sounds like he did when he shouted at the river and when he and Mama get into their arguments.

"Now, John, don't," Miss Cynthia tells Grandfather.

"I think you owe Cynthia here an apology," Grandfather tells the man.

I stare into the whipped cream on top of my pecan pie to avoid looking at Grandfather or the man. Sometimes when I feel shy, I pretend like I'm somewhere else. Now I pretend like it's a snowy mountain I can ski down, like in this place called Switzerland that Grandfather told me about one time.

Woosh, woosh. I am racing down the mountain on my skis. It's like flying, but on land. My skis make "S" patterns in the snow. I have never seen snow in real life before, but I imagine it looks a lot like this Cool Whip.

"What'd you say to me, old man?"

"I think you heard me just fine."

Zip, zip. I have zigzagged in and out of the other people on the mountain. Grandfather says you have to be careful not to hit a tree when you are skiing or you could get very hurt, so I look out for those too. The snow hits my ski and flies into the air. I catch it in my mouth. It tastes like Cool Whip.

"How 'bout you mind your goddamn business?" the man says.

"I think you'd better apologize, son."

"Maybe you and the little squirt should get out the frogging way and quit holding up the line!"

Zoom, zoom. I reach the bottom of my Cool Whip mountain; it has all but disappeared from the top of the pie, and I realize I've been scooping it up nervously with my finger.

"Now look, son, that's no way to talk in front of women and children," Grandfather says really low and gravelly, and that's even scarier than the shouting.

He looks over at me, and says, "Sarah Bell, go sit with your mama now, ya hear?"

Before I have any time to figure out what Grandfather's saying, I see him lunge forward and swing his arm at the mean man. I want to scream, but I'm too scared. Fear has my voice in her belly. The man moves to the side, and Grandfather staggers. His feet shuffle in his shoes from the home, that he always calls "moccasins." I hear them make a wet squelch and think that maybe Grandfather didn't completely dry out after he fell in the river.

"Good one, cowboy," the man says, and he does a mean laugh at Grandfather. "Come at me again, and I won't be so nice."

The man smiles, and it isn't a nice smile at all. There are black things in between some of his teeth. They look like bugs. This man scares me, but not as much as Grandfather is scaring me now. He's standing with his hands on his knees panting really hard and shaking his head as if he's just run a long race.

"Enough now," Miss Cynthia says to the man and Grandfather. "No more of this."

"Yeah, Gramps, looks like you've had enough," the man says to Grandfather.

Grandfather's bushy eyebrows scrunch together, and I see his teeth clamp down under his mustache. He lets out a

loud bellow and lunges again. This time he moves even
slower, and the man laughs as he moves to the side easily.
Grandfather slams into my arm, and I drop my tray, my
bowls of food shattering on the floor. Grandfather wobbles
and grabs the railing to keep from falling all the way to the
floor.

I am terrified. Grandfather has some of my macaroni
and cheese on his shirt. A chunk of my pecan pie sits in his
hair. His eyes are wide, and he looks like an animal in the
jungle. I've never seen him like this before.

"John, please," Miss Cynthia hollers, and rushes around
to help Grandfather. He swings wildly, and she steps back
and now I'm crying.

"I'll teach you some respect, son," Grandfather shouts,
pulling himself up and moving toward the man again.
"Sarah Bell, I said go to your mother!"

I think Grandfather is talking to me, but I'm so confused
and scared that I don't know what to do.

The man pushes Grandfather in the shoulder and puts
his face right next to Grandfather's.

"I'd like to see you try," he says, giving another one of
his scary grins.

"Enough of this, you two, I'm calling the police!" Miss
Cynthia shouts.

Without looking at Grandfather or anyone else, I hold
onto the straps of my backpack and run outside to the car.

27

LeeAnn
5 Hours Gone

"CORRINE FUCKING CARTER. CAN you believe the nerve of that woman?" I ask Sarah after they've pulled out of the parking lot. "Oh, *Danny, sweet Danny.* They went on one fucking date a million years ago, and you'd think they had this enduring love to last a lifetime. And I'm over here like the cleaning lady, making sure their royal highnesses have the perfect second date—a search party for my missing daughter."

My flip-flops thwack against the pavement as I stomp back to the SUV. They're louder than Sarah's stilettos. Despite being lathered in a thin layer of beaded sweat, I'm too angry to care about the heat. I'm too angry to care about much of anything except my anger. He used to make fun of her in school, whispering that I was worth a million Corrines. Now she's in his truck "searching" for our daughter. The image of Dan getting out of his car as the other moms fluttered their eyelashes is seared into my brain. I fling the door open and hoist myself inside, sliding across the plush leather seats. Though I wouldn't admit it, indignation is a handy replacement for dismay, and I decide to focus on the emotion temporarily to keep from caving in entirely. Besides, despising Dan and detesting the PTA are such familiar emotions they almost console me.

Samantha and Jane are huddled together, no doubt gossiping about me, while the other moms are still milling about like chickens with their heads cut off. Now that their queen has left the parking lot, they don't know what to do with themselves. One even gave me a weak smile, more dazed and confused than friendly.

"Yeah, she's a real piece of work," Sarah replies calmly, only mildly ruffled. "But as Mama would say, 'We have bigger fish to fry.'"

She's putting on her seat belt and checking her mirrors before I have a chance to let those words sink in. Out of the corner of my eye I see a faded station wagon pull into the lot, slightly rolling over the curb. The frazzled driver erupts from the car like an explosion has gone off inside. I put my hand up to stop Sarah from moving forward and make my way out of the car as Paula's head swivels back and forth desperately.

"Paula?"

"Oh my word," she cries, rushing past Samantha and Jane's sneers and wrapping her arms around me tightly. "LeeAnn, how are you? What's the latest? I'm so sorry I'm late. I was waiting on Jason to get home to watch Becky and Liam, and I swear to God that man couldn't have moved slower if he tried."

I stand there, bowled over by her unexpected embrace. This woman has never even shaken my hand before. We tend to exchange simple pleasantries when I'm picking up Gracie from her house or dropping Becky off from swim practice. True, she's never been rude to me or anything, but I always assumed she thought of me more as an irritation than a friend. I'm always late for pickups, and Gracie raves about Becky's homemade packed lunches, while I throw in a Lunchable on a good day and a five dollar bill for the school's cafeteria on a bad one.

"Oh, umm, I'm okay," I lie, stepping backward and out of her embrace in what I hope isn't an offensive manner. Her shirt has a giant picture of a kitten chasing a ball of yarn printed on the front. Cat shirts seem to be a favorite of Paula's. She seems oblivious to the other moms' judgment. I kind of admire her for it.

"I think we're heading to the river where Daddy used to go fishing a lot, just to see if they might be there. You're welcome to join us. Some of the other moms have split off to try other potential places."

"Oh my God, how terrible!" Paula says, and I'm embarrassed to see Jane doing an imitation of her behind her back. Why can't she just let me be the school leper? It would make things easier for her in the long run. She's building the worst possible alliance without even realizing it. "Bless that poor little girl's heart. We're going to find her, LeeAnn. Don't you worry. It would break my heart if anything happened to Gracie. We love her like our own."

This makes more sense than Paula feeling any strange loyalty or friendship toward me. Gracie's always had the tendency to charm the other parents. Paula's face is filled with remorse. I almost feel more sorry for her than I do for myself.

"I won't hold y'all up," she adds, giving me a tiny pat on the arm. "I'll be following right behind in the wagon. Just holler if you need me to do anything. And I mean that, Lee-Ann, *anything*."

"Thanks, Paula," I mutter, relieved to see the other moms moving away and Jane getting into Samantha's car, the sight of the two of us no longer entertaining enough to hold their interest.

I slide back into the SUV with less force this time, feeling a tendril of stress loosen at Paula's kindness. Finally, there's a friend among the wolves.

"Who was that?" Sarah asks, watching Paula plop down into her car through the windshield of the SUV. I search her tone for any notes of mocking.

"Oh, um, Paula," I say, non-committal. "She's the mom of Gracie's best friend, Becky. She's going to join us."

Sarah flips some stray curls back and pulls out of the parking lot.

"Good," she says with a satisfied smile. "I've had just about enough of these other biddies. Let's go find your girl."

In my spite-filled rage at Dan and awkwardness around Paula, I momentarily forgot to feel fear for my missing daughter. A fresh cloud of terror hovers over me now. Outside the SUV, the clear and bright sky juxtaposes my gloomy sense of dread. Reading is so small we should be able to find them, right? Despite myself I feel a mild sense of gratitude toward Corrine for suggesting we split up, no matter what her intentions might be. Having more eyes out there looking for my little girl and her mess of curly hair can only be a good thing. I wish I could burst out of the car's roof and fly over the ranch-style houses and partially working gas stations, covering as much ground as possible. Suddenly it feels like I've wasted far too much time rehashing old grudges and busying myself with people I not only loathe but who will do nothing substantial to help me find Gracie.

I turn to my sister. "Sarah, please hurry."

28

Gracie

EVERYTHING SEEMS TINY WHEN you are far away. Grandfather and I are sitting at the top of a very tall hill that is
above the town. Grandfather says it is not tall enough to be
a mountain, but it seems very high up to me. I can see the
pool and my school, but not our house because it's hidden
behind the trees.

After I ran away from the Lizard's Thicket, Grandfather
followed me very quickly even though he stumbled a little.
I think he was tired from all the hitting. I was so scared that
Miss Cynthia was calling the police on me and Grandfather
that I wanted to hide behind the dumpster, but Grandfather
told me she was angry at the mean man and that I wasn't in
trouble. But he said it's probably best to "lie low" a while
and let it all "blow over." I'm still nervous even though I'm
not in trouble, and I look around as we sit at the top of the
hill. I'm also very hungry because all I ate was Cool Whip.

There must be a game going on at the big kids' school
where my pool is. I see lots of tiny car dots, which is weird
for a day when there is no school. At first I'm worried that I

forgot about a swim meet, but then I remember that Mama wouldn't have taken me to the home if my swim meet was today. That's good, because I'm supposed to be on the Purple Team this summer and missing a meet would be bad.

"Plenty of sun up here, Gracie girl," Grandfather says.

He's right. I wonder if I should be wearing sunscreen. But I don't like putting it on, so I don't say anything. I don't think Grandfather is mad anymore like he was in the Lizard's Thicket, even though he keeps mumbling "That no good son of a bitch," which I know is a bad word.

Even though it's hot, the sun beating down on my legs makes me feel a little better. Back at the Lizard's Thicket, it felt like the walls were caving in on me. It's nice to be out in the fresh air.

"This is what living is all about," Grandfather says with a flourish of his arm. "Not stuffy homes and stupid pills and adult diapers."

I giggle. "What's an adult diaper?" I ask. "Diapers are for babies!"

"When people get old, they revert back to being babies," Grandfather says. "Sometimes they take a dump in their pants, sometimes they forget how to speak or to walk. Baby stuff. That's why growing up is a horrible trick."

I'm shocked. All my life I have wanted to be old enough, but if growing up is like what Grandfather is saying, I don't think that would be fun.

"Are you gonna forget to speak?" I ask, horrified. "How will you tell me about your adventures?"

Grandfather turns to look at me and his face goes from serious to smiling.

"Ain't never gonna happen, darlin'," he tells me. "Don't you think on it for one second."

When I grow up, I want to be smart and know lessons like Mama and go on adventures like Grandfather. But I don't know what I want to "be," which is something people ask me a lot.

"Grandfather, why does everyone ask me what I want to be when I grow up?" I ask suddenly because the thought popped into my head, kind of like a light bulb moment.

"I assume it's because they want to know what your hopes and dreams are," Grandfather says.

"Why do we have to be something?" I ask. "Why can't we just want to be *like* something? I want to be like you and Mama."

"Well, that's very sweet, Gracie Lynn," Grandfather says, and brushes back my hair. "But I suppose we all have to be something so we know our place in the world."

"What did you want to be when you were a kid?" I ask him because I realize I've never asked him before.

"Oh, I wanted to be lots of things," he replies with a far-away look in his eyes. "A railroad conductor, a museum curator, a chairman of the board, but the very first thing I ever wanted to be was the ringmaster of the Shackleford Burch Circus."

"What's that?" I ask.

"He was a man in a bright red coat and tails who wore a golden top hat," Grandfather says, chuckling. Grandfather has that starry look again like he's somewhere else, but not in the scary way like when the worm is awake, but in the far-off way, like when he's remembering moments from a past life. He lifts up his hand, and even though it's shaking a little bit, he waves his palm through the air with a flourish and in a booming voice shouts, "Ladies and gentlemen, mesdames et messieurs, the Shackleford Burch Circus would like to welcome you to our little corner of the world!"

I gasp a little, remembering Cinderella's own little corner, but Grandfather doesn't even notice. He's just sitting there with his hand raised, like he's reaching for something I can't see.

"The crowd would scream and cheer and suck in their breath as I commanded the ring, taming lions, and holding up the flaming hoop for the acrobats to jump through," Grandfather says. "When they got restless, I would subdue them. When they were scared, I would reassure them with my expertise. The ring would be my domain and its inhabitants, my loyal subjects."

I picture Grandfather calling out to the crowd in his red jacket and golden top hat, his mustache bobbing up and down across his smiling, tanned face. He's standing up tall, chest puffed out and feet spread apart in a superhero pose.

"That sounds marvelous, Grandfather!" I tell him. "But why didn't you?"

"Didn't I what?"

"Become the ringmaster of the Shackleford Burch Circus?"

Grandfather looks down at me, like he just now realized I'm there.

"Lotta things that didn't pan out, Gracie girl," he says. "Lotta dreams that never got fulfilled."

"I'm sorry, Grandfather," I tell him, because that does sound like a very sad thing.

Grandfather scrunches up his bushy eyebrows while making a serious face.

"Don't be sorry," he says, patting my hand. "All those dreams made me not appreciate the things that I actually was."

Grandfather is talking in riddles again, but I don't interrupt him. He looks away from me again and out over the hill-mountain, and he seems very peaceful. It's weird that he looks so dry when I am so sweaty. Maybe that's another superhero side effect from the worm. Mrs. Hoyt taught us in school that heat rises, so being up on this hill-mountain is very hot and there is no shade. I wish I was in the pool all the way down there, swimming the butterfly stroke in my underwater world.

"Sometimes I wish I was little like you, so I could give it another go," he tells me.

I have spent so much time wishing I was grown up that I can't imagine anyone wishing they were a kid. It's all very confusing.

"What were those books you were telling me about?" Grandfather asks.

"The *Magic Tree House* books?" I ask, pleased he remembered.

"Yes, those ones," he says. "How do they work?"

"Well, the first one is really cool," I say. "Jack and Annie are exploring in the woods, and they find this tree house, and inside are all these books. And Jack starts reading one about dinosaurs. He says he wishes he could see a dinosaur, and then the tree house takes them back in time, and they meet a bunch of dinosaurs."

"Well, isn't that something?" Grandfather asks. I don't think that's a question I'm supposed to answer. "If you wish for it, it comes true. That's always what they teach kids."

Grandfather sounds like he's making fun of the *Magic Tree House* books, which makes me kind of mad because they are my favorite books.

"I know it's just a story, Grandfather," I say. "I'm not a baby. I don't think it's real. But it would be cool if it was."

"It certainly would," Grandfather agrees.

I like Grandfather more like this. Back in the Lizard's Thicket, with the hitting and the bad words, he was scary. Scarier than I'd ever seen him before, even scarier than the night he confused hit me or when he fell in the river today. But now he seems more like himself. I close my eyes and wish that Grandfather and I could go back in time to before he had the worm in his brain. Back then Daddy was around, even though I didn't see him much then either. But Daddy used to come in my room and kiss my forehead and whisper, "No matter what, remember that I love you." He must have thought that I had a bad memory because I was little, but I remember that.

Kids are supposed to have mamas and daddies, except Rebecca Thurston who has two mommies. But I know that even if you have a mommy and a daddy, they don't always stay together. In school there is a Banana Split Club for people whose parents are divorced. Divorced means that they are still a mommy and a daddy but they don't live together anymore. They get to eat banana splits and have two houses and hang out together, and it looks like so much fun.

But my mama and daddy are not officially divorced yet, so I can't be in the club. And I've never been to Daddy's house.

Mama says she and Daddy aren't divorced because "I'm not in the mood to beg my boss for an additional benefits package."

I don't know what a "benefits package" is, but I guess it must be important.

Plus, Becky's not in the club so I don't think I'd have many friends there, and I wouldn't want to use up my one ice cream a week with people who aren't my friends or Mama.

I wish I could use my one ice cream a week now. It's so hot up here.

"That's where I took Martha on our first date."

Grandfather is pointing down to the old movie theater. Mama said it used to play lots of movies, and now it is just an empty building with old ripped-up movie posters.

"I've never seen a movie in a movie theater," I tell Grandfather.

He takes a step back and arches his eyebrows. "You're pullin' my leg," he says.

I don't know what that means, but I think the right answer is no, so I shake my head.

"I promise I haven't, Grandfather. I'm not necessary lying," I insist.

"Oh, Gracie Lynn, that is simply inexcusable behavior! That is terrible grandparenting on my part. Let's go see a movie tonight, you and me."

I bite my lip. There's nothing more I'd like to do in the whole world than go to a movie—well, except maybe going to Italy—but when it's nighttime the worm will be out, and I'm a little afraid to be in the dark night with Grandfather again.

"What movie did you go see?" I ask instead of answering.

"Hmm?"

"With Mama's mama. When you went on your first date, what movie did you see?"

Grandfather's mustache turned down into a frown as he put his thinking face on.

"Why, it was *Fiddler on the Roof,*" he says after a minute. "Yes, yes, I think it was. That musical about the Jewish people getting married. You ever seen it?"

I shake my head.

"Well, it starts off with this fiddler playing on a roof, just like the title. Martha adored it. She laughed and clapped and hummed along, even when she'd never heard the songs before. It was the darnedest thing. One time, something really funny happened, and she was laughing so hard she spilled her popcorn. She was just so beautiful and so full of life. It's not so easy to be full of life in a dark movie theater. That's when I knew I was going to marry her."

"On your first date?" I ask, surprised it could be that fast.

"Sometimes you just know," Grandfather says, and I think I see a tear bubble in his eye again. He shakes it away. "So after the movie, I climbed up on the roof of that theater just like the fiddler and asked her to marry me. She thought I was gonna fall, and she said I was crazy, but I wouldn't come down until she said yes. And she did. My sweetheart."

I smile because I can just picture Grandfather standing on top of the roof and asking Mama's mama to marry him.

"That must be nice," I say. "To have so many memories of Mama's mama now that she's dead. Because Mama says when you're dead, all that's left of you is your memories."

Grandfather considers this and smiles.

"Come on," Grandfather says. "You wanna do something fun?"

29

LeeAnn
6 Hours Gone

A MOSQUITO BUZZES AROUND my ear, soundtracking my ominous mood.

"Jesus H. Christ!" Sarah exclaims as her heel sinks into the soggy dirt on the water's edge. "I thought I'd seen the last of this shit hole."

She gingerly slides her shoe out of the mud, retreating to the dry, cracked earth on the main trail. I don't remember her ever coming down here with me and Daddy. He used to drag me to the water, which I tolerated back when he was a mythic creature to me, this God-like figure who existed on a different plane than the rest of us. Also, it made Mama happy to see us spending time together, and I'd do anything for her.

He'd regale me with stories of alligators and fishing records. He told so many tales that sometimes I wondered if he even realized I was there, if it would have been any different if I wasn't. I was hypnotized by him the same way Gracie is now, except I had a healthy level of fear associated with my awe—fear of making him mad, fear of making him leave, fear of eliciting any reaction other than approval, which I received so rarely that when it was doled out in small rations I treasured it like my most prized possession. When we were kids, Sarah liked to remind me of the month after I was born when I had colic. Daddy literally refused to come home as I wailed into a fatherless abyss. Mama stayed up with me every night, singing me songs and playing me jazz, but Daddy wouldn't set foot in the house.

"LeeAnn Abernathy, the girl who drove her daddy away as soon as she was born," Sarah used to tease me.

So whenever Daddy had a complaint or griped about anything, I took it very personally. In my early years, I turned that guilt into a kind of cult worship. The man could do no wrong. It took me a long time to understand the lesson that Sarah learned as a kid—that a girl needs her mama but our daddy was expendable. Strange that such an imposing figure could be so inconsequential in the grand scheme of things, but looking back, every milestone and core memory came from Mama. Daddy was no more a part of my story than Dan is to Gracie's. And just like I don't need Daddy, she doesn't need Dan. Though clearly I'm no Martha Abernathy in the mom department.

My sandals squish against the grassy banks of the river, as the murky water causes my feet to slip across their cheap plastic. I'm surprised the holes of my old stool legs aren't a permanent fixture here. I used to sit next to Daddy, patiently holding his lures and watching him closely for any signs that he needed my help. Even when it was hot and the bugs were biting, I didn't complain. I wouldn't dare.

I'd sit and he'd fish and every once in a while, he'd turn to me with a glimmer in his eyes and recite one of his "original" poems. I loved listening to his clever words, and would beg him to repeat my favorites whenever I could pluck up the courage to talk to him. He glowed as he dutifully delivered each line, relishing the captive audience that was my naïveté.

Once I memorized my favorite and wrote it down on the chalkboard in my room. Sarah walked in as I added the final line—"If I could just get organized"—and sneered at me.

"By John Abernathy?" she scoffed. "You don't actually believe Big John wrote that, do you?"

Cheeks burning, I decided to pick a side and hold my ground for once.

"Of course he did," I declared, with inflated indignation, remembering his mighty stance as he recited the lines. "Daddy's a poet!"

"Your daddy's full of shit," she replied, as if he wasn't her father too.

My heart broke the day she showed me the full poem by Douglas Malloch, which was written before my dad was even born. It began with the exact same line, "There may be nothing wrong with you, but I can plainly see, exactly what is wrong with me." And though he'd taken some liberties in editing it down, there was no doubt that it was the same poem.

"Daddy, why did you tell me you'd written that poem?" I later asked him with tears in my eyes, praying the book Sarah had shown me had lied, praying there was some other explanation.

The glimmer of constant amusement left my father's face, along with the idea that he was anything more than just a man. I was no longer his ally, and he was no longer my hero. I'd built him up as this larger-than-life creature, too great to stay at home with us mere mortals, but from that moment, I knew he was a washed-up fraud with great dreams and zero follow-through.

For some reason, that betrayal hurt me deeper than his absences or the various other grievances that camp themselves in my mind whenever the subject of my father comes up. It was because he had personally betrayed me for no reason I could really pinpoint other than to make himself look better. My father, the entertainer. I wanted to be more than just his audience, but no one ever was. From that moment on, I learned to question everything he said.

Even now, here we are, puppets in his play, scouring the town for any sign of him. Sarah manages to wipe the muck from her shoe, pouring sanitizer over her hands several times after she's tossed the dirt to the ground. I feel another pang of guilt knowing how thoroughly miserable she must be, but I'm afraid to suggest again that she go home, partially because I don't want to accidentally offend her and mainly because I'm afraid she'll really go this time.

Dan's up ahead, with Corrine Carter Bryant clinging to his bicep like it's a flotation device. Samantha and Jane are close behind—Corrine's loyal ladies in waiting.

"Is this the spot, sweetie?" Paula asks me, luring me back to my undesirable reality.

"Yeah, in this general area," I tell her. "He didn't tend to go more than a half a mile in either direction. The river kinda tapers off around that bend to the left, so there's not much point in going far."

Paula wipes her face and whips out a cardboard fan from her purse like the kind they hand out at church or at a funeral. I turn and face the water picturing Gracie's lifeless body following the current down to where the stream ends, her limp curls covering her face, which is bloated with the murky water. I jump as Paula touches my arm.

"Sorry, darling," she says, surprised by my response. "You doing okay? Can I get you a snack? Have y'all eaten anything?"

What a good mom.

"I'm okay, thanks, Paula," I reply, contorting my face into what I hope is an appreciative smile.

"I could use a martini," Sarah adds in a comically harassed manner.

"Well, I'll see what I can do about that," Paula answers, and I crack a small smile.

From farther down the trail, Corrine slaps her hands together, commanding the attention of the small subgroup she's assembled. She cocks an eyebrow at me as if to ask, "Well?"

I shuffle and slide through the mud and over to the grassy patch where she's standing superglued to my husband's side. He's pretending to scan the trail and water, but I know he's really avoiding my gaze. I'm thankful.

"Umm, yeah, so this is the spot," I say lamely. "They wouldn't have gone far. So I guess just keep an eye out for anything unusual. Probably a good ten minutes and we'll have an idea if anyone's here."

Corrine angles her body away from mine and toward her posse.

"And remember, ladies, let's keep an eye out for any hiding spots!" she chirps to Jane and Samantha, ignoring Sarah, Paula, and me. "We all know that little Gracie has *quite* the imagination. So let's get creative!"

She sounds like she's just encouraged them all to craft their own personal vision boards. I see Samantha and Jane pose for a selfie beside the water. Somehow my daughter's disappearance is an Instagrammable moment.

"Anything to add, Danny?"

I feel my mouth literally moving into a snarl. Dan shifts uncomfortably from one foot to the next, catches the eye of the smiling Jane, and lights up a bit, cheered by what he interprets as her approval but what is really just her reaction to getting some good light for her photo.

"Yeah, I don't think she'd hide," he says, and the other moms nod slightly, not sure if it's safe to disagree with Corrine's suggestion. "I think if she knows we're worried about her, she'll probably respond to us calling out. So couldn't hurt to shout her name a few times."

Brilliant.

"Excellent suggestion, Danny," Corrine confirms, putting her lackeys at ease. Unzipping her bag, she pulls out a tiny bottle of bug spray, pressing the nozzle and watching the chemicals fly through the air.

"Can I interest you in a squirt, Danny?" she asks.

Sarah snorts, and Paula smiles a bit too, afraid to commit to a full laugh. She's not as unconcerned with PTA politics as I thought.

"Come on," Sarah urges, pulling us away as I see Dan extend his arm.

I feel a bubble of vomit leap up my throat before I force it back down. I'm both repulsed by this woman's obvious advances and by the fact that I can physically feel time ticking away as I have to witness it all.

We walk in the opposite direction from the group, and I try to focus on searching for Gracie, not Corrine Carter and her cronies.

"Lee Lee, can I interest you in a squirt?" Sarah teases in a high-pitched voice, momentarily forgetting I'm no longer her kid sister. I roll my eyes, secretly pleased we're back on a joking level despite not being in a joking mood. It's much better than shouting about money or griping about who's going to take care of Daddy. We were never friends, but we used to at least be sisters, allies. For the past few years we've just been strangers, filled with misplaced animosity.

"How do you stand that bitch?" Sarah asks Paula.

I'm briefly embarrassed, knowing no one in the PTA is ever that candid, but Sarah has a knack for wading through the bullshit and saying exactly what's on her mind.

"Oh, um," Paula stammers, checking over her shoulder to make sure that the rest of the group is out of earshot. "Well, she can be very . . . spirited."

"Spirited?" Sarah scoffs. "She's the whole damn pep squad, if the pep squad spit paralyzing venom. I can't believe I never knew her in high school. I would have drop-kicked that bitch."

"Oh, you guys went to the same school?" Paula asks. She and her family moved from Arizona right before Gracie entered kindergarten. It's probably why Gracie and Becky are such good friends. She tends to gravitate toward the lonely without even realizing it.

"Yeah, I'm a few years older, so that's probably why," Sarah says.

It's actually because Sarah treated me like a mutant when we were teenagers and pretended like I barely existed in public, but I don't mention it.

"And I moved to Columbia for college and stayed there when I had my two kids," Sarah adds, craning her neck around some reeds, as Paula nods. "I didn't really come back to Reading for years until . . ."

Sarah's voice gets quiet, and I know even she's not willing to finish that sentence with the truth.

"Until Daddy started getting sick and all," she lies.

The reeds by the bank are stock still, unmoving in the lack of breeze. Mama used to point all the fans in the house at the couch and make us sit side by side on it, air blasting us in the worst of the summer months. August felt achingly long in the years we couldn't afford AC because of the cost of Daddy's dreams. Mama would stand nearby getting some secondhand breeze and smiling at us, offering to make us some Arnold Palmers.

"To help with the cool-down process," she'd say, patiently stirring the lemonade mixture dozens of times until it properly dissolved. "Can't have my girls in anything but the lap of luxury!"

A tear wells up in the corner of my eye at the image, but I haven't broken down yet, and I'm determined not to do it now, not in front of Sarah and Paula, and certainly not with the other, much less sympathetic crowd nearby.

We round the corner when I first hear the distant shout.

"I've got something! I found something!"

✦ 30 ✦

Dan
6 Hours Gone

THAT MOM WITH THE squished face is flailing her arms, crying out louder than Jack during a tantrum. The piercing pitch of her voice breaks through my haze of nods. Corrine has me working my neck like a seesaw, moving in a rhythmic agreement.

She'd been in the middle of telling me all about how her husband works late most nights and flashing some uncomfortably suggestive stares in my direction. As the alarm sounds, I whip around, both eager to be free of Corrine's hold and fearful of the "something" the woman—I think her name is Jane—had found.

"Over here, in the reeds!" maybe-Jane calls.

I see LeeAnn dart around the corner, ashen and trembling. It's strange—though I had a fleeting moment in the parking lot, I no longer have the desire to hold her, to go to her. She was my wife—technically still is. But something about LeeAnn in distress makes me instinctually maneuver myself as far from her side as possible. The last thing she's ever wanted in a crisis is me. It's always been best when I get out of her way.

We rush down the bank to where maybe-Jane is standing, dumbly pointing into the overgrown reeds. Careful to avoid LeeAnn coming from the other direction, I see it—a child's fishing rod. LeeAnn catches a glimpse at exactly the same moment, and I see her crumple slightly, grabbing onto Sarah for the smallest of seconds. She thought this would be Gracie. I'm not sure if she was expecting a body or our little girl, cleverly hiding in plain sight. Her contact with her sister's arm is short-lived. Regaining her composure, LeeAnn sighs quietly and takes a small step back. She has never shared her grief or turmoil with anyone, especially when at her worst. I should know.

"How can we be sure that's anything?" Corrine scolds maybe-Jane, who is immediately crestfallen. "You gave us all a real fright. I know poor Danny was quaking in his boots!"

I'm not wearing boots. They're my favorite Sperrys, which have felt like an increasingly stupid choice as our muddy day has progressed. I really wish she'd stop calling me Danny. That name is reserved for my mom, and even she stopped using it after junior high.

"That's my old rod and reel," LeeAnn says, as the entire group turns to face her, seemingly surprised she's still there. I'm amazed she hasn't taken charge of this whole thing. When it comes to Gracie, LeeAnn is always in charge. But something about these women seems to have flattened her air of authority.

Corrine walks down to where maybe-Jane is standing, bends over in a stripper-esque manner—her hourglass figure on full display in a jean miniskirt—and plucks the rod from the grass.

"So then Gracie probably used this," Corrine says, as if she's put together all the clues herself. What a modern-day Nancy Drew. "They were here!"

She lifts the rod over her head like a Miss America trophy, beaming at me as if I'm going to run into her arms, filled with gratitude. Instead, I stand there stiffly and nod again, averting my gaze. Limiting myself to looking at neither her nor LeeAnn severely restricts my options to basically staring at the ground. The group is humming with soft murmurs of excitement. The orange woman snaps a photo of the rod and reel in maybe-Jane's hands. These women are taking some kind of sick amusement in being involved in the hunt for my missing daughter. It's like this is allowing them to live out their true-crime podcast fantasies. They seem desperate to make themselves closer in proximity to potential tragedy, like they're already picturing their on-camera interviews with the local news.

"Yes, Sharon, I was there the day we found that poor little girl's body," orange woman would say through tears. "We searched high and low and then I saw her tiny little arm, and, well, that image will haunt me for the rest of my life, I promise you that. I even took a photo of her fishing rod. Would you like to see it?"

The whole thing is nauseating.

"My real-life daughter is actually lost!" I want to scream at them. But I don't.

"See, Danny?" Corrine startles me, closer than I'd realized, not looking at her and all. "She's still out there! It's all going to be okay."

"Umm, yeah," I reply, trying my best to look pleased and not disgusted as that sickly sweet smell washes over me again. "Thank God."

I take a few steps back, and Corrine unfortunately follows. "Danny, where do you think we should go next? Where do you think she might be?"

I wish she'd stop asking me. It's exhausting having to pretend like I have any clue where my daughter is or what her interests are. I have literally no idea, and I don't want to have to explain that to this woman. Though I'm sure Lee-Ann would love to hear me try.

As much as Corrine repulses me, she doesn't seem to view me as the villain in the story of my broken family, which is a rarity I'm not willing to give up just yet. I should tell her and her pack of sickos to get lost, but then I'd only be left with people who despise me, and I'm too much of a coward for that.

"Maybe we should check back at the house," I say. "I know LeeAnn and Sarah went there already, but they might have doubled back."

"Excellent idea!" she cheers with a little bounce, giving my arm yet another squeeze, her enormous beaming white teeth locked into permanent praise.

"Everyone!" she roars, magically turning her voice into a megaphone. I shudder to think of the volumes this woman could reach if anyone handed her a mic. "We are heading back to Gracie's house! Danny thinks they might have doubled back. I'll text the rest of the girls and make sure they all come to meet us there."

My cheeks flush hot with shame. I can virtually see Lee-Ann's eyes rolling all the way back in her head.

"Follow Danny and me in the truck," Corrine adds, giving me a very obvious wink.

I hope I can remember the route.

◆ 31 ◆

Gracie

"YOU READY TO LEARN something new?" Grandfather asks.

We are sitting in the middle of an empty parking lot of the old Tattered Pages bookstore. I miss the bookstore because Mama used to take me there once a month and say I could pick out one book to buy, any book I wanted. Then she said it closed down because the company went "out of business," which means you're not open anymore like the movie theater. But no other businesses have gone into business there, so now it's just an empty building with a sign in the shape of a book that's open. It seems like a waste.

"Another lesson?" I ask, excited, even though I don't know what I can learn in an empty parking lot.

"You betcha, Gracie Lynn," he says with that special Grandfather grin. It's been such a fun adventure already except for when I got scared at the river and at the Lizard's Thicket. We should have done this a long time ago. "How would you like to learn how to drive?"

I thought only teenagers could drive. Mama said that you have to be sixteen to get your license.

"And even then, I don't know if I'll be ready to let you," she always adds.

"Ummm, Grandfather, am I old enough to drive?" I ask him, not wanting to seem rude, but six is not even close to sixteen, even if I'm almost seven.

"Never too early to learn!" he tells me. "I was about your age when my Daddy took me out in a field and showed me how. Never know when you're going to need to make a quick getaway!"

That's true. As bandits we're going to need to make some pretty fast getaways, especially if we're chasing the sun.

"Did I ever tell you about the time I raced the Formula One champion at the Grand Prix?" he asks me. I shake my head. "Well, you see, I was hiding out from some tricksters I'd met at the casino in Monaco, and I ducked into what I thought was a random car. But it turns out I was on the track for one of the most exclusive driving races in the world. And once you start you can't stop or it could be even more dangerous, so I put my foot to the floor and let the other drivers eat my dust. And I'll be damned if I didn't win the whole thing!"

"Wow, Grandfather!" I say. "You must be a really good driver."

"Confidence is half the battle," he tells me with a knowing look.

I chew my lip with nerves. "Okay," I say. "Let's do it!"

He has me get out of the car and switch seats with him. I have never sat over here before. Normally, I don't even sit in the front seat. Today is a day of firsts.

It's hard to look out of the windshield with this giant wheel in the way. My head doesn't even reach over top of the wheel. Grandfather sees this and pulls a little lever to bring the wheel down a bit, but now it's right in my lap and squishing my legs.

"Okay," he says. "So you've got your gas and your brake," pointing to two pedals on the floor. I crane my neck around the wheel to see them. My feet are dangling right above them, but I think if I scooch down in my seat I might be able to touch them.

"The gas will make you go forward, and the brake will make you stop," he says. "That make sense?"

I nod. It doesn't seem too complicated. I wonder why you have to wait until you're sixteen. Maybe because I'm an advanced reader and advanced swimmer, I'll be better at driving.

"You've also got your clutch there on the left, but you'll only need to use that once when you start the car," he says. "We'll just keep it in first gear. I'll show you."

This part doesn't make much sense to me, but Grandfather said he'd show me.

"And you hold on to that wheel and turn it left and right depending on where you want to go," he adds.

I reach out and wrap my hands around the bottom of the wheel. I want to push it up a little because it's hurting my legs, but I'm afraid that if I do, the car will start moving. I'm getting that nervous buzzing in my tummy again, like when I had to hold the fish by her lip.

"So I'll be right here," Grandfather says. "And we'll just test it out. There's nothing for you to hit here."

He sweeps his arm across the dashboard, and I follow it, seeing there are no other cars here. Maybe this won't be so bad. I'm paying attention to Grandfather's hand, and I turn the wheel slightly, following it. Panic hits me, and I squeak.

"Don't worry, little nomad," Grandfather says, chuckling. "I haven't turned on the ignition yet. You're not going anywhere."

My church dress is bunched around the wheel pressing into my legs. It's pretty filthy now, but there's not much I can do about that. Maybe Grandfather can find us a bandit washing machine.

"So you want to give it a try?" Grandfather asks me. I can tell by the look in his eyes that he'll be really disappointed if I say no.

"Let's do it!" I say again, and this time it's almost a necessary lie because I'm even more afraid, but I'm pretending that I'm not.

"Okay, put your foot all the way down on the clutch," he says.

I wriggle down in my seat, flapping my legs like I'm swimming to the surface of the pool. I move further and further down until my bottom is barely on the seat, and finally I feel the pedal. I stand on it.

Grandfather turns the key to the right of the wheel and the car hops to life. I've never paid attention to a car's noises before, but the Chevy is humming, like a growling dog. I feel frozen, afraid to do anything.

"Okay, Gracie," Grandfather says. "I'm going to put it into first gear. Now this is the tricky part. You're going to press the gas with your right foot and as you do that, lift up on the clutch with your left foot."

My mind jumbles with his instructions. I secretly hold up the "L" with my fingers to remind myself which is the left and which is the right. I carefully reach over with my right foot and press down on the pedal that Grandfather called the "gas."

The car growls even louder, like it's really mad at me. I put less pressure on it until I'm almost not touching it at all.

"Okay, that was a bit too much gas," Grandfather says, and I'm embarrassed. "And remember you have to lift up with your left foot while you're doing it."

I've been too scared to move my left foot. I can't tell if I'm shaking or if it's the growling car.

"Let's try it again, Gracie Lynn," he says, chuckling because he almost made a rhyme. Grandfather's a poet even when he's not trying to be. "Just take it slowly, left foot up, right foot down."

I do as Grandfather says, very slowly, like a baby bird taking bites of food. The car lurches forward a tiny bit, and I scream and jump off the pedals. Suddenly, I am jerked forward, and the growling stops.

"Goddammit!" Grandfather angrily shouts and hits his fist on the dashboard in front of him. I jump. Grandfather is yelling like he did back at the river, and I feel scared again. He's yelled at Mama, but never at me until today. I know he said a bad word, but I don't say anything. I want to cry, but I'm trying very hard not to be a baby. The buzzing in my ears is so loud now. I keep my eyes on the steering wheel and try not to move so that maybe I'll become invisible and Grandfather won't see me.

"Sorry, Gracie," he says after a minute. "Didn't mean to lose my temper. You're doin' marvelous. You just stalled out." I don't know what that means, but it seems like the wrong thing. "The trick is not to get scared. Just take it slowly, and keep moving forward. You can't keep hopping off the pedals like a little bunny."

I giggle because even though I did it wrong, I like bunnies. I just wish I could move this wheel up. I'm basically doing a limbo under it. I did the limbo once at Becky's birthday party, and I got second place, but I still got a piece of candy even though I didn't get first. My stomach grumbles thinking about the candy.

"Okay, Gracie Lynn, get that left foot back on the clutch," he instructs me. I scooch back down and push my foot onto the pedal. I have to stand on my tiptoes to see out the windshield.

Grandfather turns the car back on and I feel a jolt of nerves. This time I'm going to get it right. Grandfather is going to be so proud of me. But I don't. We stall out three more times, and Grandfather is starting to get very frustrated. I want to do it right so badly.

"Don't get discouraged, Gracie," Grandfather says in his forced calm voice when he sees my face. "You just gotta keep trying. There's no giving up."

My teeth grit together, and my face feels tight. I want so badly to do it right for Grandfather.

"Did Mama learn faster than me when you taught her how to drive?" I ask him, wishing Mama was here now. She'd give me a squeeze and let me know it was alright.

"I don't know," Grandfather says, shifting in his seat. "I didn't teach her how to drive."

"You didn't?" I ask him, confused.

"No, LeeAnn . . . I mean, Sarah taught her, I think," he says. "I was . . . well, I'm not sure where I was. But I probably had some work I was doing. You don't have much time to spare when you're the provider."

"What's a provider?" I ask him.

"It means you make the money so your family can be taken care of," he says.

I think about that for a minute.

"So providers don't teach their kids how to drive too?" I ask him.

He looks a little sad. I'm not sure why. It was just a question.

"Just depends on how they choose to spend their time, Gracie Lynn," he says.

"Oh, okay," I say, worried about making him upset again. "Well, Mama seems like a good driver. She never stalls out, so Aunt Sarah probably did a good job teaching her that lesson, even though she never won the Grand Prix."

Grandfather smiles, and even though it's a sad smile I'm relieved because I was worried he was going to get angry.

"Can I try it one more time, Grandfather?" I ask him. I am determined. If Grandfather and I are outlaws, I have to be able to help him drive his getaway car. John Wayne probably knew how to drive a getaway car, even though I've only ever seen him ride horses.

"Let's give it another go!" he says.

I shimmy down one more time, pushing on the pedal like I've already done a bunch. Grandfather turns the key. It feels like he's injected his magic energy into it as the car roars to life. I take a deep breath and carefully push with my right foot while lifting my left. The car grumbles and moves a few inches forward.

"Now harder on the gas, Gracie," Grandfather tells me.

I push harder until I have lifted my left foot off entirely and my right is halfway down. The car is rolling forward. I did it! I'm driving!

"That's marvelous, Gracie, keep going, girl!" Grandfather says, but my bubble of excitement from the river is back, and I can barely hear him. I can't wait to tell Becky.

This must be what it feels like when Jack and Annie start the Magic Tree House before they zip through time. The car is inching past the lines in the old parking lot. I can't see where we're going so I press up on my toes to get a better view, grabbing onto the wheel to help lift me.

"Gracie, not too much gas!" Grandfather calls from outside my bubble.

The car is moving faster now and making a loud moaning sound. It moves slightly to the left where I accidentally turned the wheel. I can't remember which one is the gas. I'm fixed in place, worried that if I take my foot off the pedal I'll slide down and won't be able to see out of the windshield. And don't drivers need to see?

"Gracie! You have to slow down." Grandfather's voice is muffled by my fear and nerves.

The car is shaking again and Grandfather is saying something else I can't hear.

"THE POLE, GRACIE, THE POLE."

His words finally break through my fog, and I look up to see a tall lamppost right in front of us. It's only a few feet away, and I'm sure we're going to hit it. I scream and put my hands over my face, waiting for a crash. Grandfather reaches out and jerks the wheel toward him. I jump off the gas at the same time, and the car stalls out, thrusting me forward. My head bumps into the steering wheel, and I fall back onto the seat, trembling and relieved.

"Gracie, Gracie!" Grandfather calls to me, shaking my shoulders. I closed my eyes for a minute because everything around me was starting to get to be too much. Sometimes when things get to be too much, I close my eyes and pretend I'm back in my garden—my own little corner—or I'm swimming in the pool. Bad things don't happen there.

"Gracie!" I hear the terror in Grandfather's voice through my foggy brain and open my eyes again. "Are you okay?"

"I'm not sure I'm old enough for driving, Grandfather," I tell him.

◆ 32 ◆

Dan
7 Hours Gone

IT'S GETTING INCREASINGLY HARD to drive with Corrine practically in my lap. She's leaning over so far that I'm surprised the seat belt hasn't caught yet.

"Danny, I'm just so, so glad we get to spend time together again," she purrs. "Obviously, the circumstances aren't ideal, but I'm a big believer in all things happening for a reason. I mean, this can't be all coincidence."

I want to adjust the AC to get a little more air, but I'm afraid of putting my hand anywhere near this woman.

"I just knew we had a connection when I saw you yesterday!" she gushes, fluttering her eyelashes, her chest heaving slightly in the heat. Her movements are bordering on cartoonish. "That's why you called, right?"

I clear my throat, flustered by her obvious advances. Does she really think that because I cheated on my wife once it's open season inside my pants?

"Actually, I forgot about that one date we went on until you mentioned it today," I say, trying to sound friendly yet uninviting. "I called because you were the only parent I knew in the swim team directory."

Her face falters slightly, her pride clearly wounded. I'm surprised by how much pleasure this gives me. Normally I'm not so vindictive, but it's been a long day.

We're driving down the road with a processional of cars trailing loyally behind us. More than ever I wish to be back home with Ashley. I'd much rather be changing one of my son's diapers than sitting here next to this leech.

"Well, I'm so glad you did call," she persists. "Fate has brought us back together again."

I stay silent, considering fate. I'm not sure if it's something I believe in. After all, if fate was real, how did it account for those four miserable years after Gracie was born? LeeAnn slapping my hand away when I tried to help, to comfort? If fate was real, was I meant to cheat on my wife, to dishonor my family and make a new one? But maybe fate is what brought me and Ashley together. She was the person I needed at that exact moment, and by some miracle she chose me.

But what about LeeAnn? I picture my wife's fear on the river bank and her shame addressing those women. I should have stood up for her. I should have helped.

"Danny, I'm just *so* happy we're together again," Corrine repeats now, breaking up my troublesome thoughts. "We should hang out more often!"

I grimace, unable to think of anything I'd rather do less.

"Garrett goes on golf trips with his buddies every few weeks," she continues. "We could get Greggie and Gracie together for a play date!"

"Oh, umm, are they good friends?" I ask.

"Well, they're on the Raptors together!" she pushes. "LeeAnn doesn't really spend much time organizing play dates, but I bet you would if she let you. *You* always seem to have Gracie's best interests at heart. Like, calling me today and letting me know what was going on."

I shudder knowing how false that statement really is. I've always had *my* best interests at heart, for the last two years at least.

Turning onto the street, I mercifully spot John's old house and pull into the driveway. It looks just as looming and intimidating as ever—just like John. I remember confidently walking up to the front door to pick LeeAnn up for our first date—fries and shakes at the now-closed Fire Grill. Parents had a tendency to love me, so I hadn't been nervous, but the moment Big John opened the door that all changed.

"Can I help you, son?" he'd asked me in a tone that implied that the last thing he ever wanted to do was help. He had such an imposing presence. I was only a few inches shorter than him, but I might as well have been a member of the lollipop guild trying out for the NBA.

Even years later when he would come over to spend time with Gracie, I would shrink away. It was actually the closest I'd felt to LeeAnn in those years after Gracie was born—she looked just as unsure as I was around John. He was a stranger to us both, but one who commanded the attention of our daughter. And who were we to deny him?

Making my way out of the car and up the front walk, I realize this is the first time I've ever come to this door and hoped to find John on the other side.

LeeAnn
8 Hours Gone

THE SHAME I FELT at Sarah seeing the house again is nothing compared to my current humiliation. The pack of judgmental moms descend on our front lawn, swiveling their heads around to survey my overgrown grass and broken gnomes. Mama put those out when we were kids to "liven the place up a bit," and I haven't been able to part with them, no matter how many squirrels have used their hollowed out insides for nests.

"Does she own a mower?" I hear Samantha attempt to whisper as Corrine shoots her a furtive smile. Corrine saunters up to the front door, and I half expect her to kick it down.

"Claire, Sheila, Mary, can you go around back and check in the backyard, just to be safe?" she commands. The three women obediently half nod, half bow, retreating into the back. I want to tell them to mind Gracie's garden, but I seem to have gone temporarily mute.

"Well, LeeAnn? Shouldn't we head inside? Don't want to waste any more time, do we?" she asks, pointedly nodding toward the locked door.

I feel a fresh plume of anger waft out of the top of my head. Biting my tongue and pinching my sides, I walk in what I hope seems like a confident manner past the rest of the group and up the steps to the front door. The heat settles on my cheeks as I put the key into the lock, painfully aware of just how close Dan and Corrine are standing to me. They're the last two people I'd want to be letting into this house right now.

The door swings open, once again inviting me into the emptiness that awaits inside. I step in, suddenly aware of having turned off the fan as the still humidity pastes itself to my body, unwilling to leave me alone. This place used to be a sanctuary, my escape; now it feels like a prison.

When I was pregnant with Gracie, I'd drive here almost every day rubbing my swollen belly and complaining about my ankles as Mama ran her hands through my hair and poured me a glass of sweet tea.

"Mama, when did you know you were ready to be a mother?" I asked her, slightly self-conscious about expressing my insecurities in front of the one person I idolized above all else.

"Oh, Lee Lee, no one's ready to be a mother," she replied matter-of-factly, to my surprise. "But I know you can do this. I promise, and I've never lied to you before, have I?"

"No, Mama," I dutifully answered.

"Well, there ya go!"

Mama said I could do it, so I could. It was as simple as that. I stand here, staring at her picture on the mantle and willing it to tell me I can do this. If I could just hear the words come out of her mouth, I know they'd be true. What would she think of me now, standing here—a single parent whose husband left her and whose daughter ran away? Because that's what happened. Gracie ran away from me, no matter how many times I insist that's not the case. It's the only mercy of having Mama gone—that she doesn't have to see this.

"Gracie! GRAY-CEEEE," Corrine hollers with a faux urgency, making her way down the hall.

Jane wanders over and peers out of my stained kitchen window, running an idle finger across a patch of soot and examining it closely. I half expect her to call the health inspector.

We all know Gracie's not here. I would have mocked Dan for even suggesting it, but as much as I hate to admit it, I'm out of ideas myself. Apart from my old fishing rod, the other women turned up exactly zero signs of my father or daughter, and I haven't gotten any calls from the home.

My utter helplessness conjures up the same muted panic I felt right after Gracie was born. Dan was already back at work, or at least I think he was. Gracie sat on the changing table, her tiny face purple from screaming. She hadn't stopped crying since Mama's funeral, and part of me loved her even more for it, like she was protesting Mama's loss by refusing to be quiet. Another part of me felt like I was constantly about to be sick from the noise and realness of it all. I vividly remember just how horrible and in-my-face everything felt—the bottles leaking on the kitchen countertop, the diaper tabs sticking to everything except the diaper itself, my breasts aching with milk and my heart broken in ways I didn't know it could be. I held my screaming daughter in front of me begging her to tell me what was wrong, how I could fix it.

"Please, let me help, sweet pea, *please*," I sobbed. *Give me a reason to go on. Please.*

She just wailed and gnashed her wide mouth open and closed. I kept thinking she'd lose her voice from the screaming, but she never did. I wanted to go into the other room and put my head under a pillow, but I never did. Daddy was driven from the house when I was a baby, and I promised myself and Gracie that I'd never leave her with that guilt, with the idea that she was anything less than the person I wanted most in my life.

Paula reaches her arm around me, and I do my best not to jump. I've never been a particularly touchy-feely person. The kindness and the spontaneity of the gesture forces new emotions to barrel their way up my throat. I choke and begin to cry. It's strange that this is the first time today I've shed a tear, since I normally cry so often. But something about finally receiving a kind gesture while standing here in this house with these judgmental, useless biddies has unleashed the floodgates.

I let out a scream that sounds like the noise a wild animal would make, and now it's Paula's turn to jump.

"Jesus, LeeAnn," Sarah harshly whispers, suddenly at my side as Samantha nudges Jane and they turn in my direction. "Pull yourself together. You really can't afford to break down right now."

I look up at her through tear-filled eyes, wishing for the millionth time that she'd just comfort me, that she'd hold me like Mama and tell me it was alright. But she just stands there looking pissed.

"M—my daughter is gone," I remind her, unable to stop the tears from falling no matter how unflattering they might look.

I see Dan take a step toward me, then decide against it. I'm so humiliated, but it's nothing compared to my fear.

"Your daughter is missing," Sarah corrects me. "And you are the only person who can find her, not these idiots."

Samantha lets out a huff at Sarah's insult, still keeping her eyes locked on my breakdown. Sarah ignores her.

"You are not allowed to lose it. Not this time. I won't let you this time," Sarah says, quieting her tone ever so slightly as Corrine comes back in the room.

"LeeAnn!" she cries, in an attempt to turn everyone in the room's attention to me. As if they weren't already looking.

She makes her way across the shag carpet to me. I am the innocent canary to her hungry cat. To my horror, she reaches out and rubs my back in forceful, jagged movements.

"It is gonna be okay," she tells me in the most patronizing tone I've ever heard. "We all know you get distracted sometimes. And this time something bad happened. But we are going to find that Gracie."

"What the hell does that mean?" Sarah asks her, physically forcing her hand off my back.

My tears are still falling fast. I don't even have the energy to defend myself. Corrine looks taken aback.

"Oh, you know," Corrine vaguely replies, the cheery tone diminishing in Sarah's presence.

"No, I don't know," Sarah says. "You've been making fucked-up, snide comments all afternoon. LeeAnn is a fantastic mother. So I don't know what the hell you're talking about."

"Now, now, there's no need for that language," Corrine says, wagging a finger in front of her face. I'm surprised Sarah doesn't bite it off. "You're not around LeeAnn like we are. We see Gracie coming to swim practices late and not always having the gear she needs. We see LeeAnn struggling to get dressed properly some days. Now, I'm not blaming her! Oh gosh no, bless her heart! Being a single mother is soooo challenging. I'm just saying that Gracie could maybe use both of her parents! And LeeAnn kinda made that impossible for Danny."

"Corrine."

I barely recognize my husband's voice, it's so sharp and enraged. He's never sounded like that. It's always bitter mumbles or quiet apologies. Corrine turns her head to him, the picture of innocence.

"Yes, Danny?" she asks with a flutter of her eyelashes.

"That's enough."

His words make me shiver even as the surrounding air threatens to suffocate us all with its unforgiving heat.

"I'm just trying to defend you, Danny!" she insists. "It's not right that LeeAnn has kept you away from Gracie all these years, from being a part of her life."

Dan steps forward, his signature dimple melting into his frown. He's never looked at me with this level of disgust, though I'm sure the same can't be said for the way I've looked at him.

"I don't really see how that's any of your business," he tells her. Corrine looks like she's been slapped. "And for future reference, my name is Dan."

Corrine's giant jaw drops to the ground, appalled that anyone would ever dare speak to her like that. I'm sure it doesn't happen often. Her chin wobbles slightly at the indignation of it all.

"Come on, ladies," she says mostly to Samantha and Jane. "Let's go search outside with the others. After all, we are here to *help*."

"Actually, why don't you go ahead and see yourselves out," Dan says firmly. "I think LeeAnn and I have got this under control."

For one hilarious moment, I think Corrine is going to lunge at Dan with her manicured talons ready for attack. Instead, she struts past him, almost clipping him with her shoulder, leaving us standing there with Sarah and Paula off to the side just as floored as I am.

Jane lets out an outraged "Well, some people!" and follows her with Samantha close behind.

I watch them with a satisfied smile before meeting Dan's gaze. I don't think we've actually looked at each other all day. It seems like he's about to say something. Then his phone buzzes, breaking the moment.

"Oh, umm, I should take this," he says awkwardly, looking down. I know it has to be her. His brief good deed vanishes, and I'm left with the same loathing for him that's consumed me for the last two years.

I wipe my face, finally able to control myself. Sarah places her hand on my shoulder for the first time since my meltdown began.

"You okay?" she asks kindly, as Paula respectfully keeps her distance, pretending to amuse herself with Gracie's artwork that's littered around the room. I'm so grateful she realized she wasn't one of the women Dan was kicking out. I nod. Then I remember something.

"What did you mean 'not this time'?" I ask.

"What?"

"You just said, I can't fall apart, not this time," I recall, suddenly tired of being treated like a little kid, incapable of taking care of myself or others.

Sarah shifts uncomfortably, taking her hand off my shoulder.

"You know I think Corrine is full of shit, right?" she says. "You're a terrific mother, you really are."

I watch her quietly, waiting for her to get to the "but."

"But after Mama died, you just kind of shut down. And I couldn't let that happen, not with Gracie missing," she continues. "I know you'd never forgive yourself if something happened and you hadn't done everything in your power to find her."

"What do you mean I shut down?" I ask. "I raised my daughter. I kept a house. I did everything while you were nowhere. I had a newborn baby and no help. I had my whole life turned upside down, and you didn't so much as pick up the phone."

Now I am angry. I can't believe she'd throw Mama's death in my face like that when I am trying to find my missing daughter. She stood next to me that day at the gravesite. And then she turned away and left all of us behind again. She left me behind. In her place were Daddy and Dan, and they were no substitute for her, and certainly no substitute for Mama. They didn't even come close.

"Look, now's not the time," she says. "You're under a lot of stress. Let's just drop it for now. But eventually we need to talk about you accepting other people's help, about you allowing them to reach you."

"To *reach* me?" I say. "How could you possibly *reach* me when you got out the first chance you could get? How could anyone reach me when there was no one left?"

I'm so mad I could punch her in her perfectly arched nose, but I just storm down the hall instead.

✦ 34 ✦

Gracie

THE CHEVY IS MAKING weird sputtering noises, but Grandfather says that's not my fault. One time the front of the car started smoking, and Mama said it got overheated. When I get really hot I never start smoking, so I guess I haven't been overheated before. Plus, Mama says smoking is really bad for you.

Grandfather was really worried about me after the driving, but I feel a little better now that the wheel isn't pushing down on my legs. He seemed especially nervous about me hitting my head, but it was just a little bump, and it doesn't even hurt anymore. I have a bruise that looks like the shape of a coin, but I think my brain is fine, and it's nothing compared to the worm, so I'm not worried.

We are traveling to a different part of town now. I've been here before, but not for a long time, and I can't remember why. There are no restaurants out here, and it's far away from my school and the home, so I don't know why Mama and I would have been here. Maybe it's on the way to Aunt Sarah's house and I just forgot.

I feel a little dizzy, like the time I tried to read in the car and threw up in Mama's back seat. Grandfather lets me stay in the front seat, so I know I'm not in trouble for my bad driving. I just wish I weren't so dizzy. But it's very bouncy up here when Grandfather drives. It feels like I'm on a pogo stick. Becky has a pogo stick, and I have tried to use it, but I fall off after the first bounce every time.

I'm thirsty because I forgot to drink my sweet tea at the Lizard's Thicket. Well, technically I didn't forget. Technically I dropped it when I dropped my tray and all of my food. So now I'm very thirsty and very hungry. I wish Grandfather would roll the windows down. It feels like one million degrees in this car, which I know is not a real temperature. Mama says I like to be dramatic.

Grandfather seems worried. He keeps moving his hands around on the steering wheel. Maybe he is nervous to drive since it's been a long time. I would offer to drive, but that didn't go so well last time. Plus, I don't feel so good right now. We're back on a dusty road, which is much worse for my dizziness because there are more holes to hit in the road. I place my cheek against the window and look up in the sky. The glass is very hot on my face so I pull it away.

"Grandfather, can this be the last stop before we go on a real adventure and chase the sun?" I ask.

He doesn't seem to hear me. Grandfather sits there quietly like he's listening to the radio, only the radio isn't on. He looks different from how I have ever seen him. He is not the hunched-over wrinkled prune from the home, but he is also not the Grandfather I remember from before. It's hard to tell if it's the worm, or maybe Grandfather is changing right in front of me.

Mama says that as we grow, we change—our favorite things change and our looks change and sometimes our feelings change. That's what happened with Daddy. He loved us and then his feelings changed and he left. But I know that his feelings didn't change completely because of the secret letter he wrote me.

I don't like that Grandfather is being so quiet. It's not like him. Or maybe it is like the new him and I don't even know it yet. Maybe Grandfather is changing right here in the Chevy. Maybe he won't love me anymore and won't want to chase the sun.

Mama says that sometimes I can "work myself into a tizzy." That is what I think is happening right now. I'm having a tizzy.

Then Grandfather suddenly turns to me.

"I want you to know that even though there's a lot of years between us, I love you very much. And your mother and I couldn't be more proud of you and the woman you've become," Grandfather says. "I should'a told you more often."

That's a weird thing to say because Grandfather doesn't normally talk about him and Mama like that, and I'm not a woman. I'm not even old enough yet.

"Are you feeling okay, Grandfather?" I ask. "You're acting funny."

"There's just something I have to do before we go, Gracie Lynn," he says.

That sounds more normal, so I'm less afraid. The Chevy pulls into a long driveway that leads up to some iron gates. The gates twist into giant spirals at the top and have little flowers on them. I have been here before. This is where Mama's mama lives.

Mama says it's a bit unusual that I like cemeteries. But I think it's nice that all of the people you love who are dead are in one place where you can always come visit them. Just because they are dead doesn't mean you stopped loving them.

Mama hasn't brought me here that much, but I wish she would. I never met Mama's mama, so I like to talk to her a bit when I'm here so she can get to know me better.

"She knows you just fine, baby girl," Mama always says and then looks up at the sky. I don't know why she looks up at the sky when her mama's home is in the ground.

Grandfather drives to the back of the cemetery. Mama's mama's grave is underneath the big tree that turns yellow in the fall time. Now it's green-brown because it's so hot that the leaves are tired of being green.

He turns off the car and looks at me.

"Gracie, would you mind staying here for a little bit?" he asks. "I need to go talk to Martha alone. I—I just, I need to."

Jack never made Annie stay behind in the Magic Tree House, but I keep quiet because Grandfather looks really serious again. I nod my head and Grandfather says, "Good girl."

He gets out of the car and says, "Now don't you go any-where," and shuts the door. Then he goes up the hill to the green-brown tree without looking back at me.

The air feels still, which is weird because air is what's in a breeze so I wouldn't normally think of air as still. Grand-father looks like he is moving in slow motion. Mama has a camera on her phone that can record videos in slow motion. We recorded one of me yawning once, and it was very funny. I stretched my mouth wide, and then opened it so slowly that it looked like it was being held shut from the inside. That is how Grandfather looks now. He is moving so slowly it's like an invisible person is holding him back. The

worm is invisible, but I don't think it can hold Grandfather
back like that.

It is so stuffy in the Chevy. My legs are making sweat
prints on the seat. I hope no one thinks I peed in my church
dress. I wish I was in the pool or back in the river because
then it wouldn't be so hot.

Grandfather is standing in front of the grave now, and
his back is to me so I can't see his face. But his shoulders are
shaking up and down very fast like they were at the Lizard's
Thicket, so I think he is crying. That's two times in one day
that Grandfather has cried, which is really rare and makes
me feel kind of bad even though we are on a fun adventure.
Mama cries too when she visits her mama, but I don't
because I never met her. I hope that is okay and that Mama
doesn't think that I'm being mean by not crying. It would
probably be more mean to fake cry, which I can't even do.

I still feel dizzy from before when the car was bouncing
and I hit my head. Normally when I'm dizzy Mama lets me
drink a ginger ale, but there's no ginger ale in cemeteries,
and I don't want to bother Grandfather when he's upset.

Now he is rocking side to side under the green-brown
tree. The still air in the Chevy feels like it is pushing me
from every side. Even though I can't see it, I can feel it pressing against my face. I wish Grandfather had rolled down a
window or had gotten me a ginger ale. I could open the
door, but Mama says I'm not allowed to just get out of the
car without permission and Grandfather told me not to go
anywhere. I could turn the car on to roll the windows down,
but after I tried driving, I'm afraid of turning the car on,
especially with all of these graves around.

Everything around me feels dry like I'm in a desert. I
have never been in a desert before, but this must have been

what Grandfather felt like when he climbed that pyramid in Egypt.

I am sweating now and not just on my legs, and it's not funny. My mouth feels like all of the spit has left on vacation. I imagine spit would go somewhere tropical on vacation. I wish I was somewhere tropical like the beach from Mama's picture on her wardrobe. Maybe Grandfather and I can go to the beach once we leave the cemetery and chase the sun there. I think beaches are pretty sunny so we would be safe from the worm.

As I'm looking out the windshield, I see Grandfather sit down on the bench next to the grave with his head in his hands. His shoulders are still shaking, and they seem to be going up and down even harder now. I want to go and help him, but my head is foggy like when I'm sick.

It feels like I have so many breaths that I can't get them out in time. My breaths come out in "*hoo hoos*," even though I'm not trying to. Maybe that's why Grandfather's shoulders are shaking so much—he's trying to get all of his breaths out. But Mama says if you stop breathing you could die, so I hope that he keeps a few just in case.

I lick my lips because they feel so dry and chapped. I wish I had Mama's coconut Chapstick, which she lets me use on special occasions. I should have taken it out of her purse when I got the keys for the Chevy. This is another detail I have forgotten.

It's hard to tell how much time has passed. It feels like more than thirty minutes, which is how many minutes we have to eat lunch at school, but I could be acting dramatic again.

Hoo hoo, hoo hoo.

Grandfather's shoulders aren't shaking anymore, but he is still sitting on the bench and facing away from me. Maybe he's talking to Mama's mama about our adventure because he was married to her. When you get married you are in love, or "in theory," as Mama says. I know she is talking about Daddy because they were married, but then he stopped being in love and he left. Mama says they are still married "technically," but that does not mean that they are in love.

I don't know that not being married anymore would make Mama happier.

Hoo hoo, hoo hoo.

Daddy is not dead, and he doesn't have a worm in his brain. I know because Mama told me. But I still don't know why he went away. I wish I had solved the case before going on my adventure with Grandfather. It seems like it has been a long time since I have seen Daddy. He brought me a music box for Christmas that has a ballerina inside it. When I open the box, she spins around to the music.

"For keeping your treasures," he told me.

I open the music box every night before bed and watch the ballerina spin around and around. She never falls. Inside are my treasures—a see-through white marble I found on the playground, a chipped piece of tile from the pool, my past swim meet ribbons, and the laminated bookmark Mrs. Hoyt gave me for reading the most books in the class. At the very bottom of my treasure box I used to keep Daddy's secret letter until I brought it with me on our adventure.

Daddy also gave me a beach ball, and buckets even though it was winter time. He said they were for building sand castles at the beach. I like that sand can make castles, but I still haven't been to the beach, so I don't know how much I will use the castle buckets. The beach ball needs your breath to be a ball and Daddy showed me how to blow it up. I gave him a shy smile and said, "Thank you," and then I don't remember seeing Daddy after that. I wish I had the beach ball now because I have enough breaths to blow it up very fast.

Hoo hoo, hoo hoo.

It's a good thing that the green-brown tree is giving Grandfather shade. If he gets too hot he will be tired and need his wheelchair, and we don't have that. I thought that the Chevy's roof would give me shade, but it just seems to make things hotter.

Hoo hoo, hoo hoo.

There is a loud thumping in my chest that I know is my heart. It normally thumps, but not this loud and not this fast. It's keeping time with my hoo-hoo breaths. Grandfather seems so far away like he is at the end of a very long tunnel. I want to call out to him, but my throat is so dry and I don't want to interrupt his private time.

Hoo hoo, hoo hoo.

I try thinking about something else to keep my mind off of how dizzy I am and how hot it is. I wonder what Jack and Annie would do if they were here. The Magic Tree House would probably be in the giant green-brown tree, and we could all get inside and go somewhere else, where it is not so hot and where there is sweet tea.

Grandfather told me about a place called Iceland once. I wonder if it has sweet tea. If they do, it's probably frozen sweet tea because it's a land of ice. Frozen sweet tea doesn't sound like such a bad idea right now. We would sit inside of our igloos and drink frozen sweet tea and talk about all of our adventures. I would tell them not to go to the desert because it's way too hot. Or if they do have to go to the desert, to bring the sweet tea and ginger ale with them and to roll down the windows of the Magic Tree House.

Hoo hoo, hoo hoo.

I'm not sure the windows of the Magic Tree House roll
down. I don't remember reading about the windows in one
of the books. I want to make a note to look that up, but I
don't have my notebook anymore. My notebook is gone and
Brown Bear is gone and Mama is gone and Daddy is gone
and Mama's mama is gone, and suddenly I feel like I'm in a
tizzy again. My chest is very tight, and it's hard to breathe
even though I have a lot of breaths to get out.

Hoo hoo, hoo hoo.

I look out the front windshield to see Grandfather, but
he is spinning. I feel like I'm going to throw up, and I'm too
afraid to move. I'm crying but there are no tears coming
out. If you cry and no tears come out, are you even crying?

Hoo hoo, hoo hoo.

I look down to keep from spinning, and my arms are a
weird gray color, just like Grandfather's skin that day in the
home. Did I have an accident and not even know it?

Hoo hoo, hoo hoo.

I am very scared now. It feels like all of the breaths are
leaving my body. Grandfather still has his back to me, so he
doesn't know that I'm not feeling well. I raise my arm up to
reach for the door lock, and then things get fuzzy and I stop
remembering.

35

Dan
9 Hours Gone

COULD ASHLEY HAVE TEXTED at a worse moment? The instant it came through, I knew LeeAnn knew who it was and whatever less-than-hostile emotion she may have been feeling toward me immediately vanished.

Now I'm completely alienated from everyone here. I might as well go home.

Any updates?

No, I want to reply. Me taking action did nothing to help my daughter. In fact, if anything, I've made everything worse.

The trees are wilting in the summer heat, and I briefly notice the comforting breeze of my AC on full blast. I want to be home, watching Ashley goof off with our son. I don't want to be here. Being here makes me feel horrible. I've been running from that horrible feeling for years.

But maybe I deserve to feel horrible. I am always so focused on feeling happy and good, but what makes me worthy of such things? I was Dan Clarmont, the golden boy, then I was

Dan Clarmont, the handsome husband, then I was Dan Clarmont, the unwanted father, then I was Dan Clarmont, the
happy adulterer. At what point did I *earn* that happiness?

I watch as the pack of moms makes their way out of the
backyard, satisfied they've trampled through every inch of
beauty back there. They pass my car with their heads held
high, determined to pretend like I don't exist. When you
wound the Queen, the workers don't take too kindly to you.
Jane has her arm around Corrine and is whispering words of
encouragement to her as they pass.

"You've done everything you could for them, sweetie,"
she tells her.

Have *I* done everything *I* could?

Being with Ashley in our home has felt so good for so
long that I've blocked out the bad parts, the parts where I'm
not the hero of the story.

Suddenly I flash back to when Gracie was almost a year
old. I came home from work each day with the feeling that
most people have *going* to work—dread, resignation. But
one afternoon I walked in the living room, and my mouth
fell to the floor. My fuzzy-haired baby was tottering across
the shag carpet toward me, arms out in front of her like she
was a mummy.

"Lee! Look! She's walking!" I'd cried, flinging my bag
to the ground and rushing over to Gracie.

My startled yell had thrown my daughter off balance,
and she fell to the floor and started to cry large pearl-sized
tears.

LeeAnn rushed to Gracie's side, looking up at me, brow
furrowed like I was an absolute idiot.

"She's been walking for more than a week," she'd said,
shushing Gracie and patting her on the back gently.

"Oh," I'd replied dumbly, standing back up and backing away from Gracie.

Humiliation had washed over me at LeeAnn's words. *Why hadn't she told me? Why hadn't we shared that milestone?* But looking back on it now, why hadn't I noticed? Where had I been?

It's so easy to blame LeeAnn, the woman who drove me away, who held me at arm's length for the entirety of Gracie's life, who kept me from my daughter. But I'm the coward who let her go. I'm the coward who disrespected my marriage. I'm the father who let his daughter grow up in the background and didn't say a word. I'm the coward.

LeeAnn was someone I loved. Gracie is someone I still love. I held her tiny, perfect, helpless body in the hospital the day she was born and promised to always protect her. I just felt so alone for so long I forgot.

I wait until the other women pull out of the driveway and then I start to cry.

36

LeeAnn
9 Hours Gone

I SLAM THE DOOR to Gracie's room shut with a bang, like I'm back in junior high. I don't need any of them. I just need Gracie.

Sitting down gently on her bed, I curl into the fetal position, hugging my knees and praying for her to come home. It seems like I'm only praying in moments of desperation, which I don't think you're supposed to do, but lately my only moments of solitude *are* moments of desperation.

This was my childhood bedroom. It used to be covered floor to ceiling in posters of boy bands and my favorite TV shows. Now it's filled with Gracie's drawings and crafts she's made in school. Her books clutter the floor space as they sit in crooked towers, which I'm sure reach up to at least her hip height.

We repainted the walls last year to be different shades of purple, her favorite color.

"Luscious Lavender!" Gracie repeated over and over, obsessed with the name. She helped, in her own five-year-old way, sloppily rolling the brush up and down in uneven strokes, covering my Pepto Bismol pink walls. It was the only real change to Mama's house that I'd allowed, mostly because I was the one who'd painted the pink back when I was a teenager.

"This wall is filled with cracks, Mama," Gracie told me, pointing out the imperfections in my old paint job. "Why does the paint have cracks?"

"Time, Gracie," I replied. "Over time all of our cracks start to show."

"When our cracks start to show, do we break apart and die?" she asked me, making me regret the crack metaphor.

I brought her close and gave her a big hug.

"You're thinking of literal cracks," I tell her. "I meant that over time we learn new things about life, about other people. They aren't always nice things, but they're the truth. And we have things about us too, secrets, stuff we keep hidden. Those are our cracks."

"I would never keep secrets from you, Mama," she told me at the time.

But even she betrayed me. Because no matter how many times I repeat the opposite to everyone else, Gracie left. She chose to leave me behind. She picked him over me. I stick my face into her pillow, breathing in her familiar scent—chlorine and a honeysuckle-like sweetness—the aroma bringing me to tears again. I am preparing to start my hopeless descent into endless weeping when my cheek touches something unnaturally sharp from underneath the pillowcase.

I reach in and pull out a somewhat bent photo. It's the only one of Dan I haven't burned. It was taken a week before I gave birth, and I remember how enormous I was, though the close-up picture doesn't show it.

In the photo, I am laughing while Dan kisses me in the corner of my eye. It used to be his special place to kiss me. The corner of my eye has been kiss-free for many years now, and it certainly hasn't crinkled into a laugh in much longer than that.

But I remember the day that picture was taken more vividly than I remember going into labor with Gracie. It was a hotter June than usual, not unlike this year's, definitely not something a pregnant woman wants in her ninth month. I was wearing a loose maxi dress in the hopes that the breeze would cool off my bloated body.

"My ankles are so puffy they should be sizzled on the grill like sausages," I told him, attempting to examine the parts of my body hiding underneath my giant pregnant stomach.

"Mmm, sausage," my husband replied, reaching around my enormity to give my butt a playful pinch.

"Dan!" I squealed, pushing him away. "I don't see how you could find any of this appealing," I added, motioning to my oversized watermelon shape. "I'm as big as a house, or at least a house boat."

"Let's sail away together then," he demanded, grabbing my hand and pulling me close. "Come sail away, come sail away, come sail away with meeee."

He kissed me, taking out his phone to snap the picture. He loved capturing every moment. I can't recall the last time I took a picture of Gracie.

I can still remember his smell—an intoxicating mix of sweat and a faint whiff of his favorite Molton Brown cologne. He used to look at me as if there was no one else in the room. I'd glance away, embarrassed by how long his gaze lingered, but that never stopped him. That is, until he stopped looking at me at all. When did he stop looking at me?

"How could I not be taken with a woman who glows as much as you do, Lee?" he insisted in a tone that almost made me believe him, no matter how swollen my ankles felt. "Seriously, I've never seen a pregnant woman who's such a knockout."

"Shut up," I retorted, giving his arm a playful twist to make him squirm out of my grip. "You'll be singing a different tune when you see me all flabby and cleaning up baby poop."

"I'm glad we've established who's handling the poop," Dan grinned, giving me a kiss on the cheek.

"Oh yes, I'm not operating under any illusions about the role you're going to play in this little alien creature's life," I said, rolling my eyes and pointing to my belly.

"Hey now," Dan interjected. "You know I've always wanted kids. You're just a little better with the details. I'm, like, the fun one who will take her to her first baseball game."

"Every little girl's dream," I noted.

"Excuse me, ma'am, but we live in the twenty-first century, and little girls can be just as big Braves fans as little boys," Dan said, turning his nose up in mock indignation.

"I forgot you were such a feminist activist. So glad our baby will have you to teach her the way around the diamond."

"You know I'll do more than that," Dan replied, sounding slightly hurt.

"Like buy her her first foam finger?" I teased.

"No, I'm serious," Dan said, looking me square in the eyes and refusing to let me look away. "I'm going to be there for her. I know that's not something you're used to, considering, well . . . just considering your dad."

"Hey, as long as you manage to stay in the house long enough that she knows who you are," I said, brushing off his sincerity with my dark humor. How could I know my words wouldn't be so funny later?

Even then I just assumed I'd be the one to handle the heavy lifting when it came to Gracie. Mama always took care of us, so I would be the one to take care of Gracie. And Dan could help, in his own way. Mostly that's what I thought being a mom was. Dads were nice bonuses, the kind you bring out to kill the occasional bug and teach the kids to drive—not that mine did—but moms were necessities. I would handle Gracie's every need, every qualm, every tragedy; this was just a given.

Dan's offer was sweet, but I saw it as hollow. I knew he'd get bored with the minutiae of having an infant almost instantly. He liked the idea of having a family more than he'd like actually having one, I was sure of it.

But staring at the photo now, with the memories pouring in, I'm not so convinced. Did I really push him away from Gracie? Was I responsible for him leaving? No, he cheated. He abandoned us. Didn't he? I remember his anger at Corrine and the fear on his face at the river. I can picture the hurt in his eyes now. It was so much easier to pretend that Dan was an enemy, undeserving of my pity or anyone's love.

"Lee! I think we should get going," I hear Sarah cautiously call from the other room—yet another person I've pushed away who was trying to help me.

Did I really stop loving Dan after Gracie was born? Did I reject his help? Sarah's? Back then it did feel like nothing except for Gracie mattered, that taking care of that one tiny human was my only purpose. I was in a new motherhood trance, intent on doing my job right. And I was happy to do it away from Dan and away from Sarah, away from the world. And then the habit just never went away.

"Lee, can you hear me?" Sarah enters Gracie's room, her volume dying down as she catches sight of my face. "What's wrong?"

"Sarah, I'm so sorry," I say softly. "I'm sorry for shutting you out when Mama died. I've been so selfish. I think I thought you blamed me for . . . well, for all of it."

A moment of clarity crosses her face as she suspiciously eyes the photograph in my hand. But she doesn't ask any questions.

"Lee, I barely wanted to be around when Mama was alive." She sighs. "You closing off from the world had nothing to do with me staying away. You were the one with the new baby. I should have been there for you. I learned at an early age that life with Daddy was nothing but disappointing, and I was tired of disappointment. So I created a life and a family that didn't hurt." She shakes her head. "I was so selfish, when really it would have been in my own self-interest to have leaned on my sister. We were the only people who could have understood what the other person was going through, and we both dropped out of each other's lives when we needed help the most."

She sits down next to my circular shape on Gracie's bed.

"I'm your big sister. I should have checked up on you, asked how you were, especially after Mama died, but even now, since Dan left. It's been years, and I haven't really reached out," she tells me. "We've only talked about Daddy and the home, and you always seemed fine, so I didn't press it. But I should have. I should have known that you had no one in your corner. I should have been the first volunteer."

Sarah looks deep into my eyes, her expression so sincere and serious I desperately want to look away. But I force myself not to. Every part of me wants to run, to hide, but I won't. I can't.

"Lee, are you okay?" she asks me, and her voice has an odd tremble I've never heard before. Her hazel eyes are boring into me.

The question catches me off guard. Of course I'm not okay. Gracie is missing. How could I ever be okay? Sarah seems to translate my confused expression.

"I mean before all this. How have you been? There's so much you kept from me, so much you didn't say," she adds.

I want to defend myself, to jump in and shout, "You never let me!" but I know there's some truth to what she's saying. After Mama died, I felt like there was no one left to rely on, no one to turn to—not Dan, not Sarah, and certainly not Daddy.

"I—I . . . ," I stammer, not knowing how to finish the sentence. I look down at myself, sitting on my missing daughter's bed in tattered clothes.

"And you look so thin, sis," she adds. This time it's Sarah's turn to look away, as if her comment is shameful. "It looks like . . . like you haven't been taking care of yourself."

Humiliation like I've never experienced before washes over me. Here Sarah is verbalizing what I've always assumed she thought of me—that I'm a hot mess. True, I've started to notice I've been losing some weight; most of the time I don't have an appetite at all. I graze on Gracie's leftovers and call it a night. And in the chaos of navigating my life, sure, there've been days I couldn't find a clean outfit because the laundry had piled up. But I didn't think it was so noticeable. It isn't like I have a husband to come home to or anyone to impress. Turns out, I have plenty of people to disgust—Dan, Corrine and the PTA moms, and now Sarah.

I pinch my sides, wanting to disappear, wanting so badly to be away from all of this pain and hurt and embarrassment.

"Lee," Sarah says, and I'm surprised to hear her voice sounding not disgusted, but something else, an emotion I can't quite place. I turn slightly, not meeting her gaze, but showing her that I'm listening. "I think you need some help."

I let out a wry laugh because this feels like the understatement of the century. I need someone to find my daughter. I need someone to murder my father. I need someone to wash the dishes. I need someone to sort through the bills. I need someone to pay them. I need someone to teleport me far away from all of this so I never have to deal with any of it again.

"No, not like a maid or a babysitter, Lee," Sarah says, once again correctly interpreting my thoughts. "I think maybe you should speak to someone."

I stiffen. My cheeks flush pink at the idea that my sister thinks I need professional help. The pink deepens as I consider that maybe she's right.

"I know you don't think you can tell me things. I used to be the same way, shutting people out," she says. "Especially after Mama died. I was constantly angry, shouting at the kids, at Phil. I couldn't control it. Everything they did made me so mad."

I think about all the times I snapped at Dan, the anger that always bubbled inside me.

"One day Phil told me he was going to leave me if I didn't get some help," she continues, and I finally look up, shocked. I picture happy-go-lucky Phil with his plaid button-down shirts and his kind smile. It's hard to imagine him ever having the guts to say something like that to my sister.

"It really woke me up," she says. "I didn't want to lose him or Ollie and Iris. I wanted to be more for them, like

Mama was for me, for us. So I made an appointment. It felt so stupid. No one was going to make it right, or bring her back. But I forced myself to go. And you know what I realized?"

"What?" I ask before I can stop myself, my voice coming out in a croak.

"There were so many things I wasn't saying. I was letting my anger speak for me, but really there was so much hurt underneath it all that I had to get out."

Her words linger between us, sinking in.

"Did I hurt you?" I whisper, terrified of the answer.

Sarah doesn't immediately answer. I know why.

"For a while I did blame you," she admits. "Even though I knew it wasn't your fault and that Mama would have been devastated to know that I did. I was convinced that if you hadn't had the baby on the day you did and she hadn't been coming to see you, that she would still be here."

I start to cry again—long, ragged sobs that feel like they're coming from my core.

"I blame me too," I say, the words falling out of my mouth, each hitting like a knife wound. "Every single day of my miserable life."

Sarah pounces on me, enveloping me in a long, tight hug. It feels the way Mama's hugs used to. She doesn't say a word, she just holds me like it will solve everything. And for a minute, it does.

"It took a lot of time for me to realize that those feelings were really just my grief," she says finally. "What happened with Mama was an accident—a terrible, meaningless accident. And I could never accept it, so I was caught in this cycle of anger and grief and blame. None of it was fair—to anyone, but especially not to you."

I want to believe her, but so much of me feels like I don't deserve her forgiveness, her acceptance.

"I think you might be in that same spiral, and you need a way out," she says.

I hold onto Sarah like she's a life vest in the ocean, my fingers digging into her back, afraid of drowning.

"Maybe you're right," I tell her.

After allowing a few moments to compose myself, I take a deep breath and open Gracie's door, fully prepared to be greeted by the unpleasant sight of Corrine's followers scowling at me.

But the hallway is blessedly empty and the house is quiet. Even though I'm more alone now, I feel comforted to have them gone. Sarah's back in the kitchen with Paula, and they're writing something down on a notepad.

"What's that?" I ask.

"We're leaving a note for Gracie and Daddy, in case they come back here," Sarah explains. "Just urging them to call us and let us know they're okay."

"Sweetie, do you have the number of the home?" Paula asks. "I can call them to check in there, just to cover our bases."

Her proactive kindness almost brings me to tears again. I write down the number for her, explaining I'll be right back. I make my way outside, suddenly nervous.

I'm not sure where Dan has gone. Maybe he left with Corrine and the others, though after his display in the kitchen, I doubt she'd be willing to go anywhere with him again. Spotting his truck in the drive, I slowly approach it from the walkway, unsure of how to even broach the conversation I need to have.

I know Gracie is still out there, but somehow this feels just as important, like making amends with Dan is a key step in helping to bring her back. I'm sure it's what she'd want.

Self-consciously I pull my mousy brown hair back, trying to resemble something close to presentable. All these comments about my appearance have chipped away at any remaining dignity I possessed.

Breathing in the humidity, I am about to knock on his car window when I notice my husband is crying—not like your favorite baseball team lost tears, but real, intense, sorrowful tears. I can't take another step forward. I'm enthralled by the spectacle.

His head in his hands, Dan suddenly catches sight of me and pops up, like someone pressed an "eject" button to spring him from his seat. He wildly wipes his face with urgency and embarrassment.

"Sorry, sorry," he says, rolling down the window of his truck. I'm not sure if he can tell that I'm just as embarrassed and probably more ashamed. I don't know what my face is doing, but I hope my expression is at least amiable.

"I, um, just wanted to say thank you," I tell him. "For back there, saying those things to Corrine."

Dan looks self-conscious, never willing to meet my eyes.

"I should have said something sooner," he replies, his voice triumphantly breaking free from its signature mumble. "There's a lot of stuff I should have done sooner."

Like left us? I think, my impulse to stay bitter remaining strong.

I stand beside his truck for another minute quietly. I spend so much of my time trying to block him from my mind that I occasionally forget he's a real human being. He's not just an image in her beach photo or the villain in our history or the nuisance in my life. He's a real flesh and blood person. A person I used to love, to long for. Suddenly, I want to reach out and touch him, but I don't.

"I . . . appreciate you trying today," I tell him, and now it's my turn to look away. I don't like the idea of giving him any sort of praise, no matter how small. "I know I don't make it easy."

"I haven't given you much of a reason to," he graciously adds.

"No, you haven't," I agree, still not fully willing to commit to kindness when it comes to my husband. "But I do appreciate it, even if I can't seem to show it."

He looks up. His almond eyes lock with mine. The intensity of the gaze is excruciating.

"LeeAnn, you don't owe me anything," he says, and his tone is filled with such sorrow that I'm worried I'm going to cry again.

The cicadas around us are filling the deafening silence with their loud song. Somehow my unspoken words ring much louder.

"Dan, what if we can't find her?"

The horrifying thought has barely left my mouth when my excessively loud ringtone cuts through my words as my phone lights up with a number I don't recognize.

Ignore it, I tell myself, but then I remember Gracie.

"I'm sorry," I say, but not in the way I should mean it. "I have to take this."

I walk away from Dan's truck and toward the front of the house. I feel an impending sense of dread as my phone continues to ring loudly. No one ever calls me except for the home or Gracie's school, and this is a private, blocked number. I pause, then answer.

"Hello?"

"Miss Abernathy?" The voice on the other end of the line sounds familiar, but I can't quite place him.

"Yes?"

I realize I had been holding my breath, hoping to hear Gracie's voice.

"This is Officer Snow of the Reading Police Department. We spoke earlier today?"

My heart seizes up again as I mentally place the officer and his neat-as-a-pin buzz cut. Images of Gracie lying in a ditch swirl around me, blurring my vision. I reach out to hold onto the porch railing to steady myself.

"We still have officers out looking for your daughter, ma'am," he says. "But we received a call that we believe might be in connection to Big John."

He hasn't found Gracie's body. She's not dead. Not yet. My grip on the phone unclenches ever so slightly.

"What call?" I ask, forcing the words out, trying to urge him to get to the point.

"We had Cynthia Lawrence call from the Lizard's Thicket. She said there was a minor altercation in the restaurant earlier today. She was mostly calling to scare a man who was being hostile to customers, but she mentioned that there was an altercation between this man and a regular, a John Abernathy."

The Lizard's Thicket. Of course. How could I not have checked there? Daddy practically lived there for every meal after Mama died.

"Was Gracie there? What altercation?"

"That's the thing, ma'am," he goes on. "Miss Lawrence says she saw Big John with a young girl around the age of six or seven, and he called her his granddaughter, so we have every reason to believe they were in there. She says the girl got scared when Mr. Abernathy and the man started fighting, and she ran out of the restaurant. She says Mr. Abernathy went after the girl, and Miss Lawrence was so busy cleaning up the mess and forcing the other man out that she didn't see where they went. But there was no sign of them in the parking lot by the time she had a chance to check. She says your father appeared very emotional and confused when he was interacting with her prior to the altercation."

My familiar anger starts creeping back in as my breathing normalizes. Daddy got into a fight and scared my daughter so badly that she ran out of a restaurant and into a parking lot. She's always so well behaved, so loyal until he gets involved.

"We're still out looking for them, but we wanted to notify you with this information," Officer Snow says on the other end of the line.

"Thank you," I reply. Then, because I feel the need to seem like I've been productive, I add, "We have been searching on our end too. We found my childhood fishing rod and reel on the back river off Mill Creek Road. It was a hole my dad used to frequent, so we're pretty sure they were there too. But that's all we've seen."

Officer Snow sounds sympathetic, telling me, "The good news is that it looks like they're staying local. Hopefully, they will turn up very soon. In the meantime, please keep the police department informed if you find out any additional information and we will do the same for you."

"Thanks very much, Officer," I reply, all too aware that another conversation has ended without me knowing exactly where my daughter is.

He hangs up, and I take a deep breath before heading back over to Dan in his truck. He's watching me closely with a look of concern. He probably saw me having to steady myself on the porch.

"That was the police," I tell him quickly. "They haven't found Gracie, but she and Daddy were at the Lizard's Thicket earlier today."

I spare him the details of the fight. A look of temporary relief crosses his face, and I can tell he was expecting the worst too. It's nice to share this fear for once.

"That's good, right?" he asks.

"Yeah, I hope so. I think I'm going to get Sarah and Paula and head over there to see if the waitress can give us any more details," I tell him.

He looks slightly crestfallen, and I briefly wonder if I should have invited him to join us. I want to, but the words don't come out. We're not there yet. Maybe we'll never be.

"Okay," he replies, brushing off the lack of invitation. "I'll keep looking around here."

I don't smirk at him this time. I can tell he's trying, and I actually do appreciate it. Having someone care about your daughter when so few have in the past is an extremely comforting feeling, even if that someone is my cheating husband.

"Lee, please let me know if you get any news," he says, the stains of his tears still fresh on his face.

I nod and retreat back to the house to get Sarah and Paula. I try my best not to continue picturing only worst-case scenarios. I swear to God, if anything happens to Gracie because of my father, I'll kill him myself.

♦ 37 ♦

Dan
9 Hours Gone

I'VE COMPLETELY RUN OUT of ideas about where to go. When I was a kid I used to like to go to the movies, but I'm pretty sure the theater closed down a few years ago. I drive past the McDonald's before I remember Lee-Ann just told me they were at the Lizard's Thicket, so they probably wouldn't be going to get food again. Three right turns and I'm back where I started, in the middle of town, watching some kids skateboard outside of a Dollar General. I don't think I felt this worthless even when I was trying to help LeeAnn take care of Gracie. I consider going home. LeeAnn didn't ask me to join them. She never even wanted me involved in the first place. All I did was waste more precious time by involving those vipers from the PTA. But going home seems like I'd be taking the coward's way out again, and I can't do that. For one thing, I owe it to my daughter, and for another, Ashley would probably never forgive me either. I can't lose the one person on my side.

It's after six, but I can still feel the heat from outside beating on my windows, threatening to break in, to smother me. That's a summer night in Reading for you.

Just give up. What could you possibly do to help? What's the point?

The familiar impulse to quit lingers just out of reach. No, I can't do that. Not this time. Somewhere out there in this God-forsaken town is Gracie. And Big John. I keep having to remind myself that they're together. I try to think back to memorable moments I had with John, times outside of our home.

The only place I can think of was one we visited just six days after Gracie was born. It was a terrible, unusually over-cast summer day, but the oppressive heat felt similar to how it does now. I can see the mourners huddled around the gravesite, Gracie sleeping peacefully in LeeAnn's arms. She was wearing a giraffe onesie that looked inappropriately cheerful given the circumstances, but we hadn't had enough time to find her the proper attire. Do they even make funeral onesies? Blessedly she stayed quiet throughout the service. Sometimes kids will throw you the occasional bone. People are coming up to LeeAnn from all sides, offering their con-dolences. I can't tell if she even hears them. I wonder if she blames herself, blames me, blames Gracie. My arm is around my wife, but I don't know if she even feels it there. Big John stands awkwardly in the corner, unusually quiet for such a public gathering. We've just welcomed this new life into the world, but all I can feel around me is death.

I put the truck in drive and speed out of the Dollar Gen-eral parking lot. Cruising down Main Street, I see Larry who runs the grocery store locking up and pulling down the grate, ready to go home to his family on a Sunday evening.

Gracie used to wrap her tiny fingers around the grocery cart, holding on tight as LeeAnn pushed her through the aisles, picking out off-name-brand items and grabbing diapers. I remember wishing those little fingers were reaching out for my hand. I hope we're not too late.

The cemetery is on the other side of town. I've only been there once, so I almost miss the turn-in, catching it just in time, kicking up dust as I roll through the wrought-iron gates. It's been seven years, but I remember where to go. I know it'll likely be a pointless mission, but at least I'll have something to say I've done. I've definitely had worse ideas.

As the truck crests the hill at the far end of the graveyard, I see it. A dirty old '85 Chevy Impala parked at the base of a plot of graves. My heart begins thumping loudly. I speed the truck down to John's parked car. As I do I see an old man standing at a gravesite about a hundred feet away. He's more hunched over than I remember. The man I knew used to stand tall. He takes a few wobbly steps toward the car, looking left and right as if he's misplaced something. My truck screeches to a halt and I fling myself out like a pole vaulter.

"Where is she?" I shout, racing toward my father-in-law.

The man squints in the glow of the sunset, trying to place me.

"Whaddaya mean?" he barks, looking angry, wild. He's grown a bit of a gut in the last two years, and he's not walking well. Now I understand why LeeAnn's been so frantic all afternoon. What a difference a few years can make.

"Gracie. John, where's my daughter?"

The man takes a small step back, recognizing me for the first time, swiveling his head around in a daze.

"Gracie? Well, I . . . we left her at the river. No, she was at the restaurant. And then we were driving. Well, she went home with Martha, didn't she?"

I know he's confused, but the words send a chill down my spine. Out of the corner of my eye, I see something move ever so slightly inside the Chevy. That's when I see her, slumped over the seat belt, head swaying gently.

Suddenly, the heat evaporates. The gravestones disappear, whisking away the cheap fake flowers people have left out in the hopes that those will last longer than real ones ever would in these conditions. The Chevy practically glows as all of my attention shifts to the tiny figure in the passenger seat. In that moment, I feel like I'm actually experiencing a heart attack. I've never had one before, but my chest seizes up, my breath leaves my body, and I begin to stagger toward the car, not sure why my legs won't move faster.

I push John out of my way, desperate to reach her first, to get there in time. With a shaking hand I pull the car door open and scream.

38

Gracie

DO YOU EVER GET afraid to blink? I do sometimes, because what if I miss something very important? I know that it's a silly thought because blinks are so quick, but there are other blinks that are much longer. I am now blinking in reverse. Instead of blinking darkness, I'm in darkness and I blink the outside.

> *Blink.*
> "Goddamn car, you son of a bitch!"
> *Blink.*
> "Help! I need help!"
> *Blink.*
> "My daughter has passed out, please get a doctor!"
> *Blink.*
> "Jared, grab a stretcher!"
> *Blink.*
> "How long has she been out for?"
> *Blink.*
> "Patient is drifting in and out of consciousness."

Blink.

"I don't know, dammit! That son of a bitch left her in the car, and I found her passed out."

Blink.

"Are you the guardian?"

Blink.

"I don't know. I don't know how to tell how long she'd been in there."

Blink.

"I need to call my wife."

Blink.

"I think I know my own granddaughter's age, dammit. Why don't you stop asking me questions and help her?"

Blink.

"Sir, we're going to have to ask you to please calm down."

Blink.

"Help her! Jesus Christ, help her!"

Blink.

"We can't help her if you can't tell us what happened."

Blink.

"It wasn't my fault!"

Blink.

"Patient needs fluid resuscitation."

Blink.

"Is she on any medications?"

Blink.

"Has she had any previous surgeries or medical conditions?"

Blink.

"I'm sorry. I don't know. I don't think so."

Blink.

"Why was she left in the car?"

Blink.

"Will you stop asking me so many questions and help her?"

Blink.

"Her name? Her name is LeeAnn . . ."

Blink.

"Yes. Gracie. That's what I said."

Blink.

"Stop telling me I'm confused, dammit! Why don't you morons do your jobs?"

Then it's dark for a while longer with no more blinks in between. When I finally open my eyes, Grandfather is sitting next to my bed, looking very upset. I want to tell him it's okay, and I am fine, but I'm very tired. I don't know how I got here.

The last thing I remember was sitting in the car, and now I think I'm in a hospital. I have never been in a hospital before, but I have seen them on TV and this looks like one. There are lots of screens and machines that are constantly beeping. It looks like the inside of an alien spaceship. How exciting to go on a new adventure!

Grandfather is slumped over in his chair like he is sleeping, but his eyes are open. I'm worried the worm is awake. There are some things I heard in my quick blinks that do not make sense. Also I remember a man carrying me in his arms, but I don't know if that was Grandfather. Grandfather's never carried me like that before, but maybe he got some superhero powers from the worm.

"LeeAnn?" Grandfather asks, turning to me.

"No, Grandfather," I say, and my voice sounds very small. "It's Gracie. Gracie Lynn."

I see his eyes readjust, and he sees me for real this time.

"Gracie? Oh, thank God! Nurse! Nurse! She's awake!" I hear him shout. I have never heard Grandfather sound so upset.

A lady with a wide face comes into my room, and she has very white teeth when she smiles. They look like Greg Bryant's mom's teeth, but this lady looks nicer.

"Well, Miss Gracie," she says. "I am so happy to see you awake. How are you feeling?"

"Very sleepy." I yawn, and she laughs even though I'm not trying to be funny.

"I'd imagine so," the nurse says. Her smile is so big it crinkles her kind eyes. "Your daddy is just down the hall on the phone with your mommy."

I gasp.

"Daddy? Daddy's here?"

"Yes, ma'am, your daddy is here, so don't you worry 'bout a thing, darlin'," she says, sounding a little like Grandfather.

Was Daddy the man who carried me? I'm nervous to see him because it has been a long time. And him calling Mama will mean that I am in trouble, and that Grandfather and I can't chase the sun anymore and he'll have to go back to the home. I look at Grandfather and he smiles weakly. He doesn't seem as cheerful as the nurse. He looks scared almost, but I've never seen Grandfather scared except for the time he found out he hit me.

"Grandfather, what's gonna happen to you?" I ask him.

"Don't you worry about me, Gracie Lynn," he says. His voice, which is usually so strong, is shaky sounding. "I once arm wrestled Muhammad Ali with one hand tied behind my back. I can handle anything."

"But Grandfather, what if you get in trouble?" I ask.

He looks up at me with his serious face on. "Gracie, that's the last thing you should worry about. I've had a marvelous time," he tells me, nodding his head.

I want to cry, but I decide to be a big girl. It's the end of our adventure. The nurse checks the beeping machine next to my bed, and I notice some tubes in my arms and my nose. I would be scared, but I feel like all the energy has been zapped out of me and I can barely move. It is very hard to keep my eyes open. I want to talk to Grandfather, but I am so very tired. He's still sitting in the chair next to me, but he's not slumped over like before. The sun is still out, but just barely. I don't think the worm is awake yet.

"Grandfather?" I ask him as the nurse steps out.

"Yes, darling?"

"I'm sorry about our adventure," I tell him.

"Gracie Lynn, don't for one second apologize," he replies. "Not for one second."

"But we didn't get to go to Italy or eat gelato or climb a pyramid in Egypt or play in the snow in Iceland," I say, very sad.

"You don't have to go to any of those places to have an adventure," Grandfather tells me. "Besides, today we made it count."

When I open my eyes again, I don't know where I am for a minute. Then I hear the beeps and realize that I am still in the hospital. Instead of Grandfather, Mama is standing over my bed, stroking my hair back, and she looks so sad-happy.

That's when you're happy but you're also crying a little bit. And Aunt Sarah is there too, standing in the corner smiling. I haven't seen her in a while, but she looks the same, maybe a little tired. She has on very tall shoes, and they look a little muddy. I should remind her to clean them, but I'm too tired. I thought I'd be in trouble, but they don't look angry.

"Mama?"

"Oh, Gracie!" Mama exclaims and starts to cry a bit. But it's okay because I think those are happy tears.

"I'm very sorry, Mama," I say, even though it's taking a lot of energy to speak. "I just wanted to help Grandfather."

"Oh, sweet pea, I know you did," Mama says, leaning over to hold me without squeezing me too tight. "I'm not mad. You're here. You're okay, and you're here."

I know I'm here. But Mama seems to be doing that thing where you're saying something to make yourself feel better even though it seems like you're talking to another person.

"My Gracie girl, I was just so scared that something had happened to you," she says, and tears are falling down her cheeks now.

"You did not have to worry, Mama," I say. "Grandfather protected me."

"We're just glad you're okay, sweetheart," Aunt Sarah says. Her hair is extra shiny in the hospital light. It's golden around her head like an angel, not a ladybug angel but a real one.

Mama cries more happy tears, but there are some sad ones in there too. Aunt Sarah reaches out and squeezes her shoulder. I look around and for the first time I notice something strange.

"Where is Grandfather?" I ask, confused. He was just right there in that chair.

Mama wipes away her tears, and her face screws up a little bit like she's trying to figure something out. She looks at Aunt Sarah.

"Gracie, when we got here, he was gone," Aunt Sarah says.

I don't believe her. Grandfather would never have left me. Our adventure is over, but we can still see each other.

"I still can't believe Dan was stupid enough to leave them alone in the room together after what he did," Mama says, looking angry.

"He was calling you, Lee!" Sarah whispers back.

I still haven't seen Daddy. I wonder if he's really here.

"Your grandfather left you this," Mama says, and I turn to face her, curious for more clues.

She hands me a small ripped piece of paper. She has another one in her hand, but she keeps it. I uncrumple the piece of paper, and I recognize Grandfather's handwriting.

Gracie, I'm off to see the world. I hope you are too. All my love, Grandfather

I read it three more times. Even for an advanced reader, this doesn't make sense.

"Is Grandfather coming back?" I ask. Mama looks serious, and Aunt Sarah shifts awkwardly in the corner.

"I don't think so, baby girl," Mama says.

I picture Grandfather driving off to chase the sun in the Chevy. His skin is the color of the tan couch and the worm is asleep forever. He is never confused and he's always on an adventure. I smile.

"I think that's good," I say.

"Yeah, well, you tell that to the fleet of local officers out looking for him," Aunt Sarah says and her voice sounds annoyed.

I'm scared now.

"The police?" I cry. "You called the police on Grandfather?"

"We had to, baby girl," Mama explains. "You were missing and Grandfather is sick."

"Well, I hope they never find him!" I shout.

"Gracie, shhh," Mama scolds me.

I stop shouting.

"Gracie, sweetheart, can I get you anything?" Aunt Sarah asks kindly. "I'm going in the hallway to let your dad know you're okay."

"Do you think they have some sweet tea?" I ask her. I still feel very thirsty.

"I'll see what I can do, missy," Aunt Sarah replies, giving me a tiny wink.

The door closes behind her, and Mama sits down on the side of my bed. She picks up my hand in hers, squeezing it tight as if she never wants me to let go.

"Gracie, we need to have a talk," Mama says with a serious voice. Now I'm in trouble. But just as I start to get really scared, Mama's face gets all soft and kind, and I'm not that scared anymore.

"Did you know that when you were just born you had the biggest eyes?" Mama asks.

I did not know this. I am excited to hear a new story, so I shake my head no.

"Most newborn babies always have their eyes closed and their faces are all wrinkly, but from the moment you came out, your eyes were so big and wide that even the nurses commented on it," Mama says. I don't say anything because I don't want to interrupt her story. "You were always so alert and so curious about the world around you. I remember thinking I never wanted you to lose that curiosity. And you didn't."

I smile. I like that Mama is being nice about my baby self.

"So just know that I love the way you are and who you've grown up to be. I'm so proud of you and how smart and thoughtful you are," she says, smiling at me and brushing my cheek with her hand. "Do you know how much I love you?"

"This much?" I ask, flinging my arms out very wide because that is normally our joke.

"Gracie, I love you more than any other person on this Earth," Mama says, returning to her serious voice. "You are my entire world. When I thought I had lost you, I went crazy. It felt like I had lost my mind, like I had lost a part of me. I was terrified that something horrible had happened to you. And look, you're here, in the hospital!"

"I told you I'm okay, Mama," I insist, but she raises her hand to stop me from talking.

I fidget around and take a deep breath. The tube in my nose itches, but I'm afraid to scratch because what if it falls out and I can't breathe anymore?

"You will understand one day when you have a baby of your own," Mama says, and I'm annoyed because she is telling me again that I'm not old enough. "I know you meant well, and you wanted to help your grandfather, but what you did was incredibly dangerous, and I need you to understand that it is not okay."

I nod my head, embarrassed. I'm feeling like my shy self again. Mama takes my hand and wraps it in hers. Her hands are warm, like a cozy blanket.

"I also want you to know that what you did is entirely my fault because I was not honest with you," Mama says.

Even though I'm very tired, I suddenly feel very awake. I'm really surprised. Mama has never lied to me before. She always says lying is bad. It's why Daddy went away.

"Did you necessary lie?" I ask her.

"I thought my lie was necessary at the time," Mama says, hanging her head. She looks very upset. "But I know now that I should have trusted you with the truth. I should have trusted that you could handle it."

"What truth?"

Mama takes a deep breath and looks me square in the eyes. I can tell that it's hard for her to do this.

"Gracie, I made up the story about the worm," she says finally.

The room spins again and for a second I'm worried that I will fall back to the darkness with no blinks.

"What do you mean?" I ask, unsure of whether or not I heard her right.

"I mean that Grandfather is sick, but I invented the worm to help explain his disease," she says.

"A disease like the cancer Becky's aunt had?" I ask, remembering Becky telling me about the cancer inside of her aunt.

"Well," Mama pauses like she is trying to say the right thing. "It's not cancer. But Grandfather has a disease called dementia."

Dementia is a weird word. I've never heard it before. It sounds made up. I wonder if Mama is lying again. Now that she has told me she lied, I don't know what is the truth.

"The dementia caused all of the same side effects that I said the worm did, but I didn't know how to explain something like that to you without it," she states. "It's a difficult topic, and I didn't think you were ready for it. But I should have known that you're a very smart and very mature young lady."

I like that Mama called me a "young lady." She has never done that before. I rather like being a young lady. But I don't like that she lied to me.

"I should have trusted you with the truth, even though it was hard," Mama says. She's looking into my eyes like she really sees me. Most of the time Mama seems very distracted, but right now, she's right here with me.

It is quiet, and I'm still a little bit confused, but I don't mind and for once, I don't ask any more questions. I can tell it took a lot for Mama to tell me the complete truth. She keeps holding my hand and squeezing it tight. We sit there for a few more minutes. I don't want to talk about the not necessary lie or diseases anymore. I'm too tired. I slump my head back on the pillow.

"Mama, do you think I can have some grit here?" I ask.

She smiles.

39

Dan

"ASH, I FOUND HER!" I scream into the phone, alarming several people in the waiting area. I have no pride in being the one to find my daughter. There was nothing heroic about the way I came inches from crumpling to the ground, the way I shoved a geriatric man into his Chevy while I was sobbing and shaking Gracie with one hand while the other clutched the wheel. I knew she was dead. I knew it. I saw it.

But once again, my parental instincts (or lack thereof) were completely wrong—thank God. Ashley is so happy, but even she doesn't understand just how scared I've been these last few hours. I don't think I did either, to be honest. But now that LeeAnn's here, I have bowed out. She didn't say a word to me, except when she found out I'd left John and Gracie alone in the hospital room together. Then I got an earful.

Now I hesitate to even go into her room. My little girl, who hung limp in my arms as I sprinted into the hospital lobby, shouting for someone, anyone to help her. But

LeeAnn has dibs. She's earned dibs on holding our daughter after a major trauma. Now I stand lamely in front of the door, a stranger. I'm surprised the nurses even let me come back here—family only and all that.

Ashley would tell me to go in there, to see my daughter, to make sure she's alright. But somehow it still doesn't feel like my place. She looked so small, so helpless lying in that hospital bed. I wanted to gather her into my arms, just like I've wanted to all her life. Instead, I sit down in the stiff chairs outside of the room. I wonder how many dads have sat here, waiting for news, good and bad. Were any of those dads as big a phony as I am?

The door opens and my head snaps up, hoping to catch a flash of Gracie. It's just Sarah, but I try not to look too dis-appointed. Her heels click-clack over to where I'm sitting, and I'm grateful that her often mocking expression now looks relatively pleasant.

"She's doing good," Sarah tells me, smiling. "She's up, she's talking. She sounds like her normal self."

I'm not even sure what that sounds like anymore.

"Great," I say, trying to seem like I belong, like I'm in this, even when I feel so far removed. "Any word about John?"

Sarah's expression gets cloudy, her furrowed eyebrows casting dark shadows over her pristinely made up face. "*Daddy*," she starts in a scorn-filled tone, "seems to have skipped town."

"What?"

I keep expecting him to walk through the door. He'd been so agitated when we arrived at the hospital I'd wanted to admit him too, but he insisted on the nurses seeing Gra-cie first. Then, once I'd stepped out to call LeeAnn, he disappeared. So few traces of his presence were left behind that I wondered if he'd ever been there at all. But there was my daughter, lying in a hospital bed with largely him to blame. I've never felt so much rage toward another person. It's a miracle I didn't hurt him at the cemetery. I barely remember any of my actions after I saw Gracie lying unconscious in that car.

"The nurses aren't sure what happened," Sarah explained. "But no one in the building has seen him for about half an hour now. He left LeeAnn and Gracie some notes. I think he doesn't plan on coming back. Fucking coward."

I don't ask where her note is. Things have always been tense between Sarah and John. I always admired her for not putting up with any of his bullshit, but looking at her now, I almost feel sorry for her. She's been fatherless a lot longer than LeeAnn, kind of like Gracie. A fresh twinge of guilt hits me as I realize just how similar I am to a man I despised for so many years. The absent father. I've become such a pathetic cliché.

"Well, I'm just glad she's okay," I finish, not knowing what else to say.

Sarah sits next to me as the noises of the hospital fill the space between us. She's never been an ally to me, but she hasn't been a nemesis either, so I don't feel quite as out of my depth around her as I do around LeeAnn.

"Dan?"

I look up at her unrecognizable tone. There's a seemingly sincere touch of empathy in there, which is the last thing I anticipated would come out of her mouth.

"You know you're not so bad at this, right?" she asks. I cock my head, confused by the question. "You know, the whole being a dad thing."

I turn away, embarrassed by her words. I've never been a father to Gracie.

"We're not so different, you and I," she begins, seemingly choosing her words carefully. "Far be it for me to side with someone who cheated on my sister, but I don't think of you as such a bad guy."

I'm stunned. I have to stop myself from gawking at her.

"Obviously, if you ever repeat that, I will deny it and cut off your balls," she adds, grinning. "But, let's face it, we both left. In different ways, of course—I physically left, you emotionally checked out. And I get it, I do. LeeAnn's not the easiest one to deal with, especially not after . . . well, not after Gracie was born. And I know you have this other life and all now. I'm not saying go back to my sister or anything. I don't think that would be the right thing for anyone. But she does need you. More importantly, Gracie needs you. LeeAnn will never in a million years say it, and she'd probably be furious with me for saying it now, but she wants you to fight for your daughter."

I bow my head, ashamed. "I think it might be too late," I mumble. "There's too much I've screwed up."

Sarah grabs my shoulder and twists me toward her.

"See, that's your problem," she says, her tone less forgiving. "You're always so afraid. Maybe if you stopped beating yourself up for being such a bad guy, you wouldn't be such a bad guy. You could be a father for once. You understand that we might not even be sitting here if it weren't for you today? I don't even like to think about what could have happened to that little girl in there if you hadn't gotten to her when you did."

I don't either. The humid air suddenly feels cold as I picture all of us standing in front of another grave, one I hope I never have to see in my lifetime. Sarah's jarring words sting with the truth. What is it about the Abernathy women that makes me feel so pathetic, so worthless?

"Look," she adds, letting go of my shoulder. "Today's been a wake-up call. They need us."

Her words register, but I'm not sure I believe them. Lee-Ann has never needed me. She's made that plain.

"LeeAnn needs help, in more ways than one," she continues. And I see the same worry in Sarah's face that I felt when I first really took in my wife today. "I don't think having another parent around to occasionally help with Gracie when she needs a break or needs, you know, whatever it is she might need, could be anything but good."

I wonder if Sarah has broached this subject with Lee-Ann. I can't imagine she'd be saying these things to me if she hadn't.

"So I'm going to at least try to be around more," she says. "And maybe she'll still push us away. Maybe there's nothing that can be done. But I won't be able to forgive myself if I don't at least make an effort. Will you?"

I know she's right. But for the last few years, what's easy has felt the best. I don't know if I'm ready to switch to the route that's filled with the unknown, the painful.

"Just think about it," she says, seeing my conflict and mercifully not calling me out for it.

A doctor in an off-white coat rounds the corner and catches my eye. "Mr. Abernathy?" he asks.

To him I am Mr. Abernathy, the father of the patient, not Dan Clarmont, the estranged dad of the formerly missing girl.

"Dan Clarmont," I say, extending my hand. "Gracie's father."

"Dr. Weintraub, Mr. Clarmont," he replies, accepting my hand.

"How's she doing?"

"She'll be just fine, Mr. Clarmont," he says matter-of-factly. "She had some pretty extreme heat exhaustion. We've put her on some fluids, and she should be able to be discharged in a few hours as long as her levels return to normal." He adds: "But Gracie was very lucky. I would caution you all to make sure she's in the care of a responsible adult in the future."

I obediently nod, not taking the time to explain the total situation. It's not important.

"Thanks very much, Doctor, for all of your help," I reply in what I hope is my authoritative dad voice. It's a work in progress.

He smiles and then motions to his clipboard, going into Gracie's room with a confidence I have yet to muster. Clearly he belongs in there. The same can't be said for me. I catch the softest hint of LeeAnn's voice from inside the room, sounding cheerful and relieved.

Sarah lets out a big sigh next to me.

"Well, thank God for all of that," she says, swishing her blonde curls back and shaking out her arms to release the nerves. "Listen, I need to go call Phil and check on my kids. But you should go in there, and you know, see her."

I nod and say "Thanks," hoping the response can be used as a blanket statement for everything she's said in the past few minutes.

Sarah heads down the hall, phone already attached to her face.

I stand in front of the door.

♦ 40 ♦

LeeAnn

I'M NOT SURE I ever truly smiled before this moment. Hearing Doctor Weintraub tell me that Gracie is going to be just fine has filled me with more of a true happiness than I've felt in a long time.

"I have just a few tests to perform, and then we'll be sure to get you some Jell-O, Miss Gracie," he tells her, giving me a grin.

"Cherry flavor?" she asks.

"Let's see what we can scrounge up, shall we?" he replies with a wink.

I never want to leave her side again, but I stand up to give the doctor room to perform his checks, sinking into the chair by the window. He places the blood pressure cuff around her tiny arm.

"What does this do?" she asks.

"It makes sure you're back to being healthy again," he tells her.

"It's very tight," she says. "Is it like a handcuff for people in jail but for your arm? Is my arm going to fall off if it squeezes too tight?"

I laugh as the doctor politely assures her that she'll get to keep her arm. I never want this moment to end.

I catch sight of Gracie's bright yellow backpack next to me. Daddy must have brought it in from the car. How unusually thoughtful of him. Or maybe he knew he wouldn't be coming back.

I pick it up, examining the colorful patches I've sewn on as Gracie's swim meet ribbons swing from the outside. Inside the bag is filled, as I expected, with books and candy. But tucked into a small pocket midway through the bag there's something else. I reach down and pluck out a folded-up note from the pocket's depths. The note is written on a piece of our old grocery list paper, from back at the house we shared with Dan. I see his handwriting peeking out from one folded edge of the paper. Clearly he was in a hurry as all of his letters are jumbled in a slanty mess. Gingerly, I peel the letter open, chancing a guilty glance over at Gracie. She's preoccupied, peppering the doctor with questions that seem to overwhelm even him, and he's an MD. I feel bad for invading her privacy, but I can't help myself. I unfold the letter.

Dearest Gracie,

Today is the hardest day of my entire life. You're too young to understand now, but I hope you keep this letter and that one day you will read it and know where I am coming from. Today I made the decision to pack my bags and move out. I may be leaving, but I never want to leave you. You are the greatest gift I have ever received.

These past few years have been very hard on your mom and, by extension, me. When your grandmother died, God gave your mom the perfect, most wonderful substitute in

*you. She loves you so much, but she's still so wounded that
I don't think there's any more love left for me.*

*So I am leaving her with the best gift I can think of: I
am leaving her with you. I am trusting you, Gracie, to take
care of your mom and to be a big girl. That doesn't mean
that things won't be hard and that you won't have days
where it feels like your whole world is crumbling. Whenever
you have those days, just know that I am always here and
I will never, not for one second, stop loving you.*

Dad

My hands are shaking. I'm afraid to cry because once I
start, I truly may never stop. The doctor's voice is muffled
as the hum of my emotions grows louder and louder around
me.

Dan left his family to start a new one. The words don't
sound as convincing in my head anymore. The phrase has
been so simple, so easy to cling to. Now it feels hollow, like
an unexpected lie I've been telling myself to get to sleep at
night.

The creases in the letter are worn from years of Gracie
unfolding and refolding it. Does she understand those words
now? Has she always understood? Have I always been her
overwhelmed, grief-stricken mother? I return the paper to
its tiny square shape, cupping my daughter's most treasured
possession in the palms of my hands. I no longer feel that
unfiltered joy. It's hard to place exactly what I'm feeling.

Before I know what I'm doing, I walk out of the room,
practically colliding with Dan. He jumps back like I've
branded him with a hot poker.

"Sorry, I just, I was just wondering how she was doing,"
he stammers, taking three steps back.

Does his fear of me always keep him from her? I think, looking at his doubtful expression. This man, the source of all my blame . . . is he really the victim?

Everything used to feel so black and white—good vs. bad, right vs. wrong. Now it all feels jumbled.

"Dan," I croak, holding up the note. I'm filled with sorrow, mourning all that's been lost. There are too many things to count at this point.

He looks at the piece of paper in my hands, his expression unreadable. Then he sits down, falling back into the chair like his legs are too tired to hold him up any longer. I follow him, dropping my limp body in the chair next to his.

"Do you remember the last time we were in a hospital together?" Dan asks suddenly.

"Of course I do," I say briskly, caught off guard by the unpleasant memory.

"It was the day Gracie was born. It's still the best and worst day of my life," he continues, not meeting my eye.

I know what he means. The joy and the pain of it all are forever imprinted in my mind.

"In this one moment, I held my baby girl in my arms, and she looked up at me. She was already so awake, even just an hour after being born," he recalls as I grow increasingly uncomfortable. "And we were really, truly happy. We were a family. We were perfect. And then that call came and changed everything."

I close my eyes and picture the moment. My sleeping daughter in my outstretched arms as those horrible words lingered between us. Those words I could never bring myself to believe, no matter how true they were.

"Lee, it's your mom. I don't know how to say this. But she . . . she's gone."

I slowly brought Gracie back down to me and held her tight. In a lot of ways, I never held her out to him again. A car crash—how simple, how unworthy it had been of Mama's greatness. She had been on her way to the hospital, to me, to Gracie. But she had never made it, would never make it again. I had killed my mother.

"That was a terribly cruel thing to happen to you. And on that day," he says simply, staring at his hands clasped in front of him. "I didn't know how to handle the injustice of it all, the pain of it all."

Injustice. That was a good word for it. It wasn't just that Mama was gone. It wasn't fair that right as I welcomed a life into the world, the light went out of it. And that it was because of me that she was gone in the first place.

"I shut you out," I admit to him now. "I ruined everything. And it's taken me all this time to really see it. I couldn't see anything back then."

He looks up at me, years of apologies in his stare. "You were grieving, and I couldn't help you. I never knew the right thing to say. I never knew what you needed. No one could help you, except Gracie. It was the two of you against the world, and as the years went on it just felt more and more like I was in the way."

For the first time, I imagine Dan's pain—watching his child grow up from afar, his cold, unfeeling wife always keeping him at arm's length. Tears start to form just thinking about it.

"I hope you can forgive me one day," Dan says, refusing to look away. I don't want to meet his eyes, but it seems rude not to. "I may never forgive myself for not fighting harder for Gracie, for not being able to help you."

I notice he doesn't apologize for leaving me behind or for picking that woman over me. But I guess that makes sense.

"Forgive you? It's me who should be asking for your forgiveness," I say, surprised to find that I actually believe it. "I thought I was doing what was best, what I was meant to do. But it wasn't right, none of it."

"Yeah, but there's no excuse for leaving the way I did," Dan mumbles, and I see the shame drift across his face. "I was so hurt and there was no one for me to talk to. And Ashley and I had gotten so close."

There it is. I turn away, not wanting to hear this part of the story.

"I should have ended things with you so much sooner," he says. "I should have never done that to you. You didn't deserve it."

"No, I didn't," I say, my voice sounding colder than I want it to. "But I know I shoulder some of the blame when it comes to that. It's not me you should be apologizing to. When you left, you left your daughter behind too."

Dan looks like he's about to argue, but gives a slight shake of his head and stays quiet. I know there's more to it than I'm saying. I know that I purposefully kept him away from Gracie because I was so hurt and angry. But despite all the growth and progress we've had in the past few hours, I'm still too proud to admit it, to myself and especially not to him.

"I should have fought you to see her," he concedes finally. "I never should have surrendered so easily."

I wish I could own up to things the way Dan is now. It's making him look like the good guy again, and after years of seeing him as the villain, it's incredibly jarring. But I am defenseless against his arguments. He's right. Maybe in some strange way, we both are.

"LeeAnn, I want you to know that I genuinely thought I was doing what was best," he says, facing me again. I wish he'd turn away. He's so close I can smell him, his scent a reminder of my past life, before all the pain and the loneliness. "I knew how much you needed her. And I knew I was never much of a parent."

"I didn't give you the chance to be," I allow, finally able to relinquish some ground for him to stand on. "And . . . and if you hadn't been here today . . . I just . . . I don't know . . ."

A sob escapes my lips, and I'm mortified. I hate that he's seeing me like this. He reaches out and rubs my shoulder, then quickly puts his hand back down as if touching me burned him. I sniffle, hugging my sides.

Down the hall, I see Sarah on the phone smiling. I realize what a relief it's been to have her by my side all day. The people I've felt so distant from have all returned to me in one way or another and surprisingly it's helped.

"Dan?"

"Yes?"

"I want you to know that this isn't going to be easy for me," I say slowly. "But I want you to be a part of Gracie's life, a big part. You and your son . . . and maybe even . . . Ashley. Well, one day."

Her name comes out slowly, methodically. I'm trying not to fill my tone with poison, but also not to give my approval. It's a difficult balance. I fold my hands together, attempting to sound mature and calm. He's seen Basketcase LeeAnn for long enough; everyone has, apparently.

Dan puts his hand on my shoulder again, this time leaving it there, and my nerves cause me to jump a little. So much for keeping my cool.

"You honestly have no idea how much that means to me, Lee," he says, pretending like he doesn't notice my spasm. "We're all going to be learning, but I really hope we can just be honest with each other."

"Me too," I reply, grateful as he removes his hand. "You should go see her," I add, nodding toward the door to Gracie's room.

"You sure?" he asks. His face is filled with so much self-doubt that I suddenly feel like the worst person in the world.

"Of course," I reply. "She needs her father."

41

Gracie

D ID YOU KNOW THAT you get free jewelry when you
go to the hospital? Mama says I can keep my hospital
bracelet on until it falls off or gets gross, so I'm taking very
good care of it. It's bright yellow like my backpack and has
my name on it, and it's basically the coolest bracelet I've ever
had.

The sun bounces off it as I sit in Mama's car. I'm in the
back seat today, because Mama says it's safer and we are
going to Becky's house. I wish I was old enough to sit in the
front seat like I did with Grandfather, but after I bumped my
head in my driving lesson and stopped remembering at the
cemetery, I decided I should probably listen to Mama.

She was pretty mad when I told her about Grandfather's
lesson in the Chevy.

"Are you frogging kidding me?" she screamed.

Mama didn't say "frogging," and even though I replaced
the word, she still apologized for saying it, but then she
called Aunt Sarah and told her that Grandfather was a "frogging lunatic."

Mama calls Aunt Sarah a lot now. She even came over to our house with Iris and Ollie, who are my cousins. I've met them before, but not since I was little and I didn't really remember them that much. They are older than me, and I was scared of them at first, but they aren't so bad. Iris taught me how to make a colorful friendship bracelet out of string. It's not as cool as my hospital bracelet, but I still made one for Becky, because Becky is my best friend.

It has been three days since I went on my adventure with Grandfather and ended up in the hospital. Even though I'm still a little bit in trouble for necessary lying and running away, Mama says I can go over to Becky's house today and I can still have my birthday party this weekend.

When we get to Becky's house, her mama answers the door and gives me a really big hug, and then she hugs Mama, which I've never seen her do.

"We are just so happy you're safe, Miss Gracie," Becky's mama says. "You really scared the living bejesus out of us!"

I don't know what the "living bejesus" is, but I feel bad for scaring her and for scaring Becky. I didn't think I was going to scare anyone.

"Gracie!" Becky comes over and gives me a big hug. I'm so glad to see her. I give her the friendship bracelet I made her, and she immediately puts it on. I told you she was my best friend.

"You two kids have fun," Becky's mama says. "We'll be in the living room."

"You're staying, Mama?" I ask, seeing that Mama's set down her purse and has taken off her shoes. She never stays when I'm at Becky's house. She always goes to "run errands."

"Yeah, Paula and I are going to hang out in here for a bit," she says, looking a little awkward. "If that's okay with you, sweet pea."

"I think it's *marvelous!*" I say, quoting Grandfather.

Mama smiles and lets out a laugh. That's another thing Mama does a lot more these days—smile. I haven't seen her cry once since the hospital.

Becky and I go into her room. She has already started coloring a big flower that I know is a rose, but she is coloring it purple, which is not a rose color. I don't correct her, though, because purple is my favorite color, and Becky has done a good job.

Becky lies down on the floor and starts coloring again. She's adding shades to petals, and I watch closely, wishing I could color like that.

Instead, I pick up a cherry red crayon and start drawing a large circle. I fill it in, trying to be careful to not go outside the lines. I miss a few spots, but it mostly looks okay. Then I pick up a black crayon. I almost never use black because it's such a boring color, but I need it this time.

"You missed swim practice," Becky tells me.

Mama already told me this, but she said not to worry because Coach Grant said I can still be on the Purple Team for the rest of the summer. Becky's going to be on the team too.

"I know," I say. "But I got to go to the hospital and get this cool bracelet."

I hold up my arm, and she looks impressed.

"Did anything fun happen at practice?" I ask her.

"Not really," she says, picking up a gray crayon to shade under the leaves. I never would have thought of that, and it looks so good. "Well, Greg Bryant did another cannonball in the pool, and Coach Grant got mad and told his mommy. And Greg's mom got mad at Coach Grant for tattle telling on Greg and then she said, 'Come on, Greggie, let's go!' and they left. It was kind of funny."

"Wow," I say. "I wish I could have been there. Greg Bryant is good at cannonballs."

I tell Becky about the nurse at the hospital who had teeth like Greg's mama.

"What's that?" Becky asks, pointing at my drawing. I'm a little disappointed she can't figure it out, but maybe she's confused by the halo.

"It's a ladybug angel," I tell her, carefully coloring in the black dots.

"What's a ladybug angel?" she asks, putting her crayon down and looking at me curiously.

"Mama says that ladybugs are secretly angels, when they come to visit us from heaven," I explain.

"My grandma's in heaven," Becky says and starts coloring again.

"Maybe you could go visit her there sometime," I tell her, missing Grandfather. I wish I could visit him now.

"Mom says it's too far to visit," she says.

"That's too bad," I tell her. "Maybe when you're old enough you can go."

"I hope so," she agrees. "I've never met my grandma before."

Even though I miss Grandfather very much, I'm glad he doesn't live far away in heaven. At least he got to teach me lessons and go on an adventure with me before he left. It must be sad to have a grandparent who's too far away to visit.

"Did I ever tell you about the time my grandfather wrestled an alligator?" I ask Becky.

She shakes her head no, and I smile.

42

LeeAnn

THE STREAMERS AREN'T HANGING right.

"Sarah?" I shout into the other room. "Can you bring the tape back in here, please?"

My sister turns the corner looking slightly less glamorous than she did when she arrived at the nursing home last week. Her hair is pulled back into a ponytail—still boasting its natural curl, but more sensible than stylish. And her face is less made up. I catch a glimpse of the teenage girl I used to idolize.

"It's looking good in here!" she says. "How much time do we have?"

I check Mama's old watch that I found in Daddy's things.

"About half an hour until the guests arrive, and Dan should be here any minute," I add nervously, trying and failing to make it sound like an afterthought.

"You're sure he's actually coming?" Sarah asks. "Because it would be a shame to get Gracie's hopes up for nothing, especially on her birthday."

"He'll be here," I say, still unsure of whether or not I want that. "He's also bringing his, err, his son."

Sarah rounds on me as I try to look busy, knowing I'm guilty of leaving this key piece of information out.

"Shit, Lee! You didn't tell me that," she bursts, her tone full of accusation. "This is huge! Has Gracie ever met him?"

I shake my head. Sarah reaches back to run her hand through her hair, forgetting it's been pulled up.

"I've decided no more lies in this house," I say firmly. "They almost cost me my daughter once. That's not going to happen again."

Sarah nods, not saying anything more. I hesitate to tell her this next part, knowing that if I do, I'll have to follow through.

"And I've made an appointment," I tell her, the words tumbling out of my mouth before I have time to shove them back in. "To talk with that woman you recommended."

Sarah lights up, and I think I see tears filling her eyes. My emotions feel muddled. For starters, it's honestly a little touching to know that anyone cares about me this much. For so long, I didn't think anyone did. There's still a prideful place inside me that feels embarrassed that it's come to this, that I'm unable to handle my life on my own. But I've been treading water for so long that it makes sense I'd be exhausted enough to let myself sink under.

"Lee, I'm really happy to hear it," she tells me, careful not to maintain eye contact for too long and scare me off.

Since we returned from the hospital, Sarah's been by the house almost every day. The stark contrast between my utter loneliness the last time I brought Gracie home from the hospital and now isn't lost on me. I've told my sister to go home a million times, but instead she's insisted on having Phil and her kids over to help out. Ollie and Iris have grown into little adults while I wasn't watching. Gracie seems to adore the company, and Sarah says it's what Mama would have wanted, so I can't argue with that. Plus, if I'm being honest, having them around and having Gracie home safe are the two best things to happen to me in years.

She hands me the tape, and I apply it to the last streamer, which mercifully falls into place.

"There," I say, satisfied. I step down and survey the room. It's been turned a rainbow of different shades of purple, Gracie's favorite color. "Are all the favors set?"

"I might have eaten the chocolate in one of the bags," Sarah admits, as I give her a jokingly stern look. "Okay, maybe two bags, but kids shouldn't have so much candy, anyway."

"How noble of you to take that bullet," I muse.

"Are the games set up?" Sarah asks, gracefully changing the subject.

"Yeah, Paula brought over her karaoke machine yesterday, and I found the Disney tracks," I reply.

"If you need a duet partner on 'A Whole New World,' I'm ready to be your Jasmine," Sarah teases.

"Gee, thanks," I reply, not so secretly loving every second of our new natural back and forth.

The doorbell rings, shooting nerves up my spine. Sarah peeks her head through the curtains, flashing a small smile outside.

"That's for you," she states with a tone of set optimism.

My talk with Dan at the hospital is so surreal it feels like I imagined it. I hope the person I talked to there is the one I'm opening the door for here. Taking a deep breath, I fix a smile on my face. I actually put makeup on today, not that it matters. That's not what today is about.

Steadying myself, I open the door. There he is, the man from the Facebook photos, the man from the search party, the man who saved my daughter's life, the man who abandoned her, the man I once loved, standing right in front of me, holding the hand of a tiny little boy who is unmistakably related to Gracie.

"Hi, LeeAnn," Dan starts, graciously pretending like he doesn't notice my obvious discomfort.

"Well, hello!" I say back, a little too loudly. "Why don't you both come in?"

The little boy totters on his shaky legs, taking cautious steps inside as Dan encourages him forward. They look so comfortable together. Gracie comes bounding into the living room.

"Is that my brother?" she asks, bouncing up and down and beaming.

I told her she had a little brother shortly after we returned from the hospital, and she hasn't stopped asking questions since.

"BROTHER!" the little boy shouts, raising his hands toward Gracie. The moment is sickeningly precious.

"Hi, Gracie, can *I* please get a hug?" Dan teases, patiently smiling down at her.

My little girl looks slightly unsure of what to do, and looks at me for reassurance. I nod in his direction, trying not to revert to my signature Dan scowl. She reaches over and gives her father a half hug, afraid to commit to the full thing.

Dan kneels down and whispers, "Things are going to be different now, I promise."

I look away, uncomfortable. The scene is too simplistic. It reduces years of pain and lies into straightforward emotions. I don't know what he said to her at the hospital, but it can't make up for years of not being there. I should know, my dad was never around either. Something brushes my hand. Dan's son is trying to grab hold of my thumb. His wide blue eyes look so much like Gracie's. I pull my arm back inadvertently.

"Gracie, this is Jack," Dan says, ignoring my awkwardness. "This is your brother."

Gracie's eyes widen as she turns from Dan to the little boy to me.

"Jack?" she asks, practically shouting. "Mama, his name is Jack! I have a brother named Jack!"

She springs around on the balls of her feet, elated by this revelation.

"I take it you like the name?" Dan asks, happily confused.

Little Jack claps as Gracie continues to leap in the air with excitement.

"It's this book series," I try to explain, knowing Gracie is too filled with emotion to speak. "Her favorite books are about this brother and sister called Jack and Annie."

Dan smiles, first at me and then at Gracie. I look away.

"Well, how about that?" Dan says, and I hear that southern twang that used to make my knees weak.

"Umm, excuse me, Daddy, but can Jack and I go play in my garden with Aunt Sarah and Ollie and Iris?" Gracie asks, still oddly formal but too excited to let it hold her back. She reaches down and holds her brother's hand as if she does it all the time.

"Of course you can," Dan says, smiling. "I'm so happy to see you, birthday girl."

Gracie smiles but does not reply, racing out back with Jack waddling behind her, both in perfect harmony. Dan and I watch them go quietly.

"LeeAnn, you have no idea how much it means to me that you invited us," Dan says quietly. I'm not the only one who's nervous. "This is more than I ever hoped for."

We sit down on the back porch, watching as Gracie guides Jack through her flower garden, pointing out her favorites. Ollie and Iris are racing nearby, and our kids stop to watch them.

"It's like I said on the phone," I repeat, attempting to sound neutral. "Gracie needs you in her life. And I think it's time for me to stop being so selfish."

"I never saw it that way," Dan says. "You are one of the most selfless people I know, actually."

I'm touched by his words, even if I don't quite believe them. We sit there, watching Gracie and Jack play as an almost natural quiet settles around us. The silence is speaking louder than we can. I'm afraid to break it.

"So is Corrine coming?" he asks finally, and I surprise myself by laughing.

"Oh, you mean your girlfriend, *Danny*?" I tease him, ever so slightly, testing my limits.

He shudders and sticks out his tongue. "What a nightmare, that woman," he says. "I can't believe I actually went on a date with her once."

"I'm sure it had everything to do with her dazzling personality," I mock, picturing her ample bosom.

Sarah walks inside the screened-in porch, wiping a small bead of sweat from her brow and smiling at Dan. He tilts his head toward her in acknowledgment. It seems like they have some sort of polite pact—a cease-fire agreement. My sister hasn't said one thing against Dan since the hospital, and she's not one to hold her tongue.

"Alright, Clarmont?" she asks.

"Yeah, doing great," Dan replies, and his enthusiasm sounds pretty genuine. "Those your kids out there or actors paid to look much older than your children should be in an attempt to make the rest of us feel ancient?"

"My evil plan, foiled again," Sarah jokes, plopping down beside me on the rattan loveseat Mama reupholstered with a small daisy print when I was in middle school. "No, those two are mine, mostly because no one else will claim them. That's an awfully cute little boy you've got out there."

Dan smiles proudly. "Jack," he says.

"Yes, Gracie said his name about ten times within the first minute of introducing us," Sarah replies, laughing.

The three of us sit there, watching our kids play in the backyard surrounded by Gracie's party decorations. The moment reminds me of all the birthdays I've had in this house.

Mama making me princess dresses with layers of tulle so delicate they could have been flower petals. Sarah making fun of me but then saving me the best corner piece of cake. Daddy entertaining the room without so much as wishing me a happy birthday.

"Did I ever tell you about the time I lost my vision in one eye but still managed to beat the sultan in checkers? Did I ever tell you about the time I reached the top of Mount Everest only to discover that there was actually a taller mountain range next to it? Did I ever tell you about the time I lost my pants in a convent and had to sneak out with just a nun's habit to cover my unmentionables?"

Mama, Sarah, and I sat there, heads together, laughing and gossiping as the evening died down and guests slowly began to trickle out of the house. And like a wind-up toy that had run out of juice, Daddy began to fade into the background.

But he didn't matter; we were all we needed.

I reach over now and squeeze Sarah's hand. This may not be how I imagined things turning out, but it could have been a lot worse. She squeezes my hand back, and I know she's thinking of Mama too.

"I'm going to go see what those kids are up to," Dan says, sensing Sarah and I need some sister time. I try to look appreciatively at him as he leaves. I can tell it's going to take some practice.

"Where do you think Daddy is by now?" I ask Sarah.

She exhales, not wanting to bring Daddy into what I'm sure was a pleasant memory. "Who knows? Who ever knew where Daddy was?" she says. "He could be ten minutes away or in the Bahamas for all we know."

"You don't have any guesses?" I ask.

"I'll leave that up to the police who are searching for him," she says. "I'm sure if they ever find him, he'll manage to charm his way out of trouble. Not like I plan to see him again. And you shouldn't either."

Sarah never had a problem cutting Daddy out of her life. Why couldn't I feel the same? Especially after everything he'd done.

"Well, he's always been good with Gracie," I defend him—and myself a little. "He treated her the way I wish he'd treated us." With a jolt I realize my use of the past tense.

"Always, hmm?" she challenges.

"What's that supposed to mean?" I ask. "He took us in when we had nowhere to go. He adored my little girl."

Sarah looks pensive for a moment, as if grappling with the decision to tell me something.

"Lee, do you remember after Mama died?" she begins.

"Of course," I quickly interject, not wanting to bring up the subject of me shutting down again. I've heard it enough recently.

"You weren't the only one who cut yourself off, you know," she says. "Daddy didn't come see you in the hospital.

He didn't even meet Gracie until several weeks after she was born."

"What?" I reply, incredulous. I think hard, trying to reconstruct that time. All I see is a blur of diapers and tears. Those first few months were a haze of newborn necessities and emotional unavailability.

"Daddy wouldn't leave the house," Sarah insists. "He was either sitting alone in that very living room or out on the river. He didn't answer my calls, and he showed no interest in meeting his new granddaughter."

"But I don't understand," I say, thoroughly overwhelmed by this revelation. "He loves Gracie. He never wanted me around. He always wanted her all to himself."

Sarah seems slightly uncomfortable, looking over her shoulder as if she expects Daddy to just walk down the hall and scold her.

"He made me swear never to tell you," she says. "But I went to go see him about three weeks after Gracie was born. You both had shut me out, but I knew you needed a parent more than I did at that point. And I knew you were hurting, that you blamed yourself, more than you probably realized at the time. Dan was obviously not equipped to handle either Gracie or your grief, and I didn't really feel like it was my place to speak so frankly with him. But you know I've never had a problem speaking my mind when it came to Daddy. So I got very real with him. I told him that he'd never been much of a father, but that he had the chance to be a grandfather. I told him that Gracie had already lost a grandmother. She didn't need to lose a grandfather too. And I told him that a piece of Mama was in that little girl. I could tell it from the moment I laid eyes on her. She had that special spark. The next day you told me he had been by to see you. We never spoke of it again, but I'm always glad I went. I know he was too. It's probably the proudest I've ever been of him."

I'm stunned. The silence floats between us, the meaning of Sarah's words filling the air.

"But your children," I say, looking out at Ollie and Iris in the backyard, holding hands with Gracie and Jack. "He never paid them any attention. They never really had a grandfather, just like Gracie never had a grandmother."

"Eh, you know I've never been comfortable around that man," she says. "Phil's parents are great with the kids, and I didn't need Daddy the way you and Gracie did. I gave him this one final project, this one last dream that he could focus all of his energy on—and that was you two."

Sarah looks around and adds, "Clearly, he didn't quite master his task, but I think the fundamentals were there. You guys had the history and both reminded the other of Mama, but Gracie was a clean slate for him, a rapt audience for his stories. He could have easily blamed her existence for Mama's death, but I don't think he ever did."

My heart aches learning about this unexpected gift my sister bestowed upon me. It feels weird to think of Daddy as a gift, but he was to Gracie. I can't believe Sarah did this for me. I can't believe he listened to her and actually followed through. How did I ever convince myself that my sister didn't care about me or Gracie?

"Sarah, I'm really sorry for the past few years," I tell her.

"You know what? I'm sorry too," Sarah says, cutting me off. "I let the money stuff get the better of me. It just made me sick thinking about that man getting any of my money. He wasted so much of our money on his ludicrous schemes growing up that I wanted to be rid of the financial burden."

"Yeah, but I should have agreed to sell the house, so I could have contributed more," I admit, ashamed that Sarah has sacrificed so much while I had been busy just trying to stay afloat.

"And lived where? Out of your car? It's not like I ever offered to take you in. I learned a long time ago that you can't wish to change the past," Sarah shrugs. "You can only affect what happens in the future."

"Unless you're Marty McFly," I joke, forever uncomfortable when others are being sincere. "Then you can do both."

"Yes, yes, very true," Sarah agrees, rolling her eyes and giving me another playful shove. "Anyway, I thought you had the right to know."

"Thank you, Sarah, for . . . well, just for everything," I say, reaching out to hug her the way Mama used to hug us so tightly and putting aside my discomfort to let her know just how much it means to me.

My sister's willingness to forgive is new to me. She had always been my role model for her clothes and her hair and her sarcastic quips, but now she's earned the title for a much more substantial reason.

She twists her face awkwardly as if to imply it's not a big deal, when it's quite the opposite. I can tell she's not completely comfortable with the unnatural depth of this conversation either, and it makes me feel even closer to her.

"Anyway, Daddy will be a lot happier if we never find him again, and not to sound like a heartless bitch, but I'll be a lot happier too," she admits. "So will you, though you'd never say it."

I know she's right, but that doesn't make me feel any less guilty. I just hope that Gracie will be okay without him. Daddy was her father figure for the past few years, and if he's really gone for good, I don't know how she'll cope. I hear a small squeal from the backyard, and see Dan chasing Gracie and Jack through the flower beds. Maybe there's hope for him after all.

The doorbell rings; Gracie's party guests are starting to arrive. I stand up, motioning toward the door apologetically, and leave Sarah on the porch.

Paula is holding Becky's hand and talking to Linda on our front step. They break in their conversation when I open the door, offering up a smattering of warm greetings and reassuring hugs. I show Becky to the backyard as she marvels at the purple landscape that my living room has become.

Paula pulls me in for another tight hug, which seems to have become our thing over the past few days.

"So how you holding up, sweetie?" Linda asks me when I head back inside. "We miss you at work. Well, I miss you. Mike misses your ability to navigate a spreadsheet."

"Much better than I was a week ago," I admit. "I'll be heading back on Monday, so ready or not."

"You needed some time away, terrifying ordeal or not," Linda states, and I squirm, still uncomfortable about the references to my crappy parenting.

I pause my self-conscious train of thought, hearing the kids laughing in the backyard. The sound is so simple, so sweet. A week ago, I'd have given anything to know I'd get this moment, to know that my daughter was safe.

"I'm just sorry I haven't been more of a help to you in the past," Paula tells me. "It takes a village and all!"

"Thanks," I tell her. "But you've already done so much, taking care of Gracie when I needed extra help. I just assumed you hated my guts or thought I was an incompetent mom or something."

"Oh please," Paula scoffs. "Your kid is crazy about you. You're a single mom and your whole life revolves around Gracie even though you have a ton on your plate. Half the time I feel like the incompetent one. I barely manage even with my husband's help."

It seems insane that anyone would possibly look to me as a model for good parenting, but Paula has no real reason to lie. I always thought she was judging me like the other moms, but apparently there's a lot I was wrong about.

That night, as Gracie blows out the candles on her chocolate cake ("with buttercream icing, *please*, Mama!"), I realize this is the first birthday party of hers where I haven't excused myself while another parent watched the kids. The anniversary of Mama's death is so linked with Gracie's birth for me that I normally can't help but go into my bedroom and fulfill my tradition of crying for all I've lost.

Now, as I stand here watching Gracie animatedly talk with Sarah and Dan, I can't help but marvel at all I have to be grateful for. There, surrounded by the glow of the light of several dripping candles and the love of the people in her life, my daughter turns seven.

As I wave goodbye to the final guests, I put my hand in my pocket. Daddy's note is inside, where it's been since I found it.

It reads: *Lee—Don't forget to live. Love, Dad.*

◆ 43 ◆

Dan

"ARE YOU ALMOST READY, Ash? She'll be here any minute," I call into the other room. I've adjusted the magazines on the table four different times, as if Gracie would ever notice.

Ashley enters the room looking slightly less put together than usual. She's not wearing any makeup, and she's got a little mushed strawberry on her shirt from breakfast with Jack. I feel bad for rushing her, but she already agreed to respect LeeAnn's wishes and not be here when Gracie visits. I'm still shocked LeeAnn would even mention Ashley's name in the same sentence as Gracie's, so I'm trying to adhere to her rules, as long as I can see my daughter and Jack can spend time with his sister. Ashley understands.

"You ready?" she asks me, smiling and sharing in my excitement.

"I hope so," I tell her, glancing around the room and wishing I had more Barbies for Gracie to play with or books for her to read. LeeAnn's filled me in on some of her favorite things, but I still feel like I'm playing catch-up.

Ashley kisses me on the cheek and Jack on the forehead. He spits and drums his lips in reply. It's his new favorite sound, and I'm ninety percent sure Gracie taught it to him. I admiringly watch Ashley rush out the front door and hear the familiar crunch of the car pulling out of the gravel drive.

Only a few minutes go by before two new sets of feet are clicking up to the front door. Jack cries "BRING, BRING!" as the bell rings.

I swing the door open excitedly to find two equally anxious faces in front of me. Hoping to alleviate their stress, I up my cheery demeanor, broadly smiling, and practically shouting, "Well, hello there!"

LeeAnn looks slightly startled and Gracie softens a bit. I awkwardly motion for them to come in, and watch as my ex nervously looks around, no doubt scanning the room for Ashley's presence. I imagine she wants to bolt, but is likely conflicted about leaving Gracie here without making sure the coast is clear first. The mere idea that she would entrust our daughter to me, especially after the past few weeks fills me with gratitude.

"Jack!" Gracie calls out, rushing toward my son without giving me a hug. I try not to take it personally. We're both still getting used to each other.

Jack giggles and claps, hitting Gracie on the face in excitement. She doesn't seem to mind.

"So I'll pick her up in two hours?" LeeAnn abruptly asks me, breaking the moment.

"Oh, yeah, whenever you want is fine," I tell her, wishing it would be longer, but not wanting to push my luck.

"My appointment is supposed to last an hour, but I'll have my phone on me," she says. She told me on the phone she's going to speak to a therapist today and asked if I could watch Gracie. I was stunned—not only that she told me but that she was going at all. And I could almost hear a tiny hint of pride in her voice when she said it. I'm proud of her too, but I don't say it. I will.

She doesn't meet my eye now, instead focusing on our daughter.

"Gracie Lynn, come give me a kiss, please," she calls out, and Gracie obediently turns and walks back over.

LeeAnn kneels down, holding her daughter tight, terrified to let her go. I once again feel a rush of thankfulness that she's willing to let her stay here even for a moment.

"Now, tell me what you're gonna do," LeeAnn says in a measured voice.

"I will be good, Mama," Gracie recites with sincerity. "I will stay here, and I will never go anywhere without permission."

"I know you won't, baby girl." LeeAnn nods, reassuring herself. She squeezes Gracie's shoulder and stands up, facing me nervously. I see her hug her arms around herself, pinching her sides—a signature LeeAnn move.

"You've got my cell number and Sarah's, right?" she asks. I can't imagine the horrible scenarios she has running through her mind. She didn't even trust me to be alone in the same room as Gracie *before* she went missing.

"I've got it all," I attempt to reassure her. "We are going to stay right here, and she'll be ready for you in a couple of hours. I promise we won't go anywhere, and I won't leave her alone for even a second."

Gracie giggles.

"I might have to go to the bathroom, Daddy!" she says. My heart does a somersault at the use of the title.

"Well then, missy," I tease her. "I'll be standing just outside the door, and there aren't any windows, so there won't be any funny business."

She rolls her eyes and turns back to Jack. I see LeeAnn crack a small smile.

"Okay, then," she says. "Seriously, call me. Even if it's a small question or whatever, just call me."

"You got it," I reply, trying to look and sound as capable and reliable as possible.

She hesitantly glances back at Gracie and then heads for the door, not allowing herself to look at any of the framed photos of me with Ashley. The door closes behind her, so many unspoken words still between us.

"So," I turn, facing my two children, soaking in each precious moment. "Who wants a peanut butter and jelly sandwich?"

Gracie eyes Jack nervously, hoping he'll give her a cue as to her response. I can tell she's still not comfortable with me, but I know that will change soon. Now, we have so much more time than I ever dreamed of. My son laughs and spits, and Gracie smiles.

"I'll take one, if that is okay," she says.

"Yes, ma'am! Sit on up here then, m'lady." I point to the kitchen stool, bowing low in front of her. She smiles like she wants to laugh more but stops herself.

Gracie hoists herself on the seat closest to Jack's high chair, her feet dangling by the legs. "Daddy?" she asks.

"Yes, Gracie?" I reply, still relishing the sound of the word coming from my darling girl.

"Did you know Grandfather?" she asks.

"I did," I tell her, picturing John's all-encompassing presence filling up the room and noticing Gracie's use of the past tense.

"Do you think he loved me?" she asks, her voice wobbling slightly. "I thought he did, but now he's gone, and I don't know anymore. I'm happy he is happy, but I wish he didn't have to leave."

I watch my daughter's trembling face. I think about how I robbed her of a father in exchange for my own happiness. Once again, I'm struck by the similarities between John and me.

Putting the bread back down on the plate, I sit down on the stool next to her. I can tell Gracie is trying to be strong in front of me. She saves her tears for the people she truly trusts.

"Sometimes grandfathers and dads are a little selfish," I tell her. "I know that I've definitely been. It isn't right, but sometimes it just happens."

Gracie eyes me suspiciously, still unsure.

"But I also know how much I love you," I tell her. "And none of my actions were a reflection of that. So, yes, your grandfather loves you with all his heart, and you should never for one second think that him leaving means anything different."

She sits quietly, squinting her eyes in thought. Finally, her brow relaxes, and she faces me once again.

"Daddy?"

"Yes?"

"Do you think I could have that PB and J?"

Gracie

"SEVEN IS THE YEAR of adventures!" Mama shouts from the driver's seat. Her hair is blowing in the breeze. It whips to and fro, tickling me on my face as I laugh in the back seat.

I am seven years old now. Mama says that makes me a big girl. So far being seven is better than being six. I still have to sit in the back seat, but Mama plays me a song by a man named Elton John as we drive to our mystery adventure location.

I want to know where we are going, but Mama says it's more fun this way. I guess she's right, but that doesn't mean that I don't want to know. Daddy and Jack aren't coming on this adventure with us. Mama says it's "girls only," but that I'll get to see them next week.

It's so great to have a brother. Daddy says that Jack and I can build a tree house in the backyard at his house and that he will help. It probably won't be a Magic Tree House like Annie and the not-real Jack's, but it will still be our own little corner. I wish Jack could meet Grandfather. I know that Grandfather is off on his own adventure, and that makes me happy, but that doesn't mean that I don't miss him all the time. I close my eyes, and I see him. He's holding a squash that's bigger than a baby. He's fixing the Duomo's steps at the request of the pope. He's flying over the pyramids on the veil of an Egyptian princess. He's the ringmaster at the Shackleford Burch Circus. He's showing me the cicadas. He's pouring me sweet tea.

Elton sings from Mama's stereo, something about blue jean babies and a lady named Elle Aye.

I like Mr. Elton John's voice even though I don't understand all of the words. It makes me feel sleepy, but in a good way. I have not heard another voice like that. I must remember to ask Mama to play more of his songs in the car.

It feels like we are flying down the road. It's not like when Grandfather and I chased the sun. Mama actually knows where we are going, and this is "just for fun."

I can't remember ever doing anything with Mama "just for fun," so I am very excited. We have been in the car a long time, but I have made a vow not to fall asleep because I don't want to miss a thing.

We just keep driving and driving until finally Mama turns to me and says, "Okay, you ready to know where we're going?"

"Yes, Mama!" I say, so excited to finally figure out the surprise.

"I am taking you to the beach from my picture," Mama says. "It's the most beautiful place I've ever been, and my mama took me there when I was a little girl."

Now I'm really excited because I have often dreamed of visiting the beach in Mama's picture. I have told her this many times, but she has always said, "Maybe when we have more time."

That's almost the same as saying "maybe when you're old enough," because that means it will never happen. So now I'm so excited that we found time and are going to the beach. I wonder if Grandfather likes the beach. I never got to ask him before he went away, but I'm sure he does because he likes going on adventures.

The houses look different as we get closer. They look like they have been colored with the crayons from my box.

"What would you name your beach house, Gracie?" Mama asks.

I think for a minute.

"Probably the Magic Beach House," I say, "even though I know it's not very original."

"I think it's perfect," Mama says, reaching back to give my shoulder a squeeze. "And I bet it would be bright purple!"

"Of course it would!" I declare. "With purple shutters!"

Mama laughs and parks the car right outside some sand-covered steps. She lets me out of the back and takes my hand.

"You ready?" she asks.

"Let's go!" I shout.

I am practically sprinting up the wooden stairs. My legs are throbbing because they fell asleep in the car, but I don't care. I'm panting hard, but I have to make it to the top so I can see the beach. With every step we take I can see more and more blue, rising before me. It's the most beautiful thing I have ever seen. I have to stop.

"Well, what do you think?" Mama asks, sounding nervous.

The wind brushes against my face, and I laugh loudly. I don't know what else to do. The laugh just pops out of me. I know that I am being silly, but this is the most marvelous thing I could have ever imagined. I grab Mama's hand and pull her down to the water. I have to feel it. The sand squishes between my toes, like a less gooey version of the algae from the river. The rock in my pocket softly taps against my leg as a reminder of that day, the day we made it count.

The wave comes crashing to shore so quickly that it scares me, and I jump back as Mama squeezes my hand reassuringly.

"Do you want to swim in the ocean?" Mama offers.

"Am I old enough?" I ask.

Mama smiles down at me, and says, "You're exactly as old as you're supposed to be, baby girl."

ACKNOWLEDGMENTS

I WROTE THIS BOOK as a way to escape my own grief as I watched the impact that dementia can have on someone you love. *Sun Seekers* is for every caregiver or person who has loved someone with dementia, Alzheimer's, or any disease that robs an individual of their light. It's also for those who work in nursing homes and give our loved ones as peaceful final years as possible, especially the homes of Carriage Court in Memphis, Tennessee, and Spring Arbor in Richmond, Virginia. Being a caregiver is a thankless, heartbreaking job that can feel isolating and bleak. Never forget that you're doing your best, and that the person you care for is proud and appreciative of you, whether they can express it or not.

I have to start off by thanking my incredible agent, Liza Fleissig. She's believed in me when it felt like no one else did, and I'll never forget it. I couldn't have asked for a better first editor than Jess Verdi. From the jump, she understood exactly the story I wanted to tell, loved these characters as much as I do, and asked all the right questions. I'm also grateful for the team at Alcove Press—Rebecca Nelson, Hannah Pierdolla, Thai Fantauzzi Perez—for putting so much time and attention into getting this book out to the world.

You wouldn't be holding this book in your hands if it weren't for Brenda Janowitz. I met Brenda at a writing class when I was an obnoxious wannabe writer in my early twenties blabbering on about wanting to publish a book before I turned twenty-five (spoiler alert: that didn't happen). She was already a successful, published author, who had no reason to give me the time of day. Not only did she become a fantastic mentor, but she also became a close friend. Brenda stuck with me through the almost eight years since we first met, reading drafts, offering sage advice, support, and tough love. She never stopped believing in me, and I cannot emphasize enough the complete difference that made on kick-starting my career as a writer. I'm eternally grateful.

Every novelist should have a friend like Mary Claire Williams. She's the most passionate person I know, the fastest reader, and fiercely loyal. She has read more drafts of this book than any person apart from me. It's an honor to have her as the Rory (early years) to my Paris. Thank you also to Mehera Bonner, another extremely helpful early reader, who encouraged me to give the character of Dan his own voice. My friend Emily Plaster gave me a nurse's perspective on heat exhaustion and tended to my various ailments in college. Will Sosnowski gave me firsthand details about police officers handling missing children in the field. Lynn Messina offered invaluable continuity edits very early on that helped me keep track of the sun on Gracie and John's adventure.

Thanks to the London Writers' Café for sharing their stories and listening to mine, and the staff at my local Café Nero and the Bell & Crown pub for letting me sit for hours, typing rough first drafts.

My friend Kathy Northrop took my headshots and has been by my side since middle school, even if she doesn't remember.

Sometimes you need a cheerleader for your harebrained ideas and side projects, and, for me, that person is my friend Lawler Watkins. Your blind faith is a gift.

My mom has been with me in my writing "career" since before I could write myself. I would dictate stories to her, and she'd faithfully type them up, offering plot suggestions that were often (shockingly) better than the ideas of my seven-year-old self. She filled my childhood with wonderful books and stories that shaped the writer and reader I am today. And most of the food mentioned in this book comes straight out of her kitchen. She also never gave up hope that I'd one day reach this goal of publishing a book. Mama said I could do it, so I could. In 2016, she read this book when it was a six-page short story about a little girl and her grandfather on an adventure and immediately told me that this was what I should write.

Watching my dad write all these years taught me the importance of dedicating your time to your craft. He also blessed (or cursed, depending on who you ask) me with his sense of humor. Seeing him as a caregiver for my grandfather inspired a lot of this story. Dad, even though I might have complained about them, I knew those early morning fishing trips would pay off some day.

So much of the guilt I've felt surrounding my writing has been when it takes time away from my girls. I couldn't have written this, been a mom, and had a job without the help of my mother-in-law, Ginger Jones. Our family is blessed to have you in it.

To my Gracies—Iona and Isla—I've had a dream of publishing a book since before you were born, but you made it all have meaning. I hope you never stop trying and always give your best in whatever dreams you pursue.

It might sound silly, but I also want to thank anyone who ever listened to me talk about writing novels and didn't laugh. You allowed me to take it seriously.

Finally, when I turned eighteen, my boyfriend gave me a Moleskine notebook for my birthday. Inside, he wrote me a note saying that the notebook was to start writing down ideas for my future novel. I had never had anyone believe in me like that before. I didn't even believe in myself at that point (and still don't some days). More than fifteen years, two kids, six homes, two countries, one stinky French bulldog, and countless adventures later, I'm still so in love with that guy who gave me that notebook. Thank you, Caleb, for always being on my team, for never doubting, and for constantly choosing me and our family. All of your girls are lucky to have you.